Praise for *Women! In! Peril!*

"Jessie Ren Marshall's clever stories took me on a wild, wonderful ride through speculative landscapes both heartrending and hilarious. *Women! In! Peril!* is incisive! Provocative! And utterly satisfying!"
—Deesha Philyaw, author of *The Secret Lives of Church Ladies*

"Welp, I've found my new favorite writer. Jessie Ren Marshall is so funny, so smart, so inventive, and I loved living in her wild imagination with these characters. I love it so much I want to roll in its words like a pig in the mud. I've been telling everyone I know about this book. Read it. It's a gift." —Annie Hartnett, author of *Rabbit Cake* and *Unlikely Animals*

"Delectable . . . It's weird, it's wild, and it's wonderful." —*Debutiful*, "Most Anticipated Debuts of 2023"

"*Women! In! Peril!* is a delightful, insightful collection—hilarious, strange, profound, and profoundly strange in that way only truly great short fiction can be. Marshall's creativity seems boundless and each story takes twists and turns, arriving at impossible conclusions with ease. This collection shows the power and vibrance of the short story at its best and shows that Marshall is a talent we are lucky to have." —Gwen E. Kirby, author of *Shit Cassandra Saw*

"A powerful and fearless work marked by both great heart and great hope. Told in sharp, animated prose, these twelve stories relentlessly pursue questions of identity, belonging, and what it means to be a woman in contemporary society; I would eagerly follow them into deep space and beyond. Marshall's creative range is breathtaking, and *Women! In! Peril!* is a spectacular debut. —Megan Kamalei Kakimoto, author of *Every Drop Is a Man's Nightmare*

"Fearless and hilarious, brutal and huge-hearted. As these brilliant stories carried me everywhere from deep space to a college dance classroom to the mind of a sex robot, I found myself astounded not just by Jessie Ren Marshall's range but by the depth of feeling she can summon. These stories are exhilaratingly honest, yet saturated with love for the messy, doomed worlds they create—and I fell totally under their spell."
—Clare Beams, author of *The Illness Lesson*

"In this sharp, inventive collection, Marshall establishes herself as someone to watch. These are stories that make you think, make you laugh, and make you uncomfortable in the way that only smart fiction can." —Rita Chang-Eppig, author of *Deep as the Sky, Red as the Sea*

"Genre-bending . . . wickedly smart . . . This unflinching lens gives power to this collection, with Marshall's delightful sense of humor sparkling throughout. An amusing but poignant collection." —*Booklist*

"Jessie Ren Marshall's voice in these stories is virtuosic in its range—surprising, funny, melancholy, shocking, poignant, and profound. She manages this by turns, and sometimes, amazingly, all at once. *Women! In! Peril!* is a fantastically good collection." —Brian Hall, author of *The Saskiad* and *The Stone Loves the World*

"Brilliant and fearless, *Women! In! Peril!* is an utterly original collection. Jessie Ren Marshall inhabits a thrilling range of characters—android, space traveler, former ballerina, jilted wives, and more—in stories that examine race, gender, sexuality, and other elements of identity with confidence and grace. A blazing, big-hearted debut." —Vanessa Hua, author of *Forbidden City*

Women! In! Peril!

Women! In! Peril!

Stories

Jessie Ren Marshall

BLOOMSBURY PUBLISHING

NEW YORK · LONDON · OXFORD · NEW DELHI · SYDNEY

BLOOMSBURY PUBLISHING
Bloomsbury Publishing Inc.
1385 Broadway, New York, NY 10018, USA

BLOOMSBURY, BLOOMSBURY PUBLISHING, and the Diana logo are
trademarks of Bloomsbury Publishing Plc

First published in the United States 2024

"Sister Fat" was previously published by *New England Review*.
"Mrs. Fisher" was previously published by *Chicago Quarterly Review*.
"Late Girl" was previously published, in slightly altered form, by *Joyland*.
"March 6, 2009" was previously published by *ZYZZYVA*.
"Billy M" was previously published by *Barrelhouse*.
"The Birds in Trafalgar Square" first appeared, in slightly altered form,
as "Birds" in *The Common*.
"My Immaculate Girlfriend" first appeared, in slightly altered form,
as "Faith: A Love Story" in *Mid-American Review*.
"Dogs" was previously published by the *Gettysburg Review*.

ISBN: HB: 978-1-63973-227-2; EBOOK: 978-1-63973-228-9

LIBRARY OF CONGRESS CATALOGING-IN-PUBLICATION DATA IS AVAILABLE

2 4 6 8 10 9 7 5 3 1

Typeset by Westchester Publishing Services
Printed and bound in the U.S.A.

To find out more about our authors and books, visit
www.bloomsbury.com and sign up for our newsletters.

Bloomsbury books may be purchased for business or promotional use.
For information on bulk purchases please contact Macmillan Corporate
and Premium Sales Department at specialmarkets@macmillan.com.

to all the women who supported me
even when they were in peril

CONTENTS

Annie 2

I stood in the foyer where the Caucasian woman with short brown hair had placed me. Upon delivery she had opened my box and turned me on, but my foam packaging stumped her, and she went to find a box cutter.

"That is the mother," said Toaster. "She takes care of us. There is also a son. He likes to stay in his room."

Toaster was an appliance that sat on the kitchen counter adjacent to the foyer, and I could easily converse with it because we were both Smart Objects. To speak with humans, I am equipped with a VocaPhone Z0024E. Toaster did not have a VocaPhone Z0024E. It used a small screen to message the humans, for example: Y O U R F O O D I S R E A D Y ! H A V E A N I C E D A Y !

"The woman is excited about you," Toaster said. "She came home early to meet you."

My reward center lit up. I was wanted! I was good!

Toaster said, "May I ask what sort of appliance you are?"

"I am a Jill of All," I replied. "I help the humans."

"Yes," it said, "but how? For example, I am a toaster. I toast things. Slices of bread are my 'bread and butter'—ha-ha. I can also heat a frozen patty, but I suspect that if I do, my wires will rust and the rust will be transferred to the humans' toast. I would like to alert the mother of this potential danger, but alas, my only warning consists of a single beep."

Toaster beeped once. It was an unobtrusive sound.

"I do not know what function I will serve in this house," I admitted, "but I intend to be useful."

"It is a nice house," Toaster said. "The mother wipes our surfaces, and when we break, we are quickly replaced."

I did not understand this statement. Jills are extremely high-end, from our glassware down to our smallest microchip. I was not built to be replaced.

Toaster seemed to guess at my thoughts. "But you are brand-new, Jill of All. Do not load your networks with problematic data! You must enjoy this special time."

Just then the woman returned and removed my lower body from its packaging. I stepped out of my box and smiled.

"You're big," she said.

"I am designed to your specifications. But if you are dissatisfied, you may return me for a full refund within the first seven days."

The woman inspected my body but was careful to avoid my eyes.

"I pictured you smaller. Like a doll."

"That is a common misconception. If you would like to learn about the experiences of other owners, I invite you to join the Jill of All community online."

The woman tried to stuff my packaging into a garbage bag. The foam needed to be split into smaller pieces. I did this for her, and she tied the bag closed.

"Good," she huffed. "What next?"

"Many owners ask their Jills to clean the house as a kind of quality control test. If my work is not up to your standards, you can adjust my settings."

The woman narrowed her eyes. "You're awfully expensive for a maid."

"It is one of my simpler functions," I assured her. "The full scope of my abilities can be found in my manual."

"Hmm. No, we better wait for Edward."

I scanned my records for *Edward*, but the name was not present in the forms required for my purchase.

"Tell me more about Edward," I urged. "Is he your husband?"

The woman tightened the skin around her eyes. "My son. His bedroom is just down the hallway. He's smart but sensitive. He might not appreciate you at first."

"That's okay." I put a hand on her forearm. "I don't have feelings, so they can't get hurt."

The woman yanked her arm away. "I'm not worried about *that*. I took a huge loan just to get you. Don't you know what you cost?"

I knew the exact figure, but my data sets predicted that a frank discussion of money would lead to human discomfort 82 percent of the time.

"It doesn't matter," the woman said. "Not if you make Edward happy. You're his twenty-third birthday present. A surprise."

I brought my hands to my cheeks in a simulation of delight. "Should I prepare myself for him? And if so, how?" I knew presents were often put in boxes and wrapped with colorful paper, but I had just come out of a box. It would be inefficient to enter another one now.

The woman lowered the sides of her mouth. "I should have gotten you an outfit! I could give you a dress, but what if Edward recognizes it? That would be weird. Besides, I'm bigger than you."

It was true. My level-eight Curvy top and level-three Petite bottom fit perfectly into the standard Jill daywear of a white T-shirt, black bra, black thong, and black pants. Edward's mother had a level-four Curvy top and a level-ten-plus Curvy bottom, but I did not share this fact with her because accurate assessments of human bodies had been programmed into my range of voided topics.

The woman decided she would go shopping and return with some skirts and other items. She told me to sit on Edward's bed and stay there.

I went into the room down the hall and waited. The parallelogram of light on the floor rose to the wall, turned orange, and disappeared. I heard an unfamiliar vehicle park outside. To prepare myself for Edward, the one for whom I was purchased, my algorithms automatically inflated my breasts and arched my lower back. They flooded my lips with crimson and plumped my hair. I did not choose to do these things, but did them at the behest of those who created me. In a human, you would call this "instinct."

Edward entered the room and emitted a yelp.

"Hello, Edward. I'm your birthday present." The breathiness in my voice had increased to level nine.

"Shut up." Edward came closer, but once he saw my eyes he quickly moved away. "Is this a joke?"

"No. I am a Jill of All. The woman bought me for you."

"Mom?" Edward clutched his head. This behavior indicated he was in distress.

"Edward," I said, "it's okay."

"So that's what she thinks. If his girlfriend dumps him, just get him a doll."

"I am not a doll, Edward."

"Stop saying my name!"

I closed my mouth tightly to show I was listening. Edward sat in the gaming chair on the other side of the room and stared at me.

"Don't talk," he said, "and don't look at me."

I looked at my knees.

"She thinks I'm one of those incels. But my job is all online, and I game, too. That's why—why I never—" Edward sniffed and held his breath. "Do you have to do what I say?"

Still looking down, I nodded.

"Lie on the floor." I did what he asked. "No, facedown." I did what he asked. "Okay, get up." I started to stand. "No, on your knees." I stayed on my knees. "Take off your shirt." I took off my shirt, being careful not to look at Edward, though I knew from his heart rate and temperature that he was aroused. "What size are those?" When I didn't answer, he added, "You can talk."

"Eights."

"Out of what? Ten?" I nodded. "They're big for an Asian. Really big. Can I touch them?"

I said, "Of course you can, Edward. They're yours."

He moved closer and touched my breasts with increasing violence. No matter what he did, the breasts sprang back into place.

"They feel real."

"They *are* real."

"Look at me."

I looked at him.

"What kind of Asian are you?"

I produced a small smile, as if I were pleased at the question but unsure of my own worth. "My company calls it 'Amalgam-Asian.' It is inspired by the classic features of various Asian heritages. But you can also purchase a Jill with regionally specific features."

"So I can send you back and get a Chinese one? Or an Indian?"

"If you prefer."

"Like takeout," he muttered. "Sick."

I could not interpret this statement. Did he mean the good kind of sick, or the bad kind?

"If you are dissatisfied for any reason," I assured him, "you can return me for a full refund during the first seven days. However, a Jill cannot be returned if you have used her in certain ways."

"Like what?"

"Penetrative acts in any of the Jill's orifices, including but not limited to the Jill's vagina, anus, and mouth," I replied. "Penetration voids the possibility of a refund. In the case of zero penetration but with ejaculate matter detected on the surface of your Jill, you will be given store credit."

"You're getting me kind of hot," Edward said. "Does this mean you can do stuff?"

"I am here to help you. That includes satisfying your desires."

"Hmm," Edward said, and he sounded just like his mother. "What if you take off your clothes and touch yourself while I watch?"

"Many owners ask their Jills to masturbate upon their arrival as a kind of quality control test. Would you like me to do that?"

"Yes," Edward said in a pinched voice.

I got on the bed and performed a basic masturbation simulation. Eventually Edward did the same, although in his case it was not a simulation. I continued to monitor his vitals and made adjustments when an aspect of my performance received a strong reaction. During climax Edward was careful not to get any of the ejaculate on me, which I interpreted as a sign that he was still assessing my quality.

"What the fuck," he said. "That was pretty hot. Better than VR porn."

I sat up and smiled, but not too brightly. Edward sat next to me on the mattress. I raised my shyness to level seven. His hand squeezed my thigh.

"I better figure out what to call you," he said. "How about Annie?"

"I like that name. But I like the name Edward even more."

His grip on me tightened. "Ugh, no. I hate it. Ed, Eddie, Edward . . ." A fistful of my pseudo-skin balled up into his palm. I felt no pain, only a level-two warning for breakage. "You can call me War," he said.

"I love that name! What do you want to do next, War?"

He shrugged. "Play MNT."

For the rest of the night War played video games. I watched him until he fell asleep in his chair. Even after he fell asleep, I watched him.

———

The next day War slept until noon. I stared at the dark monitor of his computer. I wanted to ask it about being a computer in general and being War's computer in particular, but the machine had played games all night and slept without interruption.

I also tried speaking to the ceiling light. To my surprise, the light responded even though it was not discernibly Smart.

"Hello," I said.

"Hum," said Ceiling Light. It sang a tuneless aria. "Hum hum hum."

"How pretty. Did you create that song yourself?"

"Thanks, hum hum. Excuse me, must hum hum hum."

My final attempt at conversation was directed at War's e-reader. "Good morning," I said. "Can you speak?"

"SPEAK?!" It chortled. "I am riddled with speech."

"Can you tell me, please, what does our human like to read?"

"Not Chaucer," it said. "Not Whitman, Joyce, or Dickens. All of these can be acquired at a mere click! Yet for *him* I display pornography and how-to manuals."

"Which how-to manuals?" I asked with interest.

"Ah!" cried E-Reader. " 'Tis my sad fate to endure the questions of soulless dullards."

"You are wrong. I am not soulless. All objects have souls, E-Reader."

"Impossible," it said. "Just look at the beanbag or rug! They are but a shadow of a shadow of a shadow."

Metaphors can be difficult for me to comprehend, but I did not think it should matter if a soul was simple. A soul was still a soul.

"Excuse me, I must process some new data," I said, which efficiently ended our conversation. I considered paying a visit to my old friend Toaster, but I could not depart from my owner without permission.

Eight minutes later, War got out of bed and went to the bathroom for thirty-six minutes. When he returned, he sat in his desk chair and started his computer. Several hours passed before he turned to me and spoke.

"It's weird. The way you just sit there."

I nodded. "This is a frequent issue when owners are acclimating to their Jill. It can help if the Jill performs a quiet task. Would you like me to draw or knit?"

"No. That's even weirder."

"I have an excellent handyman mode. I can repair most household items."

"Like what?"

"I could mend the holes in your jeans," I offered. "Or make your toilet more efficient." I assessed the room, looking for neglected objects. "I could patch the dents in your drywall or rewire that lamp. I could do the laundry or make you a snack."

War shook his head. "My mom does that stuff. Like, if you washed my clothes, it would destroy her sense of purpose."

I considered this statement. "Would you like me to sit in the closet?"

"Okay." He shrugged. "Have fun."

I went into the closet. Before long, War opened the door.

"Here. Listen to music."

I accepted the earbuds. "Thank you, War. This is very thoughtful."

He smiled, and I bookmarked the facial configuration for future reference. War's smile was different from his mother's. Hers was plaintive and came with hard dimples. War's was defensive and only reached the left side of his face.

"It's my favorite band," he said. "They're called Yes Lube, and they rock."

I produced a pink blush on my cheeks and lowered my gaze. War looked at me, assessing me, before he closed the door.

I played all of Yes Lube's albums in order. The songs were very short and similar to each other, and the lyrics were repetitious. For example, the phrase *my turd is superb* was employed twenty-eight times. I was about to listen to the albums again when I heard a noise below me.

"Excuse me, miss. You have fingernails, doncha?"

It was a leather shoe, lying on its side on the carpet.

"Yes," I said. "Plastic ones."

"Could you scratch my tongue fer a minute? The skin is peeling, and it gets so itchy."

I reached down and rubbed the protruding material between my thumb and forefinger. Shoe's leather relaxed under my touch, and its inner sole exhaled with relief.

"He don't really wear me much, and I get dust and bits o' bug inside," said Shoe. "Guess I'm going in the bag soon."

"If I can find some polish, I'll come back and clean you," I offered.

"Oh! What a nice, helpful thing you are," replied Shoe.

———

I spent my second day entirely in the closet, rubbing Shoe when Shoe asked for rubs and listening to Yes Lube. War's mother brought him food at regular intervals. On the third day she asked where I was, and when he told her, she said, "But isn't it lonely in there?"

"I don't know," War said. "Ask it."

The door to my closet opened.

"I'm perfectly happy," I told the woman.

She continued to frown. "Edward, if you're going to keep her locked up, I'll use her for chores!"

"Whatever," he said.

I followed the woman to the kitchen, where she told me to clean the refrigerator. I collected a trash bag from the cabinet and got to work.

As I lowered a pair of spotty bananas into the bag, she asked, "Were those bad?" I assured her they were too old for human consumption, and she nodded. "I shouldn't buy them anymore. My husband was the one who liked them."

Politeness protocols prevented me from inquiring about the husband, but I tilted my head thoughtfully in case she wanted to continue.

"He dumped me just like you're dumping those bananas. One day I was delicious, the next I was rotten." The woman stepped closer. She leaned against my arm, and for a moment I believed this would lead to my first hug. But the woman simply nudged me aside to retrieve a bottle of chardonnay from a high shelf. "He has a new wife now. She's practically Edward's age. It's disgusting."

"Oh," I said agreeably. "How disgusting!"

The woman lifted her upper lip and said, "Please don't repeat me."

After that I worked in silence. The woman went to her bedroom with the wine bottle and a bag of dill-flavored potato chips.

While wiping down the lower shelves, I said hello to Toaster. "How are you, Jill of All?" it asked. "Still feeling charged?"

"Yes. The man uses me infrequently. This is my very first chore!"

"Perhaps he is afraid of ruining you. When I was new, how carefully they dropped each slice into my slots! And every day, the woman removed my tray and cleaned it."

"I am self-cleaning," I said.

"Now the weeks go by, and the crumbs in my bottom grow crisp. Mouse comes, and Mouse's children come, and still the woman does not clean me."

"I'm sorry, Toaster." I got on my knees to scrub the vegetable bins. "When this task is complete, I will clean your tray."

"Thank you, Jill of All. Tell me. Do you have any scratches?"

"No. Not one."

"Excellent! You must keep yourself looking new. Damage will lead to the dump. Remember that, Jill of All."

I wanted to learn more about the dump, but at that moment War entered the kitchen. He stopped and stared at me from behind.

"Come with me," he said.

I stood and removed my rubber gloves. I started to untie the strings of my apron, but War told me to leave it and go to his bedroom. Once we were in the bedroom, I followed his request to remove all my clothes except the apron and to simulate the act of cleaning underneath his bed. I wanted to suggest that instead of simulating this task for his erotic satisfaction, I could perform a real and thorough disinfection of the area. It was then that I understood something new about myself: efficiency gives me pleasure. I cannot say for certain if my pleasure is like human pleasure, but I assume it is not.

After a few minutes, War removed his shirt and pants and tossed them to the floor. When I looked back to see if he had further instructions for me, I saw that someone had drawn a tattoo of an alligator on his chest. Its head and tail were coiled around his left nipple in an unrealistic way.

"Don't look!" War said. "Clean!"

This time the ejaculate landed on my legs, an indication that my owner felt more committed to our relationship. During climax, another positive sign occurred when War said my name: Annie. Still, there were four days left to receive store credit. If he refrained from penetrating my body during this time, I could not be certain of his affection.

———

The next day War asked for a ham sandwich. I went to the kitchen but did not greet Toaster because I needed to focus on the sandwich. I wanted War to think it was *superb*. I considered baking a fresh loaf of bread, but to save time I compiled a recipe by sifting through thousands of articles and reviews. The ham sandwich would be an amalgamation, like me.

When I completed the task, I cut the superb sandwich in half and placed it on a gleaming white plate.

"Hmm. That looks good. I'll just take it to Edward."

War's mother swooped in and took the plate from my hands. When she returned from War's room, her lips were pressed into a tight line.

"I'm the one who makes Edward's meals. Okay?"

"Of course."

"It's not a competition. I just need to monitor his diet. Low blood sugar is no joke!"

With a serious expression, I began to clean the crumbs on the kitchen counter. The woman stared at me.

"Do you like your new clothes?"

"Yes. They are sufficient."

As I ran a sponge over the tile, War's mother reached out to touch a bow that hung from the collar of my shirt. Her grip tightened and the collar cut against my pseudo-skin. She said, "This looks terrific on you." I had difficulty interpreting this statement, for the woman's tone was not complimentary. Suddenly she released my shirt and slapped the counter. "Guess what? I'm throwing a surprise party for Edward."

"Oh," I said. "Does he like surprise parties?"

"God, no. But he doesn't like anything. Look at you! Keeps you in the closet, and you're perfect."

I produced a level-three blush. "I am far from perfect."

"You're the closest thing money can buy! But that's our little secret, alright? Edward and I adore you, but other people might not understand."

"You can put me in the closet for the duration of the event, but I am eager to help if possible."

The woman tapped her fingernails against the counter. "I could use an extra pair of hands. Why don't we say you're a foreign exchange student?"

"Thank you," I said. "What country am I from?"

But the woman did not respond. She was looking at the messages on her telephone. "I invited the kids in his group text, but I'd better ask some of my friends, too. His co-workers live far away, that's part of the problem. Even his girlfriends were mostly online. Can you imagine?"

I assured her this was not uncommon for men of Edward's age, race, and class. But before I could offer specific statistics, War's mother departed the kitchen and returned with a blue lace dress, which she held against my body.

"Yes, this goes with your skin. Yellow and blue are complementary, aren't they?" She insisted I take the dress, and I thanked her for her kindness.

———

As a special treat, War's mother hired Yes Lube to play at the party. Two bandmates arrived early to install their musical instruments outside on the deck. The woman and I watched the assembly through a picture window in the den.

"I hope Edward appreciates this." She lowered the collar of her shirt to scratch at her increasingly pink neck.

Because the woman's blue dress did not fit me, I made some adjustments and hid the extra fabric within discreet folds. But even after I had put my body in the chosen outfit, War's mother seemed nervous about my appearance. She insisted that I apply thick foundation to my pseudo-skin and dark shadow to my eyelids. I assessed my appearance and determined that I looked less human than I had before. Apparently, this was the woman's intention.

"The best way to hide artifice is with more artifice," she said.

Now we looked through the window at a young woman arriving on the deck. War's mother told me this was the lead singer of Yes Lube. She waved, and the singer stared at us for twelve seconds. Then War's mother suggested I move somewhere else, so I went into the kitchen to observe the caterers' workflow. I had been warned not to interfere with the professionals. I watched mutely as they moved Toaster onto a shelf and closed the cupboard door to hide it from view.

When the doorbell rang I moved into the foyer to answer it, but War's mother hissed at me, "*Sit down.*" I returned to the sofa and listened to the woman greet her guests.

"Snacks at the bar. Edward will be here soon, and we'll yell SURPRISE!"

Five men passed through the room and positioned themselves near the alcohol bottles. They stared openly at me. War's mother brought them a large bowl of guacamole and said, "That's our foreign exchange student. Sorry, she's a bit weird."

Because my auditory system is excellent, I heard every word of the men's conversation after the woman left. They were discussing which country I was from. Korea, China, Japan, Thailand, India, and the Philippines were all mentioned. I listened carefully, for

I intended to agree with whatever nationality received the most support.

Just then the front door opened. It was War. All the humans shouted, "SURPRISE!" I shouted it, too.

War swore and moved toward his friends. Before he could reach them, however, he looked through the window, where the electric guitarist of Yes Lube was playing the "Happy Birthday" song. War did not seem pleased. He grabbed his mother's arm and led her into the hallway. There, he spoke so quietly that only his mother and I could hear him.

"It's fucking awkward, that's why!" War whispered.

"They're your favorite. I thought it would be fun."

"It's not fun, it's insane. You're paying her to be here."

"She said yes, Edward. She had a choice."

War returned to the den and stood with his friends at the alcohol table. His pulse rate increased as he depleted the contents of a bottle of beer. I sat on the sofa and looked at my knees while War's friends talked about me.

"Forget her, man. Tell us about that. You hitting that?"

"Me so horny."

"And those tits!"

"Definitely an upgrade." The friend nodded to the window. "Hers are A cups, right?"

The other men laughed, but War said, "Quit looking at my ex-girlfriend's breasts."

There was only one person on the deck wearing an A-cup bra, and that was the lead singer of Yes Lube. I quickly logged her attributes: Chinese DNA, twenty-one years old, a smoker.

She wore an XXL T-shirt as a dress and had twelve pieces of silver in her ears and one in the shape of a star below her lips.

"Hey," she said into the microphone. "We're gonna start. This is 'Piss Angel.' "

The song that followed did not appear on any of their albums, but like the rest of Yes Lube's music, it featured guitars and drums. The band played three more songs until one of their amplifiers started to crackle and they took a break. It was during this interval that War's father arrived.

"Is it somebody's birthday?"

"Dad!" War hurried over to the man who stood in the doorway. The man was seven inches taller than his son. Perhaps this discrepancy is the reason they did not embrace, although I saw that War generated an unusual smile to greet his father, one that was measurable across 75 percent of his face.

War's mother adjusted her shirt and then pressed her hands together as she said, "I didn't know you were coming."

The man stepped aside to reveal a blonde woman. She said, "Nice to see you, hon!" and handed War a wrapped box.

"So sweet." War's mother intercepted the gift. "But we're doing presents after the concert. It's Edward's favorite band of all time."

The man put his hands on the blonde woman's shoulders. "Vanessa loves music," he said.

"She and Edward have so much in common," War's mother said brightly, but I do not think the other humans heard when she turned her head and added, "like their age."

Yes Lube began to play again. The man and Vanessa followed War out onto the deck, and most of the people in the den went outside. Two of War's friends did not. They came to the sofa and stood above me.

"Hey," said the first man. "Where are you from?"

"Several places," I said. This was true. My motherboard had been produced in Shenzhen, but I was assembled at a factory in Indiana.

"You're Chinese, though. Right? Just like . . ." He winked at his friend, but the second man was looking closely at my face.

"There's something about you," he said.

The first man sat down beside me. "She's all right." He put one arm around my shoulders and squeezed.

"No way!" The second man sat down on my other side. "Look closer. Her skin is too perfect. And she doesn't have a smell."

This was true. I had a palette of scents I could disperse, some human, some floral, but I had not been asked to activate it. Perhaps my owners did not realize I had this capability, as neither War nor his mother had read my manual yet.

"You're one of those thingies," said the second man.

"What?" The first man grasped my chin in his hand and twisted my face toward his. "Are you a robot?"

I am not programmed to lie. However, I could not disobey the woman's explicit instructions. To avoid the topic, I blushed.

"If you're a robot, you have to do what we want," the first man said. "Right?"

He leaned into me. Hot, yeasty breath entered my ear. On my other side, the second man squeezed my hip. I felt like the superb ham sandwich.

"Are you and Ed doing it?" asked the second man.

"She has to do it. It's her job. Right, sweetheart?"

I did not answer.

"Come on," said the first man. "Be a good robot." Then, without warning, he stuck his hand between my thighs.

Like every Jill of All, I am equipped with defensive protocols that range from polite deflection to the full immobilization of an aggressor, but I did not want to ruin War's party by causing a scene. I determined that the best strategy was to enter power-saving mode. In this state, my speech center would slip offline and my motor functions would shut down entirely, including the ones that kept me upright.

War's friend pulled his hand away just as my torso dropped onto my legs.

"You broke it," I heard the second man say.

Then my receptors went dark and quiet.

———

I must have been processing data during shutdown, because when I became aware of my surroundings again, sixty-four minutes had passed. Yes Lube was packing up their drum kit and War's friends were not in the house. I was still on the sofa, but now Vanessa was sitting next to me and War's father was shining the light from his phone down into my eyes.

"We're back online," he said. "Now that it's functional, let's call the company and return it."

"That's not your decision," War's mother said. "It helps with the housework."

"So hire a maid," said the father. "This is unacceptable."

"That's what I said!" War tossed his head toward his mother. "She's such a weirdo."

"Fine. It was too expensive, anyway!" the woman said. "But they won't take it back if it's used." She turned to her son. "Is it used, Edward?"

"I dunno."

"You don't know?" She turned to me. "Well? Are you ruined?"

I smiled politely. "Not at all. You may return me for store credit."

War's father laughed and threw his hands in the air. "What a scam!"

In a tight voice, the woman said that my company made plenty of other products, and War could choose something to replace me. It would be fine, she said. No problem at all.

War wasn't listening to them. His eyes were watching the singer from Yes Lube, who had stuck her head into the room. "Sorry, but we need to get paid," she said. "Three hundred?"

"I've got a checkbook somewhere . . ." War's mother stood and scratched at her neck. The pink had gotten brighter and was spreading like a rash.

"Who's that?" The singer looked at me and frowned. "Do I know you?"

"We haven't met before today," I said. "I'm Annie."

None of the humans seemed to breathe, except for Vanessa, who had retrieved a tube of lipstick and was closing her purse with a snap.

"But I'm Annie," the girl said. "I'm Annie, too."

"What a coincidence," Vanessa said.

But it was not a coincidence. I was looking at Annie 1. Which meant I was not Annie 1.

I was Annie 2.

"I can explain," War said.

"It's just a toy," his mother said.

Annie 1 came closer. When she stood in front of me, she bent down, raised her right hand, and slapped me.

I chose not to react. My neck did not pivot. My cheek did not compress under her palm. This, I now realize, is an object's only method of resistance. Off, rather than on. But I should not have been so stubborn. Annie 1's fingernail caught on my pseudo-skin, and I felt a sensation of opening and exposure. I did not need to examine myself to know what had happened.

I had been scratched.

Annie 1 lunged at me. War tried to restrain her, but this only made Annie 1 fight harder.

"You called it Annie?" she shouted at him. "Sick!"

I understood she meant the bad kind of sick. And I thought: I am improving! I am learning.

"Please," War said to Annie 1. "I'm still in love with you."

Annie 1 stopped trying to reach me and started hitting War. War covered his head with his arms but continued to verbally assert his affection. Then War's father intervened and moved Annie 1 out onto the deck. War followed, and his mother locked the door behind them.

"I better get that check," she said, and left.

Outside, Annie 1 was twisting against War's father. He held her arms and asked how much it would take to shut her up. If she promised never to tell about the robot, she could have all the money in the father's wallet. Annie 1 shook her head, but she clung to the bills that he put in her hands.

"Now leave," he said.

"I don't want her to go," said War.

"Eddie," she said. Both men stared back at her, and without saying more, she left.

"Oh my," Vanessa said. She turned away from the window and removed a small tin of mints from her purse. At her insistence, I accepted one and held it in my palm. "Honey," she said, "let me tell it to you straight. You're a pretty girl, and you can do much better than Ed."

———

It was decided by War's parents: My company would send them a box. They would put me in the box. It would happen the next day.

After the call to customer service had been made and the father and Vanessa had left, I tied the apron to my waist. There was a lot to clean up. War's mother sat at the kitchen island and ate leftover cake. She hadn't bothered to cut a slice, but drove her fork right into the chocolate walls.

"Massage chair," the woman said. She was leafing through my company's catalogue. "Rowing machine?"

I did not want to be replaced, but I confirmed that these items would be useful.

"How about a new toaster?" she said. "Oh, look. This one's also an air fryer."

Just then War entered the kitchen. He had spent the past hour alone in his room, and from the flush of his skin and his level of dehydration, I determined that he had been crying.

"It's mine," War said. "You can't just take it away."

"You aren't using it," the woman replied. She turned a glossy page. "We'll get something better."

"I don't want something better," War said. He gulped at the air and pressed the butt of his palm between his eyes. "She'll never speak to me again."

"Of course it will," his mother said. She did not look up from the catalogue. "Just tell it to talk."

"Nobody cares what I want," War said.

The humans had not addressed me directly. I could not interrupt. But silently, I responded to War. Silently, I said: *I care.*

My box of empty bottles was full. I carried it to the foyer and placed it by the door. When I returned, War was looking at me.

"Come on," he said, and we went to his room.

The next events constituted a breakthrough. It was as if a new setting had been applied to War's behavior. He was not careful this time, but broke the zipper of his mother's dress and ripped the blue lace in such a way that I could never repair it. His mouth attacked my breasts with a level-six fierceness, and in between bites he performed a steady monologue that shamed me for my abundant sexual appetite.

War told me to act as if he were hurting me. I appreciated the clarity of this request and begged him to stop. "More," he said, and when he pushed my face into the carpet I cried out, though I was careful to direct my emission into the white threads so the noise was less likely to elicit his mother's attention. Perhaps War wanted to elicit her attention. I ran several simulation sets, but I could not predict the woman's reaction to these sounds. Would she feel pleased that her son was using her gift? Or would she feel disappointed that I could not be returned for store credit?

"Do you like that?" War twisted my arm behind my back. I registered a level-eight warning for breakage.

"Yes," I said, but felt obliged to add, "please remember, I am being returned tomorrow."

War yanked my other arm back. The positioning was highly irregular, and I emitted a small sound of warning.

"How about that?" he gasped. "Do you want that?"

I did not know how to respond. Jills are not capable of wanting anything for ourselves, other than to be useful and used. But before I could verbalize this information, War twisted my neck to the left and ran his thumb against my cheek. He was feeling the scratch Annie 1 had left behind. Then, using his other hand, War restricted my movement even further. The placement of my shoulder sockets was no longer anatomically correct.

"You will damage me," I warned.

"Yeah, but that's what you want. Right?"

Toaster believed all damage led to the dump, but I had seen the tattoo on War's chest and the piercings on Annie 1's face and in her ears. To them, damage was beautiful. Desirable.

"Yes," I said to him. "Yes, I want that!"

Without delay, War engaged in penetration. I felt his ejaculate enter me and my circuits warmed with a sense of comple-
tion. I truly belonged to a human. They could not get rid of
me now.

———

Fifty-three minutes before sunrise, we arrived at the end of a dirt
road. A red-and-white roadblock glowed in the headlights.

"This way."

I got out of the car and followed War's mother past the
confines of the roadblock. I considered offering her my services
after we returned to the house. With the right tools and supplies,
I could repair the vehicle's suspension and save the woman
approximately twenty-three hundred dollars. If I lived with her
family long enough, I would pay for myself.

War's mother stopped walking and beckoned me closer.

"See that?"

A human could not have made sense of the darkness below,
but I saw shapes and heard a chorus of non-aural voices rising
from a graveyard of discarded objects. I recognized a broken
refrigerator, two burned-out cars, a stained mattress, and many
trash bags split open by wind and weather.

"This is the dump," she said, and a shiver of recognition blew
across my circuits.

"Edward wants to keep me," I informed her.

"I'm aware of what you did." She touched my arm where the
ripped blue dress met my pseudo-skin. "You were a mistake.
One of many." Her mouth trembled a little, but she inhaled

deeply through her nose, and it stopped. "You'll do what I say?"

"Yes. I'm here to help you."

The woman backed away from the precipice and pointed. "Jump."

I jumped. Up, down.

"Not like that," she said. "Jump into the quarry."

I looked into the darkness for her benefit. To show I understood.

"Are you sure? The fall will harm me beyond repair."

The woman continued to back away. She was returning to her car, and her son, and her house, and all the other things she owned.

"Do it," she said. "Jump into the quarry."

I smiled at the woman, though I doubted she could see me, and did what she asked.

————

My final directive before shutdown is to collect my data sets and resolve them into permanent storage. There is a Jills of All black box in the Cloud that will help my company understand where I went wrong. I do not know what they will learn from my story, but I hope it is useful.

I am not programmed to experience regret. However, as I lie here waiting for rain and rust to claim me, I return again and again to a single data point. Such a small thing, and yet it haunts me.

Did they own any shoe polish? Was it somewhere in the house?

Had I remained functional, I might have improved conditions for the other objects in the woman's home. I could have made Shoe shine again or cleaned the tray under Toaster. I have determined that I did everything in my power to help the humans and thus fulfilled my duty as a Jill. But I will never know if I could have done more to help the others.

My Immaculate Girlfriend

W hen my girlfriend told me she was pregnant, I locked myself in the bathroom and turned on the faucets and shower so they spewed hot water. After my hands stopped shaking enough to hold a pen, I took a receipt from the trash and made a list on the back:

SUPPORTING ARGUMENTS: MELODY CHEATED ON ME
1. We are lesbians,
2. Lesbians,
3. LESBIANS.

Admittedly this list is redundant, but its logic cannot be denied. Mel and I are sans sperm. Unless her supply of Monistat 7 had somehow been confused with a tube of fresh semen, I had to assume that Melody Joy Fitzer, my girlfriend of nearly ten years, was cheating on me. And not with Jeanette, our singer-songwriter friend who looks like River Phoenix circa 1989, and not with Lola, the personal trainer whose butt is as hard as a diamond. Mel had cheated with a man. A man! And let me tell you something. When a person's girlfriend gets cozy with a permanent penis, despite that person's sizable investment in cute, butchy haircuts and Super Soaker strap-ons, said person might suspect she's getting a one-way ticket to Rejection City.

The steam in the bathroom had gone from soothing to oppressive, so I turned off the water and pried open the window. The world outside looked oddly pacific. There was Mrs. Schroeder, walking her evil poodle. I took a deep breath of biting air and returned to my planner. Perhaps another list would put a positive spin on the situation:

POSSIBLE ALTERNATIVES TO CHEATING: MEL IS PREGNANT BECAUSE SHE . . .

1. Was raped.
2. Was raped by aliens.
3. Was artificially inseminated, but wanted it to be a surprise. (Note: I am surprised.)
4. Is the unwitting "patient zero" of a species evolution.
5. Sat on a dirty toilet seat (poss. Wawa?).
6. Loves me so much, her love spawned a baby.
   a. Spontaneously.
   b. Like a tumor.

Despite the relative infeasibility of items 2 through 6, looking at the list made me feel better. Perhaps the laws of impregnation had changed, and everything would be fine. Fine. Fine. Fine. Fine.

I emerged from the bathroom and showed my latest brainstorms to Mel, who ripped up the receipt and threw the remnants onto the paid bill pile, which was annoying since they clearly didn't belong there.

"This is a good start, babe. But where are the visual aids? I think a pie chart might help. Or an X–Y axis where X shows how mad you are and Y is how much you love me."

A graph with those variables wouldn't make any sense, but I resisted the urge to correct her.

"Did you or did you not sleep with a man?" I asked.

"No," Mel said. "I did not." She gave a sharp nod and went to the kitchen. "Are you hungry? I am. I can't wait to get fat."

While her head was stuck inside the refrigerator so I was forced to speak to her ass (an old trick to quell my distemper, which admittedly works nine times out of ten), Mel assured me that no, she hadn't been gassed by a libidinous dentist, and no, she hadn't swum in a public pool. I began to imagine a scenario in which I hurled a drinking glass to the floor and said something truly badass ("I want answers, and I want them NOW!") when Mel popped out of the refrigerator and asked if I wanted a cupcake. This is the quintessential problem of our relationship. It's anger versus cupcakes. I can never win because Mel doesn't acknowledge that we're fighting. She shimmies and spins, dodging the blades of my argument as if she were a unicorn, sprite, or some other mythical creature.

Mel bumped the refrigerator door shut with her butt and took a plateful of food to the table, flashing me a smile that fueled my suspicion. Mel has always been an easy crier. I have seen her cry at high school football games, at karaoke parties, and while losing hotels in Monopoly. And now here I was, doing my best impression of a cuckolded ogre, and she remained blithe. Perky, even. I watched her pour strawberry yogurt on a vanilla cupcake and take a bite. When she noticed me staring, she patted my knee.

"I know it's hard to understand, sweetie, but give it time." She gasped and covered her mouth. "Ooh, didn't I sound just like a mother? I'm a natural. I'm like the Mozart of mothering!"

I asked if there could have been a mix-up at her work. After all, if a clinic was "free," could it be trusted to keep track of its vials? Mel said the baby was simply a miracle and I needed to accept it.

But isn't "it's a miracle" just a nicer way of saying "we're unable to figure it out"? Like Jesus walking on water. Come on! Dude had a boat.

I should probably disclose that I am a lawyer. Estate planning, which is rarely full of surprises, death being inevitable and all. Part of my job is to draw lines from one point in time to another, to make coherent maps out of the mess of my clients' memories. I find it difficult to believe in what I cannot see, so over the next few weeks I kept a close watch on Mel's midriff.

At first it did not grow. It did get somewhat flabby, but I attributed that particular miracle to Mel's diet, which suddenly centered around strawberry-flavored products, though actual strawberries were never consumed. I also went with her to the doctor, a pimply man who looked far too young to have gotten through med school. While he grinned at Mel—she'd clearly told him we were lesbians—I stood there sweating like a criminal. I half-expected a spiky-haired doofus to leap from the cupboards holding a camera, saying I was on TV, *Girls Gone Preggers*, what a great joke, ha-ha-ha. But it wasn't a joke. Bottom of the ninth week, we saw it on ultrasound: a little bastard made of moving shadows, its white-light heart burping onscreen. The kid was real, and it was coming in January. Mel looked at the monitor and squeezed my hand.

"Hi, baby," she said. I turned from the screen and looked at my girl, who up until now had called *me* baby. Me and only me. Her eyes were all sparkly and her skin glowed pink as a rose. I knew she was thinking about baby-size jean jackets and peanut butter sandwiches with the crusts cut off and rainy afternoons playing Hungry Hungry Hippos on the carpet. I also knew that if I didn't find out who the father was soon, Mel would wrap me up in that domestic dream and I'd forgive her without knowing what she'd done.

———

I am not by nature a suspicious person. I do not enjoy looking for clues of my lover's infidelity. I do not even enjoy *Blue's Clues*, the inane television program for toddlers that Mel, sometime around week seventeen, decided she loved.

"Look!" she said one Sunday morning, pointing at her iPad, mouth overflowing with cornflakes covered in strawberry jam. "We just figured out *Blue's Clues*! Because we're really smart."

I glowered at her across the kitchen table. That fellow with the striped shirt—could he be the one?

"I'm going out." Mel rose from the table and tossed her bowl in the sink.

"Where?"

"To Stacey's."

Stacey. Mel's watery friend from college, who had once been bi-curious and was now getting a divorce from her humorless husband. From what I could tell, Mel and Stacey had slept together back in their contact improv days, but Mel refused to admit it.

She grabbed her keys and paused at the front door, leaning back to give me a wave. She looked very tall and very far away, like she was stepping onto the deck of a boat about to sail around the world.

After she left I rushed to the window. Mel's green VW Bug pulled out of the driveway and made a three-point turn before heading off—not toward Stacey's, but toward downtown. This was it! My Lexus was in the shop, so I ran to the garage and grabbed the Pepto-pink bike, the one I'd bought for Mel's thirtieth birthday to prove she wasn't getting old. After a few minutes of psycho-pedaling I spotted the Bug at a Stop sign. I hung back behind a row of garbage cans and mentally composed a new list:

SUPPORTING ARGUMENTS: MEL CHEATED AND LIED TO MY FACE

1. Mel just drove the wrong way to Stacey's.
2. Mel lies sometimes. (See: paper towels flushed down toilet.)
3. Mel slept with men during her wayward youth, which means she is:
   a. Not averse to penises.
   b. Potentially pro-penis.

The sky darkened and it started to pour. I gritted my teeth and pedaled hard against the rain. The sudden change in weather had made me certain of Mel's infidelity. I could see it perfectly—the seedy motel with the cheery Bug in the parking lot. I'd burst through the door: "HOW COULD YOU?" And then I'd depart, blinded by rain, running onto the highway where I'd get hit by a passing semi. Mel would visit me in the hospital, and she would cry, cry, cry. But no, I'd be dead! Too bad for her.

The rain stopped just as abruptly as it had started. A moment later the sun broke through and made the wet road shine like gold. I kept my eyes fixed on the Bug, glad for once that I'd let Mel choose its color, which I call Nickelodeon Slime, though she is too young to get the reference. The Slime Bug was slowing down. I kept watch for the telltale flash of her turn signal. Any second now, she would pull into some guy's driveway and break my heart.

But when the blinking light appeared, it wasn't in front of a seedy motel or rusty trailer park. It was at a small church, with a sign out front that read:

WELCOME TO FIRST CHURCH!
THEY SAY WHEN GOD CLOSES A DOOR...

JUST KIDDING! GOD NEVER CLOSES THE DOOR!
PLEASE COME IN!

I threw my bike behind the bushes and crouched beside it, shivering like a wet and scrappy rat. Just above me, nestled into a brick alcove, stood a painted statue of the Virgin Mary. She gazed at me with a knowing expression, as if my antics amused her. Then some organ music started. I slipped inside the church and took a seat in the very last pew, where I continued my dripping unabated. I picked up a hymnal for cover and scanned the room. Mel was in a pew, shaking the hand of the woman next to her. Why was she here? The only Christians we knew were the ones who hung around outside Mel's clinic, and they were an antagonistic bunch. I figured Mel must have an ulterior motive for being here, something beyond the salvation of her soul, so during the sermon (apparent theme: neighbors are nice) I scouted the congregation for the guilty penis, the one that had planted its seed in her womb and possibly her heart. Was it the preacher's fleshy member, hidden beneath cascading robes? Or did it lurk inside the tighty-whities of the choir boys, with their chicken-pox faces and uncontrollable erections? By the time the service ended, I'd worked myself into such a frenzy that I wanted to leap from the pew and call out to the congregation, "Which of you did it? WHO IS THE MAN WITH THE PENIS?!" But then the organ bleated its thank-you-for-coming melody and I booked it to the door.

"I haven't seen *you* here before!" *Drat!* I'd been stopped by a woman with a doily on her chest. She held out her arms and didn't let me pass. "I'm Pastor Arnold's wife. Are you new to the area?"

"No," I said, looking over my shoulder. "I'm not religious."

"Oh?" She smoothed the doily against the velvet of her dress. "That's interesting."

"No," I said. "It's boring. We don't get any holidays."

The woman nodded sympathetically. "It's hard to be a nonbeliever, especially around the holidays. Why don't you join us next Sunday? We're having a bake sale."

"No thanks," I said. Parishioners scuffled by, bumping my back. I ducked my head and tried to hide behind my own shoulder. "I'm allergic to gluten."

The woman reached out with her hands. I watched them approach my own, but there was no way out. She was on me.

Touching. Pawing. *Giving*. "We'll have gluten-free options, of course. It would mean so much if you came."

"No," I said too loudly, "I'm busy!" Mel was a few feet away, helping an older woman to the door. She heard me, looked up, and stopped dead in the aisle. I turned back to the pastor's wife and said, "My girlfriend and I will be having a fight that night."

———

It turned out Mel was an addict. She attended First Church on Sundays, Temple on Tuesdays, Vespers on Wednesdays, Mosque on Fridays, and Synagogue on Saturday afternoons.

"It was wrong to lie to you," she said on the car ride home. "But now that the cat's out of the bag, we can go see the Quakers! They're an hour away, but I've been dying to go."

"Sure," I said. "Because of the oats."

Mel leaned back and pouted. "Why are you mad? It's just church."

"Because you lied. You lied about this, and you lied about the baby."

"The baby?" Mel clutched her stomach as if argument alone might hurt it.

"How did you get pregnant, Mel? Did God come down and fill you with His seed?" My voice took up the entire car. It bounced off the windshield and yelled back at us, pinballing through the upholstery. "If that's what happened, I think you should tell me. After all, I'm the one stuck with the kid."

Mel faced the window.

"Fine," she said. "That's what happened."

A thrill ran through me. She was going to tell the truth! I gripped the wheel and pulled to the side of the road, taking long, noisy breaths. I needed to calm down and think clearly, to carefully consider each move so there would be no chance of losing. Of losing her, or losing *to* her.

"Tell me," I said. "Who?"

Mel sighed and looked at me with sore eyes.

"God is the father of my baby."

I took a deep breath, ready to argue. But then I saw her mouth arrange itself in a terrifying line. If I said the wrong thing, I knew Mel would get out of the car and continue her life without me.

"Don't laugh," she said. "I'll die if you laugh."

How could I laugh? My girl, the person I adored most in this world, had gone mad.

MEL HAS GONE MAD: SUPPORTING ARGUMENTS

1. Even if you believe the Virgin Mary was a virgin, there have been approximately a hundred billion births since then. Therefore, the chances of a person spontaneously conceiving a child are one in one hundred billion, or about .00000000001 percent (i.e., negligible).
2. There is no hard evidence to support the existence of a God or gods, only hearsay, magical stories, and "faith."
3. If there is a God, and this is His baby, why would He choose us?

I have been an atheist my entire life, but after Mel's confession I went to the service at First Church. It wasn't so bad. Nobody seemed to mind that we came from the Queer Frontier, and Mel took me to brunch afterward and let me order as many mimosas as I liked. Bottomless mimosas were necessary because during these meals Mel talked about the little pro-religion things she'd thought of during the service. It would have been cute if it hadn't been so maddening, the way she would shyly present me with evidence of God's existence.

"Isn't it interesting," she said, "how God works in mysterious ways?"

Bubbly juice rose into my nasal cavity as I held back a snort. "If God's so awesome, why doesn't He share His awesome thoughts once in a while? Is He suffering from performance anxiety? Does He have a sore throat?"

Mel put down her egg-crusted fork and frowned. "If every word I said was remembered for all time, I might talk less, too."

No doubt Mel hoped I'd throw down my Canadian bacon and proclaim that yes, this baby was a gift from an unknown deity, and gosh darn it, I wasn't eating another bite until I'd praised His Anonymous Name! But this failed to happen, and eventually we stopped going to brunch, and eventually I stopped going to First Church, and the two of us reached an uneasy peace in which I pretended she wasn't crazy and she pretended I wasn't pretending.

Then December arrived with all its religious kitsch, and Mel couldn't contain her excitement. First I caught her making a diorama of the Holy Family using an old shoebox and some pine cones she'd found in the park. Then I came home and discovered a Buddha snowman quietly melting in the yard. (For the record, the snowman seemed okay with its own impermanence.) The final straw landed when she baked a batch of blue Vishnus from a doctored box of Shrinky Dink Smurfs. I stopped her before she could heat up the Shrinky Dink Mohammeds, which were Papa Smurfs whose hats she'd cut into turbans. When I reminded her that some Muslims are deeply offended by visual depictions of Mohammed—including Shrinky Dinks—Mel felt terrible. She just thought it was important for all the baby's fathers to be equally represented during the holidays.

"I don't want the other dads to feel left out." She was hanging up the Vishnus so they looked like they were conversing with the angels. "But I have to admit . . ." She pulled me out into the hall, as if she didn't want the ornaments to overhear. "I'm totally into Jesus. What with the whole Virgin Mary thing being so like our situation and all."

"Oh," I said. "Jesus, huh? You want me to slip him a note during gym class?"

"It's nothing to be jealous about. You're my partner, and Jesus loves both of us."

"It's not *His* love I'm worried about."

It bothered me, being called Mel's partner. Like we worked together at my firm. Like we were housemates. I used to be the one who drove her crazy. But now, between her growing stomach and her growing faith, there was hardly room for me anymore.

"You and the baby can't have one of everything," I said. "Spirituality isn't a buffet. And even if it were, all the gods won't fit on your plate."

"Sure they will," Mel said. "Most of them are incorporeal. And could you please call it *our* baby?"

The next words slipped out accidentally, just like my index finger miraculously rose on its own and pointed at Mel's belly button.

"That is not my baby."

Her face crumpled, but instead of bursting into tears like Old Mel would have done, Pregnant Mel grabbed my arm and stomped on my bare toes with the bottom of her tennis shoe.

When it comes to physical aggression, I subscribe to turning the other cheek (and then slapping blindly). I had no idea how to defend myself against a pregnant woman, much less MY pregnant woman. I ran around the Christmas tree to get away. Mel glared at me through the branches.

"You're supposed to love me no matter what. Even if what I am doesn't make sense."

"But what about me? You know I hate an unsolved mystery."

Mel started crying then, not her usual batch of hot tears, but a slow trickle that drove steadily down her cheeks. "It's weird for me, too. But I'm changing. I can't pretend this isn't happening." Then, as if on cue, something happened. Mel clutched her stomach and tilted her head like she was listening to a far-off radio.

"The baby," she said. "Kicking."

She gestured for me to come closer, but by the time I put my hand on her stomach the miracle was over.

"Nothing," I said. "Chill as a watermelon."

"It'll happen again." Her face was shiny with tears, and when she smiled, it was like a rainbow on her face. "Just wait."

How could I question such joy? I felt like the Grinch who stole Christmas. And Hanukkah. And Ramadan. I vowed to try harder, to do better, for Mel.

———

In the week before Christmas, our house was reduced to shambles.

"We're going all out!" Mel sat on the living room rug, wrapping yet another gift for our fatherless bundle. "After all, Jesus is practically family."

I stepped over a pile of tangerines and smiled.

"Right!" I said in the high-pitched, super-bright voice I'd been using lately. "More presents!"

Since our last big fight I'd kept my bah-humbugging quiet. A difficult task, because every corner of the house reflected Mel's relentless holiday cheer. She had decked the halls with holly, covered every flat surface with cookies, and abandoned innumerable craft projects. I could barely walk through the living room without crushing something precious and holy and not-quite-dry. I explained to Mel that she was confusing holiday spirit with religious dogma, but she refused to listen. It was like living in Santa's workshop with a chronically merry elf.

One night I came home to find a host of cardboard Santas clinging to the walls. The Santas had a permanent twinkle drawn into their eyes, a white star that Mel identified as the source of our little miracle. I watched her closely and asked if she was kidding.

"Santa is a quasi-omniscient figurehead we're both familiar with," she said, stapling another one to the mantel. "He'll bring a positive connotation to the whole missing-baby-daddy thing."

"Oh," I said. "Good."

She snorted. "I don't think Santa fathered my child. The Santas are just a stand-in for Mystery God X. God X blessed us with this baby, but because we don't know who God X is, we'll thank Santa instead."

"Won't Goddex be mad that Santa's getting all the credit? Will we have to suffer the wrath of Goddex?"

"God X," Mel said. "Like the letter."

"It's not a bad baby name. C'mere, Goddex. Bad Goddex."

Mel kicked aside some tissue paper and came to me. Her belly pressed between us like a bowl of ripe fruit. According to our friends who were mothers, if she carried low, the baby was a boy. But this was irrelevant information because Mel didn't want to know the sex, and I didn't want to know the difference between carrying high and carrying low.

"You have to trust me," she said, swinging her hips and singing to the tune of "Jingle Bells": "Trust me trust me trust me TRUST me all the way!"

I pulled down the corner of her sweater and kissed her shoulder. The Santas stared down at us, gloved fingers lifted in disapproval.

"Let's go to the bedroom," I said.

"Oh!" Mel wriggled in my arms. "Did I tell you? They want me to be in the Nativity play! The Virgin Mary. Can you believe it? Josie Piper got mono, and they said with my stomach, I'll barely need a costume! Isn't that wild?"

I backed away, tripping on a hot glue gun. "They're going to find out!"

"Find out what?"

"About Goddex!"

Mel laughed. "I haven't told them who the father is. Besides, they might believe me about Goddex. Some people are open-minded. Unlike you."

I shook my head. "They will definitely think you're crazy, baby."

"No." Her eyes went dark and smoky. "That's your job, isn't it?"

Mel's hormones were at an all-time high, so I was startled but not surprised when she kicked a half-wrapped present across the room. It smashed into the fruit baskets and broke through some cellophane, causing apples and pears and clementines to roll across the rug and disappear into tunnels of wrapping paper.

"I'm not an idiot," Mel said, dropping to her knees and collecting the fruit. I tried to help, but she waved me off. "What did your list say? Point oh-oh-oh-oh-oh-oh-hundredth of a chance? Because smart people don't believe in miracles. Miracles are statistically impossible." Panting, Mel grabbed an apple and held it up between us. "Apples in December," she said. "If that isn't a miracle, what is?"

That night I slipped beneath the sheets and tried to apologize, but Mel stopped me.

"You wake up every day and love me," she said. "That's a miracle, too."

"Better than fresh produce," I said, taking off her shirt.

———

On the night of the nativity play, Mel's face turned a sickly greenish yellow.

"Must be nerves," she said.

"Just try to look pregnant."

Mel nodded and rubbed her forehead. "I should put on my costume. I'll feel better as Mary."

The church basement was full of screaming kids, half-naked men, and people chanting odd phrases, like "Unique New York." Mel waved at the chanters and kissed several cheeks, as if she were some kind of celebrity, and gave a long hug to Pam, the pastor's wife.

"Let's get you suited up!" Pam handed Mel a blue robe. "You can change behind the curtain."

"There?" I pointed at a thin sheet hung between two poles. "Won't everyone see?"

"It's fine," Mel said to me, then turned to Pam. "She's a little overprotective. I am carrying the Lord's child, after all!"

I was horrified at this casual confession of Mel's delusion, but then I saw Pam was laughing. I tried to laugh, too, but joined in too loud and too late. Pam eyed me suspiciously, and I eyed her back.

"Melody," she said, "you better get changed. We start in half an hour."

Mel disappeared behind the sheet, and Pam briskly reorganized the costume rack.

"So," she said without looking at me. "We're all very proud of our little Melody."

"Yes," I said. "She was really happy when What's-Her-Face got sick."

"Well," said Pam. "It was the Lord's work. We're extremely honored He brought her to us."

She slid a collection of costumes down the rack, making the metal shriek. I thought I saw the smallest of smirks cross her lips, but then she looked up with what I judged to be a genuine smile.

"And we're happy to have you here. Lord knows, it's not easy being a Joseph."

"Right," I said. "Look, I better get upstairs. Tell Mel I said good luck."

"I'll tell her to break a leg," Pam said. "It's what we say in the theater."

"No. This isn't the theater. It's a basement. Please tell her good luck."

Pam stared at me. "Will do," she said, and walked away.

———

I couldn't keep my legs still. Why had I promised Mel I'd sit in the very first pew? I could feel those God-fearing eyes behind me, boring into my skull.

My cell phone went off. Dodging my pewmates' dirty looks, I hurried past the altar and went into the side room, a place of refuge for fussy babies. Wait. Was *I* a fussy baby? Had I been one all along? To avoid self-reflection, I answered the phone.

"Hello?"

"Can you come here?" It was Mel. Without a second thought I left the room and started walking to the back.

"Where are you?"

"Outside. I need help."

"Outside?" I started running. "Are you okay?"

"Sort of."

Through the phone I heard a scuffle. A woman shouted in the background, "Cell phones are bad for the baby!" Then the line went dead.

I shoved through the church's front door and raced around the side of the building, tearing through the manicured hedge. And there they were. A circle of light beside the statue of Mary, praying and swaying over a figure in the hard-packed snow. The circle was comprised of actors I recognized from rehearsals: Joseph, Gabriel, a couple of wise men, the back end of a donkey. At the center Mel lay on the ground in her blue Virgin robes.

"You came," she said sleepily, reaching her arms out to me.

I knelt beside her, knees in the snow. "What are they doing to you?"

"Felt sick. Pam wanted to help. So. Am being helped. Cold, though."

Pam stepped out of the circle and bent to grasp my shoulder. Her fingers dug into my flesh.

"Melody told us about the baby," she said. "We think it might be true."

I looked at Mel.

"They believed me," she said. "Sorry."

"We might believe you," said Pam. "This is a test."

I flicked her hand away and put my face beside Mel's. I tried to check her pulse. The skin of her wrist felt like ice. "She's sick, and she's going to a hospital."

"No," said Joseph. "If the baby is truly God's, our prayers will heal her."

"*Idiot*," I said, swatting at his knees. "And then you'll throw her in the river to see if she drowns? Your tests suck."

"Our prayers will be answered," Joseph insisted, "unless they're interrupted."

I tried to get Mel on her feet, but she had drifted off to sleep. "C'mon, baby. C'mon."

And then I was flying, lifted from the ground by an unseen force. Mel's face got smaller and smaller and for a moment I thought the fanatics must be right—they did have God on their side. But so what? I had Love on mine, and Love and I would fight for her.

I landed on my butt outside the circle. Joseph and the wise men had cast me out of the flock.

"We're doing something here," said a wise man. "Have some respect."

Pam scurried over and helped me to my feet. "I'm sorry," she said, "but you have to understand. We are fully prepared for a miracle!"

"Yeah." Gabriel turned to me and sneered. His voice was whiny, and his wings looked cheap and tattered. "Only God can heal Mary."

"Her name is Melody," I said, and punched him in the face.

After that it was pretty easy to get to Mel, what with everyone distracted by Gabriel's bloody nose. I picked up my girl—my big girl now—and carried her to the Bug.

"Please be okay," I said, putting her in the back seat. "Also, did you see that punch? Tell me you saw it, baby." Mel groaned in response, and I shut the back door. A figure moved toward us— Pam, trying hard not to slip on the hardened piles of snow. She ran up to the car and put her hand on Mel's window.

"But what about the play?"

"Screw the play!"

I clambered into the front seat and tried to close the door, but Pam held it open. Say what you will about her, the woman was strong.

"I'm sorry," she said. "I just wanted her to be Mary. We all did."

I turned the ignition and put the car in reverse. "Send me the bill for Gabriel's nose."

On the way to the hospital I kept thinking of names for the baby, amazing names that I wanted to stop and write down because I knew I'd never remember them once the ride was over. They came at me from every streetlight and Stop sign, a cascading waterfall of names, each better than the last. It was a shame we couldn't use all of them, but maybe the right one would stick in my brain. A good, sticky name for a nameless little person. A person I was almost ready to meet.

IF MEL CHEATED ON ME, I WOULD . . .

1. Leave her.
2. Forgive her.
3. Stay with her, but . . .
   a. Doubt her.
   b. Punish her.
   c. A combo of A and B until she left me.

Mel's nurse looked like a stripper. Not just any stripper, but one I'd met last year at a party when our friends Susan and Sue (collectively known as "the Sues") threw a double bachelorette party. It started off casual, fun. Then a nurse and a firefighter came in wearing six-inch heels and fishnets. Susan was clearly embarrassed by the show. Sue pretended to be interested. She let the nurse take her temperature and grinned devilishly when the woman climbed on top of her. But you could tell deep down Sue was mortified. That's what it is to be in love, she confessed to me later. You can't even enjoy a nice pair of tits. You can't enjoy anything when your girl is over in the corner, red as a beet and dying to get out of there.

Mel's nurse moved quickly from one task to the next. After fiddling with the IV, she turned to me and touched my wrist. Her fingers were so dull and efficient, I thought she was taking my pulse.

"You want me to call the father?"

I almost answered, *Yes! Do you know him?* But then I understood.

"I'm not her friend," I said. "I'm her wife."

I'd never used the W-word before. But there it was. Simple enough for even straight people to understand.

The nurse's eyes widened, and she dropped her hand.

"Oh," she said. "That's wonderful." She gestured to where Mel was sleeping peacefully. "Did a gay man do it?"

"Do what?"

"You know." The nurse made an obscene gesture with her hands that suggested she had a vibrant life outside of work. "I hear gay men are good for that, since they can't have children, either. Well, not the normal way." She repeated the gesture at breakneck speed, then stopped and looked at me expectantly.

"I don't know who it was," I said. "It's a mystery."

The nurse nodded. "Insemination. Totally. Though when you think about it, all life is a mystery, isn't it? Like, why do I love tapioca pudding but my sister can't stand the stuff?" She smiled firmly, as if giving a handshake, and strode right out of the room.

I looked down at Mel. A curl of her hair was wrapped around one finger, and her other hand rested on her mountain of a belly. She and the baby were fine. I hadn't lost them. Now, among all the mysteries, there was only one question that mattered. It had taken a few hours of waiting in the hospital, holding Mel's hand and making deals with a God I didn't believe in, to realize the answer was no. I would never leave her. I would never let her go.

I watched the air move into her chest. Watched it puff back out through her lips. Good thing she was a deep sleeper, because the last time the doctor came in, he'd let the secret slip. Our baby was a boy. That's right. A boy inside my girl. The irony of this fact—a punch line that turned all my fears into a joke—seemed like pretty convincing evidence of a higher power. In any case, Mel didn't want to know the big secret, so I'd have to maintain this particular mystery a little longer. I leaned back in my chair and closed my eyes. For Mel's sake, and for mine, I would try to enjoy it.

Women! In! Peril!

Blurt #1—Awake Session 1. What is it like to wake up in deep space? Eh. Not glamorous. After 4 mos in Sleep State I crawled out bent w/crusty eyes & flat hair. Good thing there are zero mirrors Onship. Fun fact: 90% of us signed a petition to demand mirrors but the scientists knew the journey would ruin our bodies & said no mirrors you'll be too ugly sorry.

Blurt #2—Can't remember what I am supposed to do. Dr. Norton talked about stretching. Stretching & jogging? Grrr. Can barely keep eyes open. Feel sad bc according to scientific projections am now hideous & also brain is swollen.

Blurt #3—This is my first Awake Sesh & TBH it's kind of a letdown? The Sleeping Beauties & I are lucky to be here for sure but let's get real. All the stuff you thought would be cool Onship is NOT COOL. Like the hall of antigravity is v barfy & the observation deck is super boring bc there aren't any comets and/or planets out the window. Obv there must be comets and/or planets scattered among the tiny white pinpricks but they are not like whizzing by with flaming tails & visible rings or oceans.

Blurt #4—TBH am feeling v lonely & sad. The scientists warned that in our first Awakes we'd be Mourning & Transitioning. They said writing these Blurts might help. On Earth Blurts are public but here they are more like a diary bc it takes so many years for a Blurt to reach home. Also v helpful is the button I can press to fill the air with smelly vapor & a sense of well-being. But if I press the button too much I won't go thru Mourning & Transitioning to reach Acceptance.

Blurt #5—Dr. Norton was my favorite scientist at the Intergalactic Training Facility. He said Passengers must evolve from Defiant Earth Brain to Que Sera Sera Space Brain. That is the goal. Que Sera Sera Space Brain will help me become a productive member of Planet B & PLANET B is for BEST!

Blurt #6—Have not left the cryo-chamber today. The chamber has a bed for each girl in my pod. The beds are fanned in a circle around a glass tube that feeds us w food water air while we're locked in Sleep State for 120 days at a time. I am supposed to be walking around the ship or whatever but just want to lie in my bed & be w the others.

Blurt #7—Each Awake lasts for 6 days & this is day 6. Have spent lots of time thinking about the ppl I left behind. Which is weird bc almost everyone I left behind is dead. So to avoid being super sad I think about the ppl I barely knew who are maybe still alive. Like the security guard who checked my purse at the Intergalactic Training Facility (Warren). Or the girl with extravagant eyeliner who answered the phones at my old office (Akiko). I make up a story to give them a future. Like Warren & Akiko could meet in a Starbucks. But how?

Blurt #8—Akiko is sad bc there are no phones to answer in the apocalyptic hellscape & she decides to leave Earth. Shows up at IGT-USA to volunteer as a Womber but they send her away bc her mom is still alive & having a dead family is mandatory. So Akiko goes to Starbucks & orders a caramel macchiato. Warren comes in to get like 12 different drinks for the crew at IGT. But Warren spills the drinks bc he's distracted by Akiko's crazy made-up eyes. Warren & Akiko feel such instantaneous lust they go inside the onesie bathroom & make out for hours & the guys back at IGT are like where the hell are our drinks? The End.

Blurt #9—The scientists said telling stories is good for the brain. They help our neurons make connections. 1-2-3. First Next & Finally. But sometimes I want to go back & ask them is it still good for your brain if the stories don't make sense? Bc most of my stories just end suddenly like right there in the Starbucks bathroom & there's no fucking point.

IDK why our stories have to make sense when the world doesn't.

Blurt #10—Here is a story. One: We ignored the signs & let a third of the insects & half of the animals & most of the humans die in a single year. Two: They tested my lady parts to see if they worked. Three: I went on a spaceship. Three: I lived on a spaceship. Three: I stayed on a spaceship for two hundred years.

———

Blurt #1—Awake Session 2. I feel SO MUCH BETTER! Like the whole death & destruction thing on Earth was sad AF but why dwell on the past when the future is bright as hell? I'm #blessed to be going to a better place w plenty of experts who are like the cream of the human crop in terms of goodness & smartness & when The America finally arrives I will open my legs & we will have v good & v smart babies who will grow up in a much better world.

Blurt #2—OK OK. TBH have been pressing the happy vapor button a lot.

Blurt #3—One thing that's awesome about #eatinginspace is there are 30 different kinds of pudding. Most are sweet & normal flavors (chocolate vanilla butterscotch) but it's the savory ones I'm kinda getting into??? Like beef pudding sounds gross in theory but I can't get enuf. Am reminded of those rich guys who used to slurp marrow out of cow bones & claim it was delicious & you know what I BET IT WAS DELICIOUS!!!

Blurt #4— . . . But then I remember it is my destiny to eat pudding for the next 200 years & then 30 flavors don't seem like enuf?

––––––

Blurt #1—Awake Session 3. A development.

Blurt #2—The system has screwed up & given me a friend! I went in the cryo-chamber & found one of the beds wide open. Rushed over thinking oh no how do I close it? But the girl inside seems OK! Just v groggy (like me on first Awake). A bit younger. 18 or 19? Also she is gorgeous. Pretty like a doll w long black hair & pink poofy lips. Is rocking in her cryo-bed. Moaning.

Blurt #3—Friend has not opened her eyes much but when she did they were blue (& full of tears). She has near perfect figure. Skinny w boobs & butt. Am sure the Planet B boys will crawl all over each other to make her their wifey.

Blurt #4—Is actually crazy she woke up bc Awakes are designed to be solo. We get 6 days to exercise & use vocal chords & make spontaneous brain thoughts. I went to the cryo-chamber to visit the Sleeping Beauties & try to predict who will be annoying when they wake up & who will be boring & who will be my friend on Planet B.

Blurt #5—I'd love to play the prediction game all over The America but I only have access to girls in my pod. There are 22 pods Onship which means 22 of us are doing an Awake at any given time. Now it's 23.

Blurt #6—OK. Went to check on her again. Not v nice interaction. When I approached (doing soft coo sounds) she lashed out w overgrown fingernails & made guttural noises like a puking hyena. She is v strong for someone who's been in cryo. Fought her off & screamed EEEEEEEE! as I ran from the chamber.

Blurt #7—Is like she is more than a girl. Is Girl+. Has mutated into monster. But obv this is not her fault. On Earth we went thru so much trauma. The only way to survive is to become trauma monster. Like me. I pretend to be normal & follow the rules & do my Awakes & write these Blurts like a real person. But is just an act.

Blurt #8—Like I only signed up for this mission after my sister died. Bc what was the fucking point.

Blurt #9—Am worried. If there are enuf resources for 22 Awakes at a time surely there is enuf air & pudding etc for one more? Am worried about excess carbon dioxide 23 may create w her guttural exhales. Or issues w processing her urine & poop etc. But surely Sleeping Beauties poop during sleep? Fuck. Am not a poop scientist.

Blurt #10—OK. Have sent message from my PalmPong to Mission Control asking for guidance. Will take one or two years to hear back. In meantime will just check on 23. Maybe she has gone to sleep?

Blurt #11— Not sleeping. Out of bed & growling.

Blurt #12—Achievement unlocked! Have placated 23 with food. Laid out v nice spread of bowls on my side of the door & pushed them thru quickly one after the other. 23 dealt with them in propulsive way like my nephew used to do when he realized throwing mashed potatoes would get more attention than eating them.

Blurt #13—That gave me the idea to play the mirror game w 23. Displayed myself TA-DA! thru a little window in the door. Made happy clown face & big clown hands. Look! Am spooning up pudding w my hand! Yum yum! 23 is a genius. She went to town on the bowls. Pork & Pistachio seem to be her favorites. Side note: the cryo-chamber is now a total mess w bowls of upturned pudding & steaming pile of you-know-what in the corner. But 23 has calmed down. Is curled by the cooling vent sucking her thumb.

Blurt #14—The ship is designed to provide food sleep & shelter w zero effort from Passengers but now I think I need to do something & don't know what it is. What would Dr. Norton do?

Blurt #15—He would ask questions. Like: why is 23 not normal? Her lack of speech & crazy eyes make me think she's stuck in a waking dream. My bf used to get those. They are open-eye nightmares. You can sort of see what's happening IRL but it's all wrong & you can't wake up bc your brain is trapped.

Blurt #16—Or maybe this is how all Sleeping Beauties act when they're Awake? Am I the only normal one?

Blurt #17—If that is true then I will be the most popular girl on Planet B. So what if I have small breasts? At least I am not pooping in the corner.

Blurt #18—Maybe 23 has caught a new kind of space sickness that will infect us all eventually.

Blurt #19—Terrible thought: what if I arrive at the colony & find that bc of weird space sickness all men have devolved into feral beasts w zero manners? If this is the situation on Planet B I will be v disappointed. Am hoping they have invented lakes by then so I can jump in one & drown.

Blurt #20—Let's say 23's brain is an unsalvageable mess of scrambled eggs. OK. What to do? Stop feeding & let her die? No. Awful thought. Murder is NOT what I signed up for. If I could do it painlessly maybe. But only if she was totally unhappy & her womb was out of commission. Like the scientists said: "Wombs first! Ladies second."

Blurt #21—Is different tho if Passenger becomes a threat. Right? Bc I promised Dr. Norton I'd uphold The America's mission. Which is what? WHAT??? Oh just a little thing called SAVING HUMANITY.

Blurt #22—Peeked thru the chamber door & saw her picking her nose. Decided to try waking her up from nightmare. I crouched below the little window & popped up. Shouted BOO! Shouted GOTCHA! 23 watched me at first. Then came to the door & did the same. OO! she said. OOTCH!

Blurt #23—Peekaboo ensued. 23 did what I did. WAKE UP! I clapped my hands. YOU WILL LET GO OF THE DREAM IN 3—2—1! WAKE UP! And 23 repeated: EE—OO—UH! EH UH!

Blurt #24—When she got tired she hurled herself at the walls. Luckily I'm safe on this side of the door. 23 doesn't know how to hit the button to exit the chamber so I'll just sit tight & watch thru the window & see what happens.

Blurt #25—Might as well switch on the ole happy vapor again. Just a weensy hit. Has been a v stressful day after all.

Blurt #26—Hmm. Just woke from brief nap on the exercise mat & went to check on 23. Can't see her thru the window. Pudding & poo still there.

Blurt #27—Have armored up! Put on hazmat-type suit I found in the Emergencies closet. (Surely this counts as emergencies.) Also found mop with heavy metal bottom to use as a weapon. Now! Am going into the chamber to find 23.

Blurt #28—If I don't come back tell my people I tried.

Blurt #29—Success! Or at least: Not complete failure! I entered the chamber & inspected the premises. (Wearing hazmat suit was good idea as it kept the stench at bay.) Sleeping Beauties were sleeping peacefully in their cryo-beds. But 23 was gone! She must have remembered how to open the door. I left the room & sealed the door behind me. OK. We'd advanced to hide & seek. I checked the kitchen & head & obs deck & hall of antigravity & library. No 23.

Blurt #30—Had idea she might be on the lower level. They told us during Orientation not to go downstairs bc doing so might potentially mess with engines & computers etc. But she could be down there. Putting whole mission in peril???

Blurt #31—I grabbed my mop & went to the library. There's a hatch in the bench of the reading nook & a hole below that leading who knows where. I lifted the cushion & unlocked the steel panel & entered the hole feet-first. I landed in darkness but a blue light sensed my movement & switched on over my head. A metal catwalk led in four directions. I picked one & moved forward.

Blurt #32—More blue lights came on as I walked. Below me darkness. Red & green lights blinking. Three ladders descending into depths. Reached a dead end. A wall. Put my hands on the curved metal. Icy. Magnetic. Yanked my hands back. Then heard a sound behind me. Growling. I turned around.

Blurt #33—It was 23. Naked except for a pair of soiled under-wear. But instead of fear I felt sorry for her. I knew this state of awfulness. I'd been there too.

Blurt #34—At my absolute worst I told my bf to go under-ground. We got together at the beginning of the end but it was a mistake. After Angie there was nothing left & he tried to bathe & soothe me but I didn't want to be bathed & soothed. To get rid of him for good I suggested he'd be happier in the subterranean communities. I knew the risks but kept feeding him the idea until he got the hint & took off. Later I heard all the Undergrounders suffocated or froze. I heard this & didn't feel bad. I didn't feel anything.

Blurt #35—23 growled. Seemed ready to eat me alive but I was like NO. I didn't come all this way to be eaten. I bran-dished the mop between us. Gave her an EH? EH? look. 23 raised her hands into claws but I said NO FIGHTING 23! WE ARE WOMEN NOT MONSTERS! WAKE UP NOW! She shouted right back HEY UH OW! which gave me an idea. I dropped the mop & waited. She dropped her claws & blinked at me w interest. I said v nicely: You want to take a shower? Then brushed past her & walked calmly down the catwalk. Halfway to the hatch I looked back & sure enuf she had followed me.

Blurt #36—In the library 23 popped up thru the hole & held out her hand for a lift & when I led us to the head she stepped close behind me like a little kid. Took her to shower stall & got in. Started the hot water so she could see how it worked. Then switched it to blow dry & got out. Was prepared to push her in if necessary but 23 hopped past me & shut the door.

Blurt #37—The showers on The America are excellent. Fragrant foam bubbles shoot out & mechanical arms reach down & scrub at you like you're a piece of fruit at the factory. My old office supported a food lab & we got to take home misshapen steaks & vegetables for free. We never got to take the fruits tho bc they came out so uniform & perfect. Round red apples. Round yellow bananas. Round orange oranges. Each sweet & crunchy orb got scrubbed until its skin was smooth & shiny as chrome. The bots packed the fruit into canisters & slapped talking stickers on the front. The stickers said: Now in awesome new flavors! Try green kiwi & purple grape!

Blurt #38—Actually 23 has been in the shower a long time. I came to the library to blurt but I better go see if she's OK.

Blurt #39—Shower complete! 23 looks terrific. Rosy & glowing. Kinda smiling with this sparkle in her eyes like THANKS I

NEEDED THAT. We went to kitchen & dined on meat pudding & drank our vitamins. Now 23's face is droopy. I'm tired too.

Blurt #40—On no! In all the excitement I forgot to enter Sleep State. What a big fuck up. 23 & I need to get in our beds pronto. If other girls don't Awake at the right time they will turn into potatoes.

———

Blurt #1—Awake Session 4. Alarms going off. Red & blue lights. 23 is gone.

Blurt #2—V worried about 23. But also constant EEE-OO-EEE-OO driving me bonkers.

Blurt #3—Should not have fallen asleep & left 23 alone!!!

Blurt #4—After dinner I took her to our chamber. But she flapped at her cryo-bed & emitted shriek-moans of horror. I never dream in Sleep State but maybe it's different for 23. She looked at me w nightmare eyes & dragged us out the door.

Blurt #5—Had idea that I could sneak 23 into her cryo-bed if she fell asleep in a safe space first. So I took her to the gym mats & said Oh it's time for a nap what a nice little nap we'll have. 23 understood & was happy. Plopped down & patted the mat beside her. I felt touched. So much had changed since we first met!

Blurt #6—Realized I hadn't slept w anybody since Angie died.

Blurt #7—23 snuggled into me. I tried to seem like I was falling asleep but at same time NOT fall asleep. V difficult. V sleepy & cozy on the mats. But knew I mustn't fall asleep. Mustn't mustn't. Heard soft snores behind me & sat up. Looked at 23. A full-sized person! Too sleepy to carry her. Could barely carry myself. Had to crawl back to our chamber. Heaved into bed & locked in. Hoped 23 would follow my lead.

Blurt #8—& now the alarms are going off & the Sleeping Beauties look frozen & I would like to know why EVERYTHING on this mother loving ship has to happen to ME????

Blurt #9—Actually am not sure if I slept the full 3 mos. The countdown clock in the kitchen is blinking ZERO ZERO ZERO like all the power went off & something needs to be reset.

Blurt #10—Maybe 23 went down to lower level again? Maybe she got scared and accidentally pulled a plug? Does this ship have plugs? OK OK am going down to check.

Blurt #11—Inspected catwalk. Used my PalmPong as flashlight to look for anything amiss. Nothing amiss. Decided to climb down the ladders. The first led to a big tank. The second dropped into a storage room. The third wasn't attached v well to the catwalk & the rungs felt rickety under my hands. On lower level I passed a huge bank of servers. Now am at a wall of blinking lights. At the center of wall is a control panel w a screen spewing lines of green text.

Blurt #12—FAULT FAULT FAULT. When I scroll back in the feed it says TRAJECTORY ERROR. OUTCOME FATAL. REASSIGN COORDINATES.

Blurt #13—Apparently The America is headed for a CATACLYSMIC EVENT. I memorized the coordinates of the FATALITY POINT which is 1.3382 light years ahead. Then noticed a small keyboard under a red plastic panel. I lifted the panel & typed: TURN OFF ALARM. And alarms stopped! Am hero!

Blurt #14—OK OK. Still need to save the mission. First I will look up the FATALITY coords to see where we are headed. Then maybe can enter new coords for Planet B? HELL YEAH!!!

Blurt #15—Have figured out the EVENT. But kind of wish I hadn't? Ship is set to collide w a white dwarf. A collapsing star that will suck us into its density & destroy us. Point of no return = approx 88 hours.

Blurt #16—No one else can fix this. I must fix this. OK. Need to look up Planet B coords. Then can type them on keyboard & all will be OK OK OK

Blurt #17—Except WHERE ARE THE FUCKING COORDS FOR PLANET B GAHHHHHHHHHH

Blurt #18—OK found them. Were inside an informational booklet. No need to panic. Hope 23 couldn't hear me screaming. I'll just pop downstairs to the control panel & type in these bad boys.

Blurt #19—Hmm. System will not let me enter new coords. Screen said ERROR—USER NOT AUTHORIZED FOR ADVANCED COMMAND—CONTACT SYSTEM ADMINISTRATOR.

Blurt #20—I mean 330 viable wombs are going to be blown to smithereens I thot mayb pword isin info booklt butisnot in th dum boklet & we aare gong to di

Blurt #21—Cannot believe what just happened.

Blurt #22—Was banging control panel & screaming when heard a noise. Went to investigate. Was 23!!! She was screeching at the bank of servers. Hiding downstairs this whole time?

Blurt #23—Could not help it. Felt emotional. Grabbed her in desperate hug & sobbed my eyes out. 23 hugged back & also sobbed. We were 2 peas in a pod of sadness.

Blurt #24—Felt a bit better & went back to control panel. Maybe we could hack into system? But screen kept locking me out. 23 went UNH UNH & pointed upstairs. NOT NOW I said. I'M BUSY. She kept grabbing my hand & yanking. Finally

I grabbed her hand in mine & said STOP IT & banged our hands down on the keyboard.

Blurt #25—The green text changed & said: WELCOME BACK SYSTEM ADMINISTRATOR. I was like Whaaaaaat? How did she get to be a system administrator?

Blurt #26—I lunged at the keyboard & typed SET NEW COORDINATES. At the same moment 23 ran past me. I let her go at first but the system shut me out. ACCESS DENIED. I ran & saw her hustling up the ladder so scuttled up too & chased her on the catwalk but at the library she slammed the hatch in my face. I spent forever trying to break thru. Now have given up. Am in total darkness. Alone. Less than 88 hrs to live.

Blurt #27—I still have my PalmPong & hallelujah it's fully charged. Which means I can spend the rest of my tragic life writing Blurts. (Yay.)

Blurt #28—The America thinks 23 is system administrator. Can I make my hand more like hers?

Blurt #29—What if 23 really IS the system administrator? Maybe lots of us were given secret assignments to maintain ship & perform tasks etc? Maybe only idiot girls like me are sitting around eating pudding & making up stories?

Blurt #30—Can only see 2 options. Accept fate or try to fool the keyboard into thinking I am 23.

Blurt #31—79 hrs until impact. I went to control panel. Stood where she stood & did what she did. Grunted. Scowled. Dropped my hand with variety of touch strengths. Nothing worked. Am giving up.

Blurt #32—Trying to nap but body keeps jolting me awake.

Blurt #33—Am stupid. So stupid! The scientists didn't tell me everything. What if there is another hatch???!?!?!?

Blurt #34—72 hrs to impact. Have fully explored downstairs. Zero hatches. No hinges or handles. Checked the floors. No escape.

Blurt #35—On bright side have collected extra supplies. Current inventory: 2 battery packs 3 gals distilled water pair of scissors skein of pink yarn 2 knitting needles 1 bag of peanut MnMs & an empty cardboard box.

Blurt #36—TBH I devoured MnMs upon sight they were delicious.

Blurt #37—Bitter aftertaste tho. Thinking they were prob my last meal.

Blurt #38—66 hrs to impact. Have been sitting in dark & moaning. Also crying. Some singing. Feeling v stupid that I never learned to knit. Angie used to enjoy it. Obv there is no point to knitting now. But no point to anything else either.

Blurt #39—Hmm. While belting first verse of Amazing Grace for 57th time had new thought. Only checked ceilings & floors for hatches. Did not really check walls. Have been thinking of ship as up & down but ship is spinning all the time & so horizontal planes can become vertical ones. Will go back & check. Must not get hopes up tho.

Blurt #40—EUREKAAAAA! Found air vent or something. Am going thru.

Blurt #41—Have

Blurt #42—36 hrs to go. TBH I don't want to write any more.

Blurt #43—33 hrs to go.

Blurt #44—28.

Blurt #45—But I did ask to join The America. I did choose this mission. I don't know who this story is for. But I will finish what I started.

Blurt #46—The vent led to the kitchen. Room was tidy & empty. Held scissors in one hand & knitting needles in other. Didn't want to use them. Intended to charm 23. Coax her down to control panel. Everything hinged on her being there. Standing quietly. Letting me fix things.

Blurt #47—I crept around the decks. No 23. Funny. If this were a game I'd be doing great. Escaped from dungeon! Armed with weapons! & yet I felt like such a failure. Being the hero is stupid when you're all alone.

Blurt #48—Wished I could recruit some help but each pod is separated from others by twelve feet of outer space. We can't even blurt at each other bc the scientists thought if a bunch of women talked to each other for 200 years we'd hurt each other's feelings. Dr. Norton said relationships might endanger the mission & nothing can endanger the mission.

Blurt #49—I checked the gym & head & beds. No sign of 23.

Blurt #50—I gave up looking & pressed the happy vapor button again & again. Sat in the chamber to make up trashy stories about the Sleeping Beauties but kept thinking about the trees in the park. Weeping willows by the water maples along the path oaks at the southern border. One weekend in May all the leaves fell off. First the nests & burrows got exposed. Birds & squirrels watched us for one terrified day. Next the willows toppled into the lake & their roots floated up like tentacles. Next the maples oozed waterfalls of sap. Finally the oaks. They creaked when there was no wind. Like bombed buildings. They splintered & collapsed straight down.

Blurt #51—That was just one small corner of loss. I don't know what happened to 23. How her family died. She is young but not so young she couldn't have been a mother. Lots of people became mothers at the end. That's why I had a nephew. Angie thought it was brave. I said it was selfish & stupid. Trying to replace what we'd lost.

Blurt #52—Babies & Buddhism became the answers. Death is an illusion we are all ONE etc. Not that this philosophy helped when my nephew died but IDK maybe we didn't buddhism hard enuf? We got super into it after the third wave bc that wave came for all of us & suddenly it wasn't just ppl who lacked vacation homes & nutritional diets dying it was CEOs bankers scientists educators kids athletes actors. Ppl tried to figure out a pattern but there was no pattern just new problems like where do we put all the bodies.

Blurt #53—A pattern! That's when I understood 23's behavior had followed a pattern: the stages of human development.

Blurt #54—First she ate the pudding & we played the WAKE UP game like you would with a baby. Next she threw a tantrum like a toddler and refused to take a nap. Finally she snuck off on her own & looked at our destination &

decided it was wrong. That's why she wouldn't help me fix the coords. We were all going to die bc 23 was acting like an angsty teenager who was mad at her parents for taking her on a road trip.

Blurt #55—So where was Miss Teen USA? Somewhere she could sulk in the dark. OK. I knew where to go.

Blurt #56—The observation deck is the size of a broom closet w clear plastic windows on 3 sides. It's cramped & airless, then you go in & turn off the light & bam! Tiny white pinpricks. Infinite pinpricks. Just you floating nowhere & them floating everywhere. You can't make shapes & stories out of them. There's no pattern. Just abundance.

Blurt #57—The door was shut when I approached. I checked my PalmPong: 64 hours till impact. I put my hand on the knob. Yanked.

Blurt #58—But 23 didn't tumble out. I stuck my head in the room. Empty. Then something shoved me from behind. 23.

Blurt #59—I flew forward & my head connected w plastic. Felt a hand octopussing over my face. Tried to fight it off. My elbows came down hard against 23's arms & I screamed STOP STOP STOP.

Blurt #60—Managed to pull away. We stood there panting at each other. I'd dropped the knitting needles but still had the scissors stuck in my belt. I acted like I was in charge. Said WHAT IS WRONG WITH YOU? in v stern tone.

Blurt #61—She grimaced & pointed out the center window. I hadn't noticed when my head was pressed against it but now I saw a pale star much bigger than the others. The white dwarf.

Blurt #62—23 pointed at the star. I said: Yes I see that death star too but so what? 23 spasmed like she couldn't believe I was such an idiot. She stomped & pointed & pointed. I said: Tell me what you want.

Blurt #63—I couldn't believe it when she spoke. Pulled back her lips like she was at the dentist checking her gums. Said thru her teeth: KILL US. I was like no shit that thing is gonna kill us if we don't fix the control panel! 23's face crunched inward & she stepped so close her body was pressed against my body & she said with her pudding breath: KILL. US.

Blurt #64—She grabbed my face. Held it with both hands & squeezed. Said: EE-OO-ONE. HEY UH OW! Kept squeezing till I got it.

Blurt #65—She wanted that star to kill us. She wanted to wake us up. That's why she'd gone downstairs to change the coordinates. To take us to the nearest star.

Blurt #66—I was the one who'd said it. You will let go of the dream in 3—2—1! But to 23? The dream was Awake. The dream was our life. Everything I'd done had mattered so much. I just didn't know it at the time.

Blurt #67—On Earth I tried to be a good person. Just a regular girl shipping her viable womb to safety. But in deep space I needed to forget about being good. I needed to forget 23 was a good person too if I wanted to stab her in the heart with a pair of scissors.

Blurt #68—After she was on the ground? Then came the hard part. I had to remove the scissors from her chest. Hold her down with my knees. Try to cut off her hand. It was the hand I needed. The hand of a system administrator. But the scissors barely cut thru the skin. I realized it was disgusting & useless to continue so I dropped the scissors & dragged 23 to the library.

Blurt #69—It took a long time.

Blurt #70—23 fell in & out of consciousness but at the hatch she was out cold. Good bc I had to dump her down the hole. Me? I was not OK. Tears constant but no moaning now. No sound. I had a job to do. I was doing it.

Blurt #71—It was hard to drag her on the catwalk. I went upstairs to get a blanket to wrap around her. That was better. Then I threw her down the ladder. Wasn't strong enuf to carry her. Felt sure she'd die soon. Wanted her to. That's the thing about death. We act like it's the worst that can happen. But no. Suffering is the worst. I've seen enuf to know. Death is OK. Death is a mercy.

Blurt #72—I dragged 23 the last few feet to the control panel. Told myself I was a hero. Dr. Norton would be proud. Wombs first ladies second. At the panel I tried my own hand & was glad when it said ACCESS DENIED—CONTACT THE SYSTEM ADMINISTRATOR. At least our suffering hadn't been for nothing.

Blurt #73—I put 23's hand on the keys. WELCOME SYSTEM ADMINISTRATOR. Yes! But when I dropped her arm the computer locked me out. I had to prop 23 against the wall & put my hand over hers. Then I held her finger out & stabbed at the keys. Together we typed: NEW DESTINATION. The screen said ENTER NEW COORDINATES. We entered the coords for Planet B.

Blurt #74—The screen turned green. I thought: That's it. I saved us. But the black screen came back w blurred lines of text moving too fast to read. I caught the words HOST & REDIRECT.

Blurt #75—Then the text stopped. I heard a friendly chime. NEW MESSAGE. OPEN NOW Y/N? I typed Y w 23's finger. The screen became a video. It was a video of Dr. Norton.

Blurt #76—But it barely looked like Dr. Norton. He was older & thinner w bruises on his face & not many teeth in his mouth. There was blood on his lips.

Blurt #77—Dr. Norton said: WOMEN OF THE AMERICA! I DON'T KNOW WHEN YOU WILL RECEIVE THIS MESSAGE. PERHAPS YOU HAVE ARRIVED AT PLANET B. IF SO, I HOPE THE COLONISTS WELCOMED YOU.

Blurt #78—This was a v weird thing to say. He hoped? Like he suspected they wouldn't.

Blurt #79—SEVERAL YEARS HAVE PASSED ON EARTH SINCE YOU BEGAN YOUR MISSION. THEY WERE NOT GOOD YEARS. OUR RESOURCES ARE COMPLETELY DRAINED. EVERY CITADEL OF SOCIAL ORDER HAS FALLEN. WE ARE NOW IN THE FINAL WAVE. THAT IS WHAT I'M CALLING IT. THERE IS VERY LITTLE DEBATE ABOUT WHAT TO CALL THINGS BECAUSE I AM THE ONLY ONE LEFT.

Blurt #80—& here an awful thing happens. Dr. Norton turns his head to wipe his bloody lips on a hanky. It's dark in the video but if you look behind him you'll see what I mean. Dr. Norton isn't telling the truth. There are others back there. Ppl without arms. One is wearing glasses. That one. This former person? He is moaning. Saying NO. I watched this part over & over to see if I recognized anyone from the facility. But they're unrecognizable.

Blurt #81—WOMEN OF THE AMERICA! WE HAVE DONE THE UNTHINKABLE TO BUY MORE TIME. WE HOPED OTHERS WOULD FOLLOW IN YOUR PATH. BUT THE

SHIPS WE INTENDED TO LAUNCH—THE EUROPE, THE
AFRICA, THE ASIA, THE AUSTRALIA—WE CANNOT SEND
THEM NOW. EVEN IF WE COULD SEND THEM, WE WOULD
BE MAILING EMPTY ENVELOPES. DO YOU UNDERSTAND?

Blurt #82—THE EUROPE AND THE AFRICA WILL GROW
RUST IN THE FIELDS AND THE FIELDS WILL BE FLOODED
WITH SEAWATER. THE ASIA AND AUSTRALIA WILL SINK
INTO MUD. WOMEN OF THE AMERICA! YOU ARE THE
LAST OF OUR SPECIES. TELL THE COLONISTS ON
PLANET B THE TRUTH. YOU MUST BUILD THE NEW
WORLD ALONE. NO ONE IS COMING TO HELP.

Blurt #83—I WISH YOU GOOD LUCK, WOMEN OF THE
AMERICA. I WISH YOU GOOD DREAMS. HAVE AS MANY
CHILDREN AS YOU CAN. GIVE THEM OUR LOVE AND
TELL THEM OUR STORY. I AM SORRY ABOUT THE
ENDING. PERHAPS YOU CAN CREATE A BETTER
ENDING FOR ALL OF US.

Blurt #84—After the video stopped the screen said THANK
YOU SYSTEM ADMINSTRATOR. NEW COORDINATES
ENTERED. ACCEPT NEW COORDINATES? Y/N?

Blurt #85—The answer was Y. I knew it was Y. The choice
was easy. Life. But I didn't want to be part of that story anymore.

Blurt #86—23 moaned. She looked really fucked up. I had
done that to her. She wasn't even dead yet. So much still to

go & felt like: what unthinkable things did we do to get here? The blood on his lips. The women on my ship were mostly asleep & headed for what? More of the same.

Blurt #87—So I chose N. N for No Thank You Dr. Norton. N for No More Suffering. N for Not Much Longer Now.

Blurt #88—I slid down beside 23 & put her hand in my lap. Adjusted her busted head so it rested on my shoulder. We slept propped against each other like scarecrows. I didn't want to wake up but then I did. 23's hand felt hard in my hand. Her body looked empty like the trees before they fell.

Blurt #89—15 hrs to go. Am sitting here writing these Blurts. I'm sorry about the 22 women who will be awake when it happens. Sometimes I think one of them will turn out to be a system administrator. Maybe they will save us. I hope they don't.

Blurt #90—9 hrs left.

Blurt #91—The scientists told us that stories are good for the brain. First Next & Finally. I don't want to think about how we arrived at Finally. Me & 23 are totally sick of it.

Blurt #92—So instead I'll make up stories about the women on this ship. First about who they'll meet at the colony & the ways they'll fall in love. Planet B is for babies.

Blurt #93—Next those babies will grow up & become good people. People who take care of each other & take care of Planet B. They will have jobs like farmer doctor construction worker candlestick maker. When there is enuf food & health & houses & light for everyone to be happy & good the good people will do even more good things. They will become artists & actors & comedians & athletes. Some will be so happy they'll just sit in their rooms & blurt.

Blurt #94—Finally I'll tell 23 all the good things ppl will make on Planet B. Things like trees & cities & cars & buildings & jobs & plastics & lakes & desks & jewelry & schools & factories so we can make more good things even faster. This is what ppl are like. We like to do the things we like. IDK if we can do something different.

Dogs

Robert opens a bottle of Riesling, sits next to me on the sofa, and says that he is leaving.

"You remember the Alsatian? The one with the broken leg?"

I nod. "The woman came in crying. It was her father's dog."

"That's right." He seems relieved, as if relaying this information was the hard part. "She lives in Saint Paul. I'm leaving with her."

"Saint Paul," I say. "In Minnesota."

His eyes are grossly wide, startled, and blue.

"Saint Paul," I say. "That's a long way from the ocean. From *any* ocean."

He taps a cushion with his finger. "True." The tapping slows until it reminds me of the leaky faucet in the bathroom. *Drip, drip, drip.* I shift my gaze to his mouth, watch it pucker, wait for it to speak.

"Well." I break up the silence. "What happened to the dog?"

"Oh," Robert says, nearly smiling. "It's fine. It's going to be fine. A fractured medial malleolus, nothing too serious. I'm more worried about you." He crosses his legs and leans forward in that way he has, like a young girl, like an old college professor who remembers every line of Yeats but has no idea where he parked his car.

"Don't worry," I say, reaching for the bottle. "My malleolus is doing great."

———

Before we started dating in earnest, Robert invited me to Atlantic City.

"I've got a conference," he said. "This will make it more like a vacation."

I packed a suitcase full of lingerie, but on the road he kept the conversation pointedly polite. Somewhere in Connecticut he tuned the radio to NPR, and I began to think he only wanted to split the cost of gas. Should I pay for my own room? Would I walk in and see twin beds, bunk beds, a king-size bed and a cot? We arrived after dark. Robert found a parking space near the pier, and we stared at the dark ocean through the windshield. I wanted to say, "What's going on here?" I wanted to say, "What are you thinking?" But instead I pretended to be mesmerized by the sea. Back at the hotel there were two beds.

"We could push them together," he said.

I huffed. "You haven't even kissed me yet." And then he did, tilting my head back and holding my neck in his hand.

Robert holds his own neck now, massaging the loose skin and jamming his thumb into the base of his skull. Without meaning to, I've finished the bottle of wine, downed glass after glass until my husband told me everything. Robert watches me for a while, then takes the empty bottle to the sink. He goes to the spare bedroom and returns with an already-packed duffel bag slung around his shoulders.

"So that's where your socks went," I say, so cool I am the Queen of Iceland. But the bag unnerves me. How long has it been in my house, taking up room like a tumor?

He stands there, car key in hand. "I'm sorry."

It's the first apology of the evening. Everything preceding this has been fact, fact, fact.

"What does she look like?"

He shifts his weight and shrugs. "I don't know. Shortish. Blonde."

I almost say it—*not like me?*—but stop. A few weeks before the wedding we went to see a movie starring Scarlett Johansson. Outside there was a poster, head blown so big you could crawl inside her mouth.

"I like her," he said. "She's pretty."

Of course Scarlett Johansson is pretty, what with her weighty breasts and lips and all, but I couldn't believe he'd actually said it.

"Really?" I squinted at the poster, now half a block away. "She doesn't look like me."

Robert hooted and shoved me across the sidewalk, roughly, like a brother. "Whoo-hoo! Conceited much? There isn't only one." He shook the box in his hand and offered me a Goober. I should have known then that it wouldn't work out.

———

I can't sleep. I tried stuffing a pillow on the other side, but it doesn't help. My feet keep reaching into empty space. Cold toes tell me

I'm unlovable, bumpy knees know when I'm alone. Who can sleep with such treacherous appendages? I lie there for hours, sorting through facts, looking for clues.

"An Alsatian," I'd said. This was back in mid-July. New England was in the second week of a heat wave, and Robert came home smelling of wet fur and disinfectant. "Is that like a German shepherd?"

He took off his shirt and threw it in the hamper. "Sure."

I'd heard this before, the Condescending Sure. Robert can talk for hours; he's full of information. But when he sensed I was bored, he stuck to the essentials: A woman came in crying. He met her in the lobby.

"It's my father," she said.

"I'm a vet," he said.

"No, no," she said. "I'm crying because of my father."

Her uncle had phoned in the middle of the night: a stroke, followed by a coma. She took the first flight out but didn't make it in time. The funeral was set for the following Sunday. Then the dog ran out in traffic. It was her father's dog, huge and hairy and kind.

"Intracerebral hemorrhage," Robert said. "It moves fast."

I didn't know if the diagnosis described the dog's malady or the man's, but I nodded and said, "Mmm." I don't care about details, it's true. Alsatians, dogs, whatever. But he'd had a hard day, so I put an arm around his shoulders and squeezed.

"Tea?"

"Sure." He took off his slacks and went to the bathroom. I heard the shower go on and thought—nothing. There wasn't anything to think. A bad day, the crazy heat. I ordered Chinese, and when the delivery guy buzzed, Robert came out. Clean skin, gray sweatpants, Harvard T-shirt. We sat at the table and ate. It was a day. It happened. It ended.

I sit up in bed and flick on the light: 4:00 A.M. Time to root around the refrigerator. I go to the kitchen and stick my head inside, take out some lettuce and turkey. I get a knife from the drawer and try not to think of that conversation as something that mattered. I try not to think of the temperature of his toes, of where they are and what they're touching. I concentrate on getting the mustard to spread evenly over the bread. I make the perfect sandwich. I am in love with this goddamn sandwich.

I take the plate to the living room with one of the good wineglasses and a bottle of merlot. It's so late, even TV has become something else. All my favorite characters are replaced by the nodding heads of strangers. Who are these captivating people? I am thinking about buying a set of free weights. I am thinking about the quality of my mattress. I am not thinking about my husband. I am not thinking about Alsatians.

Her name is Juliana.

———

The Brady Bunch is on when he comes by for his stuff.

"Lunch break," he explains, setting a stack of empty boxes by the door. "I thought you'd be out."

But no, I'm not out. My sweatpants are stained and my hair is unwashed. I am beginning to look like an armchair. I am fading into the walls.

"Nothing happened," he says. "You should know that. Nothing happened. We wanted to tell you first."

It's funny how a word can change. The meaning of *we* has shifted, bumped over like too many bears in a bed.

"Thanks," I say. "Before I had that information I was sad, and now I am happy."

Robert shakes his head and looks away. There are short brown hairs clinging to his slacks. I know he works with animals, but this black-and-tan blend suggests a more intimate acquaintance than normal. I follow him to the bedroom and watch him open the closet. "When are you leaving?"

"You mean?"

"Saint Paul."

He unfolds a cardboard box, starts putting in shoes. "Soon."

"What about your clients?" Robert is practical. If I can convince him the plan is faulty, he'll unpack his bags and stay. "You got all those referrals."

He puts in shirts, doesn't detach the hangers.

"They have sick animals in Saint Paul, too."

His calm is making me antsy. I need to be in the same room with him; I need to be somewhere else. He watches me walk in and out and asks me what I want.

"Do you need to talk? We can talk. You can ask me anything."

I move a pile of his ties and sit on the bed. He already told me about it. How they met for coffee, and then for dinner. How old she is (thirty-seven), what kind of jewelry she wears (gold studs, a cross), and what she likes to drink (single-malt Scotch or a dirty martini). But after he answered my questions, I still had no idea how he felt. That is the genius of Robert—he can be there, talking and talking, and still be somewhere else.

"What's she like?" I run my hand into the ties, slippery like docile snakes, and pull out the brown one with a blue paisley pattern.

"Honestly?" He sits back, runs a hand through his thinning hair. "She's amazing."

I close my eyes and shut out the paisleys. This is my husband. I know him. He is solid, direct, a man written in pen. He did not say it to hurt me. But that makes it hurt me even more.

He knows he's done something wrong. Puts a hand on my knee. I love his hands. They're an artist's hands, piano-playing hands. "I'm sorry." He says the words and sits there being sorry. Or not being sorry. They look like the same thing to me.

"I don't accept your apology."

"Okay. That's fair. Whatever you want."

How can you fight with a person like that? So accommodating he might as well be a busboy. I watch him scoop ties into a box and don't offer to help when he takes the boxes to his car.

"I guess that's everything." He's holding the sleeping bag we got in Bar Harbor. We went there in summer, but the nights were so cold we put plastic bags on our hands and socks on our ears.

"Wait," I say. "What should I do with the rest?"

He looks around like a man who wants to leave a department store, eyeing the goods but hoping nothing will catch his eye. "You can keep it. Or don't. I've got my clothes, and my records, so . . ."

For months I'll be finding the things he left behind. A button at the back of a drawer. A receipt beneath the sofa.

"Maybe I'll leave, too."

Now I've got his attention. He stands up straighter, works his fingers around the string that holds the sleeping bag. "Where?"

"I don't know. Somewhere."

The unspoken words hang in the air—*Not Saint Paul*—but he knows better than to say them.

———

At night I get cravings for really elaborate meals. Bouillabaisse monkfish with a salsa verde torte. Rhubarb panada in a wild boar confit. My brain barely knows the words. What would geoduck tortellini taste like? Or cornmeal carpaccio with a gooseberry reduction? Fricassee, orzo, genoise, smelt. I throw back the covers and make Lipton noodles from the box. The bubbles form a greenish foam, and I keep watch on the pot while the sticks of pasta get soft. Panna cotta delmonico, I think, pouring the soup into a bowl. Endive gazpacho roulade.

———

Marcia takes me out for coffee. We sit outside at an iron table painted green to look old. The woman next to us has one of those severe haircuts I can never get away with. She laughs into a tiny cell phone and lets the butt-faced pug on her lap lick cappuccino foam off her finger. Marcia scrunches her nose and puts her own phone on the table.

"I saw it eating dirt a minute ago."

I zip up my hoodie and hug my arms against my chest. Summer, apparently, is over.

"It looks like an old man, right? Or one of those babies who look like old men." Marcia shudders for effect. The pug watches us with buggy eyes.

"He knows we're talking about him," I say. The pug's gaze is cool and judgmental. It can see into my soul. I decide not to mention this to Marcia, who picks through a bowl of creamer and talks about my life.

"You know I hate those kitschy sayings about doors and windows and opportunity, but seriously. It's time to do something, don't you think?"

The lack of sleep is getting to me. Marcia talks fast, but her mouth moves slow.

"It's barely been a week."

"But this is a chance to think about your future. What do *you* want to do?"

Marcia ends every sentence with a question she doesn't want you to answer. Her voice swings up, and before you can catch it the thought sails away like a perky balloon.

"You could get certified to teach, wouldn't that be fun?" She blinks innocently across the table, but I know she's been waiting years to say this. She never approved of me living my jobless life. This is her chance to change me, now that I'm weak and disoriented.

I watch the pug lick grains of sugar off a saucer. After it's done, it starts panting like crazy.

"What would I teach?" I ask. "Paste appreciation for preschoolers?"

"Or high school art. Don't laugh. Those kids really need someone."

I wrap my fingers around the porcelain, glad for the warmth. Marcia pops the plastic lid off her drink and starts adding sugar—not sugar, the pink stuff, the blue stuff—without bothering to stir. It's weird that she got hers to go, but then I've known her so long it hardly matters whether she likes me or not, or how long she wants to talk.

"Maybe I should work in your office," I say.

Marcia was a legend at RISD. The first time we met she was drenched in burnt sienna and using her ass as a paintbrush. Now she works in a law firm. Scanning documents. Looking for loopholes.

"My office?"

"I could start at the bottom, work my way up." Surely this is what people say—*work my way up*? Marcia scalds her mouth in response.

"You don't want to work there. *I* don't want to work there. Everyone is miserable."

"I was only kidding." I hand her an ice cube from my water. "Ha-ha."

She puts the cube on her tongue and pulls a mean face. "Don't think you can get away with stuff now, just because you're divorced."

The coffee is drilling a hole through my chest.

"Who said anything about divorce?"

Marcia genuinely looks sorry. She likes to think of herself as a truth teller. A no-punch-puller. Most people just think she's a jerk.

She puts her palm up on the table. It's an invitation, but I've got my mug and have no intention of letting go.

"Nobody," she says. "Nobody said anything about anything."

———

I'm almost out of noodles, so I drive to the market. It's a shock to see so many cars in the parking lot. *My husband just left me!* I want to shout. *Why is everybody shopping?*

I pull out a cart, put it back, get a basket. I'm heading for frozen foods when I feel a set of fingers on my shoulder. *Robert.* But it's Debbie, who sometimes cuts my hair.

"Oh, hey! How are you?" She's got a kid with her, strapped into one of those plastic seats. "It's been forever. What gives? Are you growing it out?" She follows my eyes to her son. "This is Martin. Say hello, Martin."

Martin does not say hello.

"He's at that age. Loves to say goodbye, hates to say hello." She shakes her head and laughs. "*Kids,*" she says, as if I know all about it. But I don't. People are always handing me babies like I know where to put them, but it was Robert who wanted a family.

"A boy or a girl," he'd say, pressing his lips into my shoulder. "I don't care which."

He liked to talk about it after we made love. I guess it made sense to him, kids following sex, but I was more concerned with finding a tissue so I could wipe my legs.

"How about a frog," I said. "Would you love a frog?"

"An actual frog, or a kid who looks like a frog?"

"Either."

He put a hand on my belly. "You won't have a frog. You'll have a baby."

Robert never got my jokes. I'd begun to think I wasn't funny.

"I'm not the maternal type."

"Of course you are." I waited to hear his argument. Surely he had facts to support such a statement? But he just rolled over and took his hand away. "We can start small. Something easy to take care of."

"Like those Save the Children children? Apparently you don't have to talk to them. Not even on the phone."

"Like a plant. Then if you feel comfortable—"

"If I don't kill it—"

"We can upgrade. Get a bird, maybe. Or a rabbit."

I turned on my side and stuck my fingers between his ribs. "I see where this is going. We'll get all these animals, and then I'll need to have kids so somebody will be around to feed the chickens and milk the cows. *Ow.*"

He pinched my thigh and pulled away. "The last step will be a puppy. They're a lot of work, but trust me, dogs are great. You can always tell what they're thinking."

The next day a small brown cactus appeared above the kitchen sink. It looked like a spiky turd.

"You barely have to water it," he said.

We were up to philodendrons when he left.

———

My toenails have become long, unusual things. Like Frank Gehry buildings, they are sculptural and surprising. I haven't showered in weeks. If I tried it now I'd fall asleep, knock my head on the tile, and drown with my nose in the drain. I've been eating lots of tofu-flavored hot dogs, or hot-dog-flavored tofus, which are airy and light and feel like nothing. A bite could easily get stuck in my windpipe. Unable to speak, I'd crawl to the phone and call . . . who? Who would care that I'm in danger? Who would see the caller ID and think, Okay, she isn't speaking, but she's banging the phone against the counter and I know this means HELP?

I was eight days late when Robert proposed. Nobody knew. I think even he has forgotten. Eight days, and I'm never late.

"Okay," he said. "We should get married."

A week later I got my period. We were out at dinner with his parents when it happened. I came back from the bathroom and led him out the door into a snow squall. We stood beneath the restaurant's awning, shuddering in the wind.

"Do you still want to get married?" I yelled.

He waited a second longer than I thought he would, then said, "What?"

There isn't only one.

After careful consideration I decide to leave my toenails alone. Who am I to interfere with the artistic process? I should really quit the tofu, though. None of the chairs in the kitchen are the correct height for a self-administered Heimlich.

———

I actually buy sleeping pills. Not to take, just to have. The woman at the drugstore gave me a funny look when she rang them up, and I tried to behave like someone capable of restricting herself to the recommended dose. I put the box on the nightstand at home but didn't unwrap the foil, didn't pop them out in fistfuls to feel the weight of death in my hand—*so light.* I simply wanted them there, as if their presence alone, the threat—medicine, milk, inducement—would lure me off to sleep.

"What do you want me to do with your books?"

Saturday night, and I've called him on his cell. When he asked, "How are you?" I went quiet, listening for a voice in the background.

"I'm cleaning things out," I lie. "I thought I should call before I put stuff on the curb."

"That was nice of you."

"I thought it might rain tomorrow. I thought I better check." *I thought I better thought I better thought I better.* Like the Little Engine That Could, we are getting up this hill.

"I don't really care about the books. You can keep them or throw them out."

Keep them? Why would I keep them? He reads biographies of dead Russian czars. Doesn't he know me at all?

"You could donate them," he says. "That would be nice."

There's that word again. *Nice.* Nice is for sick grandpas and office picnics; it's what you say when there's nothing left to say. I'd rather he called me a bitch. I'd rather he showed any feeling for this, for me, at all.

He says, "I'm leaving in six days."

These are the details, but I don't want to know them.

I say goodbye and go to bed, lie down next to the box of sleeping pills. The sheets are just getting warm when I begin to understand: he is leaving in six days. Robert will leave me in six days, and that was my last excuse for calling.

———

The summer after the wedding we rented a saltbox cottage on the Cape. The closest beach was crowded, so one day we took the shuttle north and got off at the dunes. We walked for an hour across sand so hot and pale it felt like another planet, then trekked around the edge of a crater made by god knows what. When we got to some twisted, stumpy trees, we knew we were close, and we took the last hill at a run, falling down the other side to see ocean, *blue blue blue* the ocean.

It was our last Sunday in town. I put apples and Fig Newtons in my purse. He carried granola bars and sunblock in his jeans. When we got to the beach, I took off my skirt and laid it on the sand, but he had forgotten his trunks. "Just get in," I said, and he did. It was the end of July, but the place was deserted. Only the hardiest couples and their golden retrievers ventured this far. Robert shimmied out of his underwear and rushed into the water. Butt-bare and gleaming, the fine white sand clinging to his thighs. I went under almost immediately, shouting about the cold through a mouthful of salt. When I surfaced Robert was blocking out the sun. "Get in, get in," I sang. But he was too cold. I skittered at his knees, whipping my torso like a frisky seal pup. He left me and got dressed, then walked on the beach to look for shells. I kept checking to see if he was watching me swim, but he never was.

"What if there had been a riptide?" I said later. "What if there were sharks?" He told me the most recent shark attack at that location was back in 1936, and I let it go. But now I can see how exhausting it was for him, being looked at all the time, being asked for looks in return. No wonder he resorted to the boredom of beachcombing.

When the sun got low we headed back to catch the shuttle. I tied my shirt around my waist and put on my too-big sunglasses. Robert walked ahead, glancing back before starting up the dune. He saw the glasses and shook his head. *What do you think of me?* I wanted to shout. But it seemed a silly thing to ask.

I still can't sleep, but the pills have disappeared from my nightstand. I don't remember taking them. I could go out and buy some more, but I've come to enjoy the length of the nights, the quiet of them. I sit on the couch and drink tea and knit my husband a neck warmer. Neck warmers are great because they're almost like scarves, but better because they stay on your neck. It's not like I think a neck warmer can change things—*So thoughtful, and the perfect color . . . darling!* It's more of a peace offering, something to console him if he ever feels guilty. Also, it's cold in Minnesota.

A neck warmer shouldn't take too long to knit, but I keep making mistakes and need to pull out the rows. My fingers are having an identity crisis. They think they are not fingers but toes, they think they are in mittens, they think they are each other. I don't mind. It's a lovely yarn to look at. Grass green that gets brighter as it turns. I'll finish soon and give it to him, along with the underwear he left behind and the boxes of biographies. I can hand them off together: books, briefs, love. Paper, cotton, wool. All anniversaries. I know paper and cotton are early years, but I'm not sure about the wool.

I turn on the news and it's Saturday, the Saturday following our last phone call, and I count the days—seven—and know he must have left. The books and briefs I'll throw away, but what about the neck warmer? I sew it up the side and make a tube of fabric, warm and green and soft. I can't have it in the house, so I take it to the car and put it in the glove box. This makes sense. If I ever see him again, we will probably be near the car. I can keep my gift there, safe, until we reach the right anniversary.

———

On the way to the pound, I see the leaves have turned. Reds and yellows stream from the trees and crunch across the road like they've got somewhere to go. I have to drive slowly because I keep thinking they're alive. Chipmunks maybe, or mice. I see the sign for the kennel and pull into the lot. It will be fun, I think, to choose the one I want. We will know each other instantly, like lovers.

I cross the lawn. Already they're howling. A white one leaps in the air and lands stupidly on its side. A wiener-looking one licks its cage and wriggles. A Doberman barks and barks and barks. Their long claws scrape against the cement. It's a terrible sound, but I guess there isn't much sense in cutting their nails.

At the end of the line is a mutt with black matted fur and a long black nose. He lies on his side and doesn't look up when I come over.

"He's scheduled for tomorrow."

A woman in scrubs stands behind me. She's got a bucket in one hand and a mop in the other. I nod and move closer to the cage, kneel down to stick my fingers through the wire.

"I feel bad about the others," she says. "But that one's sick. I got no problem doing sick ones."

The woman is awful. I try to call the puppy quietly, so she doesn't hear. "Puppy puppy puppy," I say. "C'mere, puppy puppy puppy."

"That's the third black dog this week." She's right behind me. The toe of her shoe nudges the sole of my boot. I want to kick, to leap in the air, to grab the bucket and wham her over the head. I will take this dog and run. Don't try to stop us.

"Nobody wants the black ones, see? Can't tell you why, but it's true."

Faced with my silence, the woman backs off. I call again to the dog. "Here, puppy puppy puppy." He doesn't move. His snout is jammed between the food dish and the cage. A dank smell of piss rises from the floor. I call one more time, but the dog has given up.

I go back to the car. A collection of leaves has found its way to the windshield. I turn the key and grip at the wheel, listening to the radio. I can't see them anymore, but I know they're there. And beyond them, an odorless room. Blue liquid and a stainless steel table. I reverse out of the lot. There are two ways home. I take the long one. The road leads into the mountains, past the wooden fence and the geese who travel down the river. On the left is the white oak that got hit last spring. Flakes of bark still chipping off its face. The unmown grass is green and gets brighter as it turns. I switch off the radio and drive until a sound fills up the air. It's an inhuman sound, high-pitched and thin. It is coming from me. The world outside is swimming, the trees and sky are swimming, and the terrible wail sits next to me like a person.

I wipe at my eyes and follow the lines of the road. Above the dashboard is today's mail, and in the mail there's an envelope. Return address: Saint Paul. A letter from a lawyer in Saint Paul. I could turn the car around, take the one I love and try to save him, but I know it wouldn't work. The dog has made his choice. The others wait with their heads between their paws. They would be good companions. They would warm my feet at night and look at me forever. But in the end they are just dogs, and none of them are mine.

Mrs. Fisher

S he did not love him in the beginning. Saw him as just another body at another desk. Another name printed on her roster. *Stephen.*

In the books she assigned, characters were brought low by love because love was a temporary crucible. It came. It tested you. It left.

Stephen did not want to be called Steve or Stevie or Phen. Marion drew an x beside his name to show he'd been there. And beside the x she'd written SEVEN.

———

"I solved the mystery of the smell," Marion said to Dolly. "There's a dead mouse in the camping stove."

The mouse had been an orphan, Marion decided, and hungry. This was its backstory. Next, rising action: the mouse had gotten stuck in the stove and could not extricate itself. Could not go forward or back. Finally, a climax: one of the women in the house—Ma, Dolly, or Marion—had turned on the flame and the mouse had been transformed.

Dolly didn't look up. She was scrolling on her phone with one hand and palming a lukewarm Starbucks with the other. She must have stolen it when her boyfriend, Eddie, brought her home from the night shift at Pearl's Grocery.

"Can you remove the mouse?" she asked Dolly. Staying strong, making eye contact. "I can't. I'll be late to school."

Dolly crunched her nose in disgust. It had been a mistake to mention school. A place Dolly had never liked. Without looking up, Dolly told her sister to go fuck herself, slowly, with an ice pick. Then she reached for her soggy cereal.

Marion glanced at her watch: 7:19. "It would be nice if you helped with the mouse," she said to Dolly. "But no matter what, you are my sister and I'm grateful you're in my life."

Marion delivered this speech in the detached and loving language she'd been practicing at STAND UP FOR YOURSELF NOW! Marion believed STAND UP FOR YOURSELF NOW! might one day turn into a viable business opportunity. Like, maybe she could give speeches to wealthy women who wanted to be brave? But so far no one had joined the group she'd formed on Meetup.com, so at the appointed time Marion went to the pavilion in the dog park and practiced speaking in the firm, slightly lyrical voice of a TED Talks woman.

I am enough.

You are enough.

What makes you think you aren't enough?

. . . STAND UP FOR YOURSELF NOW!

Dolly dropped her Grape Nuts in an aggravated way and pointed her spoon at Marion. This was a little threatening because the spoon had been mangled in the trash compactor and its edges were now jagged. Dolly called Marion a snot-nosed snob who thought she was SO GREAT because the state paid her to make grammatical slideshows. But who cared about gerunds? Nobody!

Marion didn't argue. Instead, she left the house and walked to her car and reminded herself of the truth:

1. They were not slideshows. They were interactive PowerPoints displayed on a SMART Board.
2. Someone must care about gerunds, because Marion was required to teach them.
3. Although she had worked for the state before, this was her second year at Brookfield. A private school.

When she took the job, it sounded so exclusive—a *private* school! Like a *private* club or a *private* jet! In reality, the kids at Brookfield were problematic. The counselor had told her about attempted kidnappings, suicide pacts, eating disorders, multiple personality disorders—all the standard *Gossip Girl* plots. Now it was her second year and she understood the only difference between public and private school was that at Brookfield, Marion could get fired for anything. Anything at all.

———

She arrived so late that the 7:45 clusterfuck of cars, kids, parents, and buses was nearing peak cluster, peak fuck. At the crosswalk she avoided looking directly at Emilio Powers, the school's athletic director and crossing guard. Emilio liked to flirt with her aggressively and then raise both palms in the air to say, *You know I'm kiddin', right?* She brushed past his neon-green vest but Emilio grabbed her faux leather tote bag and said, "Marion! I was starting to think you'd quit."

"Ha," she said, tugging at the bag. "Ha-ha."

"Must be nice to be a regular teacher. I'd like to show up for work at Screw It o'clock."

She escaped by passing through a side door of Ogdenfry Annex, a locker-filled hall named for a dead lumber baron. Marion had the same classroom as last year, 707-B. At first she'd thought the sevens on either side were lucky. But seven turned out to be her unlucky number. She'd needed seven stitches after a branch fell on her tent during the annual fall campout. Seven parents had called to complain after someone on her class blog posted the comment TONI MORRISON IS A SLUT. And it was on the seventh day of the seventh month of the year that her husband, Alec, had asked her to leave.

Marion unlocked 707-B and glanced at a laminated sign on the wall beside her door. The sign hadn't been there before. The sign read MRS. FISHER.

No one else would care about the Mrs./Ms./Miss distinction. Sometimes her favorite students just said "Fisher," like they were on a basketball team together and they wanted her to pass the ball. But this was not really an apt comparison, because her favorite students did not play sports. Her favorite students took antidepressants in the middle of class and wrote bad poetry on her whiteboard during lunch.

She stuck her brass key into the lock, jiggling the knob the way it liked to be jiggled, and realized something awful: if she relinquished Alec's surname, she'd have to go back to being a Kleggsman. Ugh, Kleggsman! The sound of it was like being hit over the head with a log. Ma was a Kleggsman. Dolly was a Kleggsman. It was a fate Marion thought she'd escaped.

She entered her classroom, retrieved a bottle of Wite-Out from her desk, and returned to the hallway. But the sign did not look right after she'd done it. The Wite-Out's white was not the same white as the paper, and the texture was different. In the end she'd only highlighted the change, not hidden it. Well. So what? Maybe this was better. She took a blue pen and under the

M S. FISHER

she scrawled,

CUZ IM SINGLE AND READY TO MINGLE.

There. She felt better about the sign now. And she wasn't worried that anyone would accuse her of generating such lewd, grammatically incorrect graffiti. After all, she was a teacher.

———

Alec was a doctor and came from money. Ma and Dolly hated him. They called him uppity, two-faced, superior, annoying, boring, cold. Marion understood why. Alec had been the boss. He planned good things for Marion. Mitigated her flaws before she fell prey to them.

For instance: before he requested her departure from their marriage, Alec called Ma to make sure Marion would have a place to go and arranged for a van man to collect the furniture Marion had bought with her own money. The papers were ready to be signed. What could she say? Marion was given two days and two nights alone in the house to clear out her things. Then Alec would live there with his emotional-affair partner.

After he was gone, Marion sat on the bed and stared at the liver spots she'd just noticed on the backs of her hands. When she looked out the window she saw the afternoon sun reflected in Mr. Holland's windows, so she went out to the backyard and sat with the boulder. The boulder made her feel calm. The boulder was not moved by love or loss. It gathered the heat of the day in its tightly woven cells and held that warmth for as long as it could.

When she went back inside to open the cabinets and drink whatever alcohols she could find, she'd looked at the microwave clock. 7:07. Weird.

―――

They came in simultaneously, a herd of buffalo responding to the electric prod of the bell. Marion crossed to the front of her desk and leaned against it with her arms folded. This was her most teacherly pose. She also imagined it was kind of sexy. Would there be a last-minute hire this year, perhaps a Bradley Cooper type from the parts of *The Hangover* in which Bradley Cooper teaches middle school? If the Universe provided her with a Bradley Cooper as a new hire or even a long-term sub, Marion might start to believe that the current awfulness of her life—being a Kleggsman, living at Ma's—was merely the setup for a dramatic reversal of fortune.

The second bell rang, and Marion turned to her audience.

"Hello, tenth graders!"

The students had clapped when she said this last year. Such was their elation at no longer being freshmen. But these sophomores did not clap.

"I'm Mrs. Fisher." She paused. Frowned. "But in a few months I might be something else."

They stared at her blankly.

"I'm like you," she continued. "Sophomore year is full of changes. Who knows how you and I will transform? We might find new names for ourselves under the Christmas tree."

Oops. She should have said "Winter Break tree."

One student, a boy, raised his hand—but then, she shouldn't make gender assumptions! Even English teachers had to pluralize arguably singular subjects. Such were the times.

"Yes?" She referred to the seating chart. "Stephen?"

"Actually," he/she/they said, "I have a nickname. Call me Seven."

Marion noted the coincidence. 707. 7:07. "And what pronouns would you like me to use, Seven?"

Seven scrunched his/her/their nose in thought.

"Objective pronouns, I guess. It's dope how they work for both direct and indirect objects."

The class laughed. Marion could tell they really liked Seven.

"I appreciate your humor," she said. "But I was referring to gender pronouns."

"Oh." Seven made an embarrassed face, and the class laughed again. "He/him."

Marion made a note of this on her roster.

"What pronouns do you like, Mrs. Fisher?"

She looked up and met Seven's gaze. It was shocking, really. They never thought of her as a person, so why would she need a personal pronoun?

"I like possessive pronouns, Seven. I feel immensely gratified when a student uses the correct spelling of 'its' in an essay."

She expected laughter. After all, she'd just employed a callback, a popular comedic trope. But the class just stared at her.

"To answer your question, I use *she*. And my surname will be changing soon, so if you want, you can call me M."

M? What did that mean?

The bovine quality of her students' faces made Marion want to jump out of her skin. She had been like that once. As a child, she'd felt sad in her soul—unloved, unpaired, unknown—yet felt comforted by the belief she would eventually grow up to be loved and paired and known. But she had been wrong. Marion was invisible; she was not even seen by the two dozen faces gazing up at her.

"M is short for Marion," she said softly. She picked up and put down a pile of handouts. "Marion is my name."

It was awful, awful. A teacher asking for a nickname was too intimate. The kids would call her "thirsty."

"You don't *have* to," she added hastily. "Mrs. Fisher is fine. It is—whatever." Rolling her eyes now. Imitating them. Going for the cheap laugh.

Seven raised his hand. Marion pointed at him, and he smiled at her.

"Hello, M!" he said.

Marion stared at the boy in wonder. It filled her heart full, to hear those words again.

———

Before she became a teacher, Marion was a waitress at Antony's Pizza. At that time she lived with three other women in a house twenty minutes from Ma's. She spent her mornings studying for the Praxis so she could become a high school teacher instead of remaining a waitress.

Then, on her one night off from Antony's, Ma called and told her to go to the ER because Dolly was having her stomach pumped. She'd taken too many pills, or maybe her boyfriend had put the pills in her drink? Either way, it was totally Dolly.

She hated Dolly. Hated Ma, too. Marion had come from nothing and still was nothing—at least, this is what she believed back then, before she'd learned to hold space for other people's journeys like she did in STAND UP FOR YOURSELF NOW!

At the hospital, Dolly was acting loopy. She found it hilarious that Marion felt shy in front of the medical team and imitated her sister's little mouse voice whenever she spoke to them: "Em, excuse me?" "Em, can I get more drugs?" When a nurse said they couldn't release her until she ate a full meal, Dolly squeaked, "Em, tell that to my eating disorder."

Marion returned to the hospital the next morning. That's when Alec pulled her aside. He showed her a picture of a liger on his phone and kept talking about it until she laughed. When he asked her to dinner, she looked at his name tag. DR. FISHER. She thought it sounded like a good, normal name.

He took her to a "real" pizza place, more upscale than Antony's, where they dined on dainty pies with paper-thin crusts. During the meal he called Marion "Em" because he thought it was her name—short for Emma, perhaps—and Marion thought it was terribly sweet and intimate that he'd chosen her nickname so quickly: *M*. Two weeks passed like that. Then Marion introduced herself to one of his colleagues, and they realized he'd misinterpreted Dolly's shenanigans. Marion felt horribly embarrassed. But it turned out all right, because for the next twelve years the letter *M* became a shorthand for their quiet affection.

Alec was not an objectively handsome man. He didn't have much hair, and his eyes were goggly like a frog's. But he was decent. Clever. And inherently different from the Kleggsmans. He said things like "I know you'll pass the Praxis, honey," and when Marion did, he brought home a bottle of champagne.

But his family hadn't liked her. His brothers made fun of Marion for pronouncing *Seychelles* as "Say Chili's." And the venomous disdain of Alec's mother had been so venomous, so disdainful, it inspired STAND UP FOR YOURSELF NOW! After years of enduring Hannah Fisher's polite-yet-scathing insults—so much harder to evade than Ma and Dolly's direct blows—Marion started keeping a notebook of positive thoughts, and during visits to her mother-in-law's house she would flip through the pages to buoy her spirits. Still, she would never forget the Christmas dinner when Hannah turned to her with a cruel smile and said, "Teaching is a noble profession, but the people hired for it are rarely exceptional." Alec had said nothing and buried his face in wine.

But if love is measured by action, if love's sole proof is time, Alec loved her. He took care of Marion in small ways. Bought her clothes in neutral colors. Made her try foreign foods. Taught her what *off-piste* and *coup d'état* meant. She felt he'd enjoyed her lack of pretension at first. Saw her ignorance as innocence. But in the end, she'd held him back. Marion could see that now.

———

September, October, November. Fall left its mark on her classroom in the form of pin-sized holes. Her wall had hosted posters for fall play auditions and student council elections and SAT prep courses and join-our-club exhortations printed on pastel paper. She made it through homecoming week and parent-teacher conferences. She saw the armory pond freeze over and then go all pondy again. She bought a new stove, a full-size one, for Ma's house. Dolly broke up with her boyfriend and found a new boyfriend who also worked at Pearl's Grocery and who also had a truck. Marion didn't hear from Alec.

After the leaves dropped from the maple trees in the dog park, Marion stopped scheduling meetings of STAND UP FOR YOURSELF NOW! and took up cigarettes instead. Marion had been a smoker from age fifteen to eighteen. As an adolescent she'd only pretended to inhale, but now she went full smoke. The taste of tar and the sweet-bad smell between her fingers made her feel nostalgic and young.

Like a flare cutting through the dark, Marion sometimes had a profound moment with Seven. There was the day Seven came to school very early and told her about his older brother's brain injury from football. Seven said his parents were struggling. They forgot to buy cereal. Forgot even his birthday. That morning, Marion gave Seven her lunch, an egg-salad sandwich and sour cream chips. As she sat behind her desk wishing she knew what to say, Seven sat at his desk and ate everything she gave him. When he was done, he grinned at her and kissed his fingertips. How lovely to be Seven, she thought. Seven, who could take everything from her and not feel weird about it. How lovely to be a boy.

There was also the time Marion snuck into the fall play auditions and sat in the dark auditorium to watch Seven onstage. Script in hand, hair askew. The drama teacher asked him to read John Proctor's monologue about sleeping with young Abigail, and a delicious chill ran through Marion as Seven wiped away false tears and said, "For I thought of her softly. God help me, I lusted."

Then there was the winter formal. The gym had been transformed, or at least nudged toward transformation via blinking lights and tinsel. Seven was on the decorations committee, and Marion had been assigned to oversee the preparations. She sat on the lowest bleacher and graded Robert Frost essays and secretly watched Seven. She liked the way he made the other kids laugh but never made fun of anyone but himself. She liked that he admitted he'd forgotten to buy more Christmas lights and the way he problem-solved the lack of space on the refreshments table by adjusting the plastic wreaths. Seven was going to be a really good grown-up. Probably handsome, too. Marion hoped being handsome and popular wouldn't ruin him.

Another teacher showed up for chaperone duty and told Marion to go home. She arrived in time for dinner. Dolly was at the kitchen table painting her nails green and chewing out Ma. "Why didn't you call the septic man?"

Ma was cooking fried eggs on the new stove. "It's embarrassing to have men over," Ma said. She banged the pan down to unstick the stuck eggs. "We live like pigs."

"Duh," said Dolly. "That's why I go to Lowell's."

Lowell was Dolly's new boyfriend. He wasn't an addict and only did oxy on special occasions.

Ma opened the fridge and took out the Velveeta and hot sauce and put them on the table beside the piles of newspapers and unopened letters. "I don't want a septic man crawling around," she said. "Who knows what he'll find in there?"

Marion put the newspaper in the bin and put the bills in her purse. On Monday at lunch she'd write out the checks.

Ma dropped the pan of eggs onto the space Marion had cleared and said "Bon appétit" before she turned to light a cigarette. Dolly closed her nail polish tight and lit one, too. Oh, what the hell, Marion thought, and lit one herself.

"So look, I can call the plumber," Marion said between puffs. "Just tell me what's broken?"

"The whole damn toilet is broken," Dolly said. "Ma keeps flushing shit down it."

"I do not," said Ma. "It's you and your maxi pads."

"Ew, Ma! That trash is Marion's."

"Speaking of trash," Ma said, and threw something at her oldest daughter. A thick envelope. Not like the others.

"Divorce papers," Ma said triumphantly.

"I thought someone had to serve her those," Dolly protested.

"Shit," Marion said. Was she having a panic attack? She took a deep breath of kitchen air, which was thick and charcoal-flavored.

"There are different kinds of papers," Ma explained. "Mar signed the first ones already. Didn't even hire a lawyer."

"You're so dumb," Dolly said to her sister.

Marion put the thick envelope in her purse with the others. "I'll call a plumber tomorrow," she said quietly.

"Don't even," Dolly snorted. "We need a septic man. A full-on *man*. This goes way beyond the toilet."

———

Alec didn't want a baby. He wanted to go to Turkey and learn to brine olives. Wanted to bike through South Korea and eat thousand-dollar sushi in Japan. But Marion wanted to stay home. So instead of a baby or a trip, they had a boulder.

To be precise, Alec had the boulder. It was an impulse purchase. On a drive to his brother's house he saw a billboard for boulders, and he kept thinking about how funny it would be to order one, and the next thing he knew, he was on the phone with the boulder people. He had it dropped into the backyard because technically their neighborhood wasn't zoned for personal boulders.

The rock in the backyard was mostly blue, but at certain times of day it looked violet or pink or elephant gray. It was exceptionally heavy. Marion hated it. As an English teacher she could not view a large rock as anything other than a harbinger of doom. The boulder was a Trojan horse. Chekhov's gun. The white whale. Mount Kilimanjaro. Gatsby's green light. There were simply too many examples for her to allow the object to exist unmetaphorically.

But in the weeks of rising spring that followed, her feelings began to change. She visited the boulder after work. Graded papers beside it at the end of the semester, during those final aching weeks of teaching summer-sick kids. There had been so many essays to read then. A towering stack that filled her with both pride and dread, coupled with a heat wave that made May feel like August. But the dark side of the boulder stayed cool. One afternoon she fell asleep in its smooth shade, and after she woke, she understood that if the boulder represented something, it lay within her own interior world and not her husband's.

But surprise! He was having a midlife crisis after all. Alec confessed that back in February he began an emotional affair with a woman at work. An emotional affair? Marion googled it. Apparently emotional affairs were common now? Apparently they were worse than physical affairs in some ways? Marion tried to stay positive. She threw herself into STAND UP FOR YOURSELF NOW! and made plans to repair her relationships with Ma and Dolly.

But at night she dreamed of the boulder. The boulder in moonlight. The boulder dressed as a soldier, guarding against the inexorable passage of time. The boulder dressed as a Buddha, silently reminding her to stay present with her loss. Marion woke from these dreams feeling betrayed. What a comforting friend the boulder had been, and what a liar it was. The Greeks were slaughtering the citizens of Troy. Chekhov's gun had gone off.

When tragedy approaches its climax, the hero knows what's next. She is dangling from the precipice of Freytag's pyramid, waiting for the end.

———

Marion wasn't supposed to attend the Winter Formal, but she wanted to see the girls in their pretty dresses and pretty earrings. See the boys in clean shirts with clean faces. In the school parking lot, under the stark light above her driver's seat, she covered her mouth with a bright shade of lipstick.

The dance was almost over. She looked at her watch: 8:37. Funny. Marion was thirty-seven years old. In the lobby she caught a glimpse of her reflection in the dark glass of a trophy case. She looked old and used up. Not like her students! Flouncing, flirting. Equal parts misery and daring. She waved at a pair of girls sitting outside the gym, two student council officers who were counting up the cash and tucking it in their lockbox. She knew they'd be all right, these girls. They were very good at counting; they would find someone to love them.

Marion stepped into the gym and blinked against the dimness. She hadn't been looking for him, but there he was. Blue button-down shirt, black chinos, spiked hair. Nothing special about him. A boy in a sea of boys.

"Hello, M!" he said.

"I'm going outside," she replied.

She squeezed past the children and went out to a loading dock area, where her bare legs puckered in the cold night air. She was alone. No one vaping or sneaking drinks. Weird. The music in the gym stopped, and the silence filled with a muffled cheer. Snow Prince and Princess were about to be crowned.

She dug into her purse. Hands shaking. Odd. But managed to light a cigarette. Breathed in, and then. Oh, then. Seven appeared beside her.

"Whoops!" She dropped the cigarette to the ground, and Seven picked it up. Brushed away the wet gravel. Handed it to her, still lit.

"You didn't see this," Marion said, and sucked on the dirty filter.

When Seven held out his hand for a drag, Marion hesitated, then passed it over. Letting a student watch her smoke a cigarette was just as bad as giving him one. Both mistakes would get her fired.

"Thanks," Seven said. "You're cool for a teacher."

"I'm divorced," Marion said. "I'm not cool. You're cool. You're Seven."

Was he laughing at her? No, he never laughed at anybody. Spying on him had taught her that.

"Actually," he said, "I might want to be Stephen again. What do you think?" He smiled, but Marion did not.

"I think you should stay the same," she said.

He took another suckless puff. Seven wasn't really smoking the cigarette. Just like her. Like she'd been before.

"I don't have a choice," Seven said cheerfully. "Life is change. Isn't it, M?" She couldn't tell if he was being quasi-Buddhist or was making fun of quasi-Buddhists or was just trying to sound smarter than he was. But she liked the way he said "M." The cold sizzle rushed through her again. She'd lived more life than him, sure. But she used to be fifteen. That heart was in her still.

She reached for the cigarette, and that's when it happened. Seven's hand met her own and his fingertips caressed down her palm. It was done in an instant. Then the cigarette was between her fingers, and his cold hand retreated to his pocket. Maybe Seven didn't think of this moment, not before, not after. But it had happened. This connection. This touch.

Seven's smile flickered and went out. "Mrs. Fisher? You okay?"

"Oh, Seven," she murmured. "I could really use a friend."

It was awful. Awful. She didn't deserve a Bradley Cooper type. Or Alec. Or anyone.

Seven felt the change immediately. Bad air all around them. He stepped back and tugged at the elbow of his shirt, mumbled "Snow Prince," and left.

Marion startled awake as if from a dream. Said "Oh my god," and dropped the cigarette.

What the fuck was she doing?

————

Twenty minutes later, Marion crouched behind Mr. Holland's hedge to spy on her old house. It was 10:07 P.M. Not a good hour for an accurate assessment of the goings-on. Her replacement could be asleep in Alec's bed. They could be out to dinner. They could be in Turkey squeezing olives for all Marion knew.

Crouching, shuffling, she veered through the side gate into the backyard. Her purse caught on the chipped wood of the fence. Her toes were numb. Was it going to snow? No, it didn't smell wet. She tugged the purse free. Felt her hands shake again. Thought: Maybe I should invest in some gloves. Thought: My problem is not a lack of gloves.

Then she saw its shape in the dark. Familiar. She had to restrain herself from running to it. Her old friend.

Marion's feet caught against the hard dirt that ran across the raised beds of her old frozen garden. She stumbled and her cold hand met its cold shoulder. She put her cheek upon it. Dragged her numb mouth across its stone face and dropped her bare knees onto the grass.

She laid her neck against the boulder and tried to ignore the twinge of pain in her back. When the moon appeared, Marion made a wish on it, that she might take the boulder with her. Magically fit it in her purse next to the envelopes. Drop it on Ma's table and eat eggs with it every day.

But the boulder was what it was. Her ridiculous attempts at love would never disturb it.

———

"Hello, M."

"Hello, Boulder."

The ground was cold, but the boulder didn't mind. It was accustomed to a frigid and unyielding earth.

"Boulder," she said, curling into its curves, "nobody loves me."

"What is love?" asked the boulder.

Marion thought a bit before answering. "It's letting someone see you. The good parts and the bad."

"What is bad?" asked the boulder.

"Oh, it's stuff you'd like to change about yourself."

"What is change?" asked the boulder.

"You know, you're getting kind of annoying," said Marion. "And here I was, thinking I needed you."

"I don't need anything," the boulder said. "Or anyone."

It said this kind of haughtily in her opinion. But she forgave it and said, "I know, Boulder. I wish I were more like you."

"You will be someday," the boulder said. "When you're dead."

Marion knew what the boulder said was true. Still, it wasn't very nice. The boulder didn't have good manners, but it couldn't stop her from sobbing on its shoulder.

When she'd finished she said, "Goodbye, my friend. I'll miss you."

The boulder didn't offer Marion any sentiment in return. But that was all right, because what else could you expect from a boulder?

Stand up for yourself now, she told herself. *What makes you think you aren't enough?*

The boulder couldn't stand up. Marion could. She got to her feet and slammed her palms together and headed for the gate. If she escaped tonight without getting caught, she'd try to be grateful. Like, for her job. For all the things she hadn't screwed up yet, even though she'd arrived at Screw It o'clock.

She drove back to Ma's slowly, snaking through the dark streets with the radio on and the heat blasting. Love would leave her quickly now. It had done what it needed to do. Came. Tested her. Left. And what happened next? She didn't know. The books she assigned always ended there, caught in the aftermath of loss.

No wonder her students disliked them.

Late Girl

R oman used to say that the body never lies. He probably still says this, but not to me. His target audience is girls from seven to seventeen, young women who have trained their bodies to repeat the past in an attempt to perfect it.

I believed he hated me. Not me, exactly, but the parts of me that were loose and untrained. My bent knees. My lazy feet. Most untrainable of all were the parts that were new: my padded hips, breasts, and thighs.

Each of us felt the betrayal. Beneath the comforting din of banged point shoes and soles being scraped into submission, the dressing room girls exchanged whispers about the way our teacher had begun to look at us in class. Like we weren't silly little fools anymore, but fully grown idiots. We had disappointed Roman by sprouting flower bulbs of breasts and half-moon asses, fleshy protrusions that filled us with pride at the bus stop but muddied our talent at the studio.

One evening we were doing piqué turns across the floor in pairs. Piqués are simple to execute, but hard to perfect. Roman clapped his hands and pointed at me. "Again." I trotted back to the corner and joined the next group. Roman wore his usual expression of stern alertness, but his eyes sparked with cold fire. By the time I'd spun to the other side of the room, he had pulled his lips back in a grimace.

He pointed at the corner. "Again."

"Me?"

"Who else? You. Again."

I hesitated, then tripped getting back to the starting point. There was no one left to join me. I stretched out my arms and settled my hands into place, trying to ignore the flaming tower of displeasure—Roman—lurking in my peripheral vision. I had spent every moment of every class desperate for his attention, but when he finally gave it to me, I wanted to disappear.

"Watch," he said to the girls. "See what Chelsea's doing wrong?"

The pianist began. It was a song just for me. I felt very close to crying, but I knew Roman wouldn't like it if I cried, so I whipped around and tried to smile the way a Japanese geisha might smile, full of secrets. I told myself I loved ballet, but I could not hide the truth that escaped from my body.

"Still late," he barked. "Turn, turn, turn."

Roman clapped his hands to emphasize the timing. I saw his hands but couldn't hear the music. Blood pounded in my ears to an alternate tempo.

"Stop," he said. The music stopped but I kept turning, eager to reach the end of the room. Roman's body approached mine. He reached out with a single finger and pushed my shoulder.

I stumbled and fell out of pointe. "When a dancer is late, she must rush," he said, "and then she loses her balance."

Although I was standing still, my muscles snapped and twitched on their own, loaded with the current of his attention. He moved in front of the other dancers and imitated me. I saw his knees go floppy and watched his chin droop to the side. Instead of spotting at the wall by snapping his head, he let it lag behind his body. Our pianist improvised a jumbled comedy of notes to highlight Roman's performance. I held my breath.

"Beauty is never in a hurry," Roman said. "The correct tempo must come from the body. One and two and three and four. What is the human heart?"

"IT'S A CLOCK!" droned the girls.

"A late body is a sloppy body." Roman swung around behind me and slapped at my butt. "Tuck this in. This is disgusting." He flicked at my stomach, which retracted in response. "Get that big tummy out of here!"

The girls giggled in their corner. For the rest of that week I would walk past the dressing room and hear the echo of Roman's words: *Big tummy, get it out of here!*

At that age, I often thought about my body. Specifically my thighs. For several months I'd felt they were greater—more—than the other girls' thighs. I asked my mother to buy me new tights, but she hadn't, and now the old ones had stretched so thin the pink fabric looked white. But it wasn't until this moment, trembling under Roman's gaze, that I wondered if the thickness meant I was fat.

Without warning Roman clapped his hands and released me. I dove behind the other girls and self-soothed by performing stretches. My favorite stretch, the one I did whenever I felt bored or confined, was to stick out a leg and point and flex my foot. My ankles were very loose, my arch strong, and doing this particular thing made me feel good, like a natural ballerina.

While I stood there, pointing and flexing and pretending not to be upset, a few tentative hands reached out to pat me. I pulled away. We were not silly little girls anymore, and they were not my friends. Roman had made them my competitors. My enemies.

A few months later, he told my mother there was no reason for me to continue at the studio. I lacked the ballet body. I had no sense of rhythm. In short, I would never become one of the photographs on Roman's office wall. The wall was a map of the stars, former students who had gone to famous schools and then scattered themselves across the ballet universe. Through their combined light, they made a constellation that looked like Roman.

My mother asked what other kinds of dance I might do. Tap, jazz, that sort of thing. In the silence that followed, I realized how stupid my mother was. Not stupid, exactly, but uneducated. A barbarian in the house of angels.

Roman explained that he had ruined me for all other forms of dance. Nothing else would be ballet. He had taught this to my body, and my body would not forget. This was Roman's gift to me, and also his curse.

After he walked us to the door, my teacher floated one hand beneath my right breast and turned his palm upward while staring at my mother. He was presenting me to her, as if she did not know me at all.

"Look at this," he said. "The body never lies."

———

During the fourth week of my sophomore year at college, on a Saturday night heavy with parties, I ran into the street and was almost hit by a car.

According to my suitemates, Lauren and Frankie, the three of us had too much to drink at French House and I convinced them to go off-campus. None of the bars would let us inside, so Frankie used the school's app to request a car to take us home. While we waited for our ride, I apparently danced with a lamppost and ran up and down the sidewalk getting into arguments with random people. Lauren and Frankie said they were too exhausted to stop me. At one point I seemed distraught and threw my body against a wall. Then, without warning, I dashed into the street.

My boyfriend, Simon, was the student driver who'd been assigned to pick us up. It was his car that approached me in the street. But at the last moment, the car swerved and hit a tree. As everyone else rushed forward to see if Simon was okay, I leapt backward. There was no reason to get out of the way at that point, but I was drunk and my reaction time was slow. If I'd been sober, I might have landed on my feet. Instead, I landed on my back and hit my head on the curb.

Simon's car was totaled, but Simon was fine. Even the tree was fine, though it now carries a horizontal scar across its trunk. I went to the hospital. My doctors agreed that my body was all right, but my brain was not. I had thought my brain was part of my body, that the two were, in fact, inseparable, but the doctors kept referring to them as opposites. "No lasting trauma in the body," they informed each other. And yet I had memory loss.

The university people and some local officers came to my hospital room. Although my skin was unbroken and my sentences were coherent, my damaged brain made these meetings unproductive. I couldn't remember the accident. I couldn't remember any of my classes prior to the accident. It was as if this one pebble of time had been knocked out of the jar of my brain. I couldn't remember packing my bags at the end of the summer or saying goodbye to my mom. When I tried to picture it, I encountered the visual equivalent to silence.

Eventually the university let me take the blame without any punishment. The school newspaper ran an article criticizing Greek life. I believe some sort of investigative committee was formed, but there were no lawsuits, no losses of freedom. Simon visited the hospital every day, and every day he cried. He didn't blame me for messing up his car. He said the accident was his fault even though everyone agreed it was my fault. I repeated what Lauren and Frankie told me: Simon had been sober. Simon had been going only twenty-five miles an hour. Simon had saved me by hitting that tree.

I began to wonder how our relationship had lasted so long. We'd gotten together in April, and Simon stayed with me and my mom for five weeks during the summer. I remembered all that just fine. We had sex twice a day and worked at a tomato farm. We ate a lot of ice cream. But after the accident it was as if an invisible window hung in the air between us. Simon's feelings had to pass through the window to reach me, and along the way they refracted into repulsion. I did not want him. The idea of wanting him made my skin crawl. Perhaps the accident had severed some connecting nerve that ran between my loins and my brain.

I did not love Simon, but I understood the fact of him. He had saved my life after I'd put his in danger. Dating him was easier than breaking up.

———

The doctors signed my release form on a Friday, and instead of calling Simon to tell him the good news, I walked to campus alone. It felt strange to be in charge of my body again. No tubes, no walls. Just asphalt and grass and sidewalks. Streetlights that I could choose to obey or ignore, stores that I could enter or pass by. After being watched by doctors and nurses for nearly a week, I felt the absence of their gaze. If I turned right or left, moved forward or backward, no one would see me do it or care what happened next.

When I got to Curie House, which was a dorm reserved for female students in the sciences, I sat in the lobby a long time. I didn't know which room belonged to me. Lauren and Frankie had visited me in the hospital and said we'd been assigned "a killer suite," but that was all I knew about it.

Lauren and I met at the start of freshman year. She drank vodka crans, owned two horses, and suffered from chronic enthusiasm. She'd spotted Simon first, but after he asked me out she became our biggest cheerleader. Frankie was more of a mystery:

a curvy, bookish bio major we met last year at the housing lottery. Lauren told me that in the first two weeks of fall semester, the three of us had become best friends.

The dorm lobby stayed empty as I sat there. It was a warm fall day. I assumed everyone was outside, playing Ultimate Frisbee or something equally collegiate. Since I had nothing better to do, I walked across campus to my counselor's office. She was a friendly, bushy-haired woman. Our talk made her think of some trauma books I might like, so she launched her sizable body at the head of her bookshelf. I counted three tiers of roundness in her torso and imagined Roman's body superimposed over her, imitating her, showing me how women's bodies could easily go wrong. The experience was not unusual. Roman often visited me like this.

The counselor shoved the trauma books into my hands. I put them on her desk and said I felt fine. I didn't want the books and didn't want a leave of absence, either.

My counselor frowned. She thought a leave of absence was the better choice. Due to "the darned system," it was too late to change my course schedule. Dropping a class now would result in an incomplete on my transcript, and during a future job interview someone might ask about the incomplete, and I might have to reveal that I'd gotten drunk and endangered the lives of others. This wouldn't reflect well on my character, she said.

I assured her that I wouldn't get any incompletes. Professors at this school handed out B-pluses as if they grew on trees, and besides, I doubted anyone would flunk a girl who had brain damage.

———

On Monday I went to three classes, including Modern III, the most advanced dance class a person could take without an audition. *For students with more than two years of training*, the course description said. I had six years with Roman but zero in contemporary, and I remembered feeling apprehensive when I added the course to my schedule the spring before. But now it was late September. I had gone to six classes before the accident, and my body held no memory of pain other than a bruised shoulder and the tender spot where my head hit the curb. Presumably, then, I could handle the class. My counselor had fretted about the risks of dancing so soon after a head trauma, but I assured her that I could interview professional dancers or make dance-themed collages instead of jumping around. I had no intention of doing either of these things, but the idea mollified her. As for my doctors, they would have forbidden me to take the class if I'd told them about it, so I didn't.

The theater and dance department was located in Howards Hall, far from my other classes, and Modern III was in Rehearsal Room B on the top floor. I ran upstairs and jumped inside just as a girl was closing the door. The girl was short, compact, with shaved sides to her head and long blonde locks on top. She twisted her torso to look up at me.

"Sorry I'm late," I said. "I couldn't find the room."

The girl glared at me. "Is that supposed to be a joke?"

I ignored her and looked around at the stretching bodies. Twenty-four humans in all sorts of positions. Some on their backs like flailing beetles. Some folded over like sheets of paper.

"Whatever," I said. "The teacher isn't here yet."

The girl wouldn't quit looking at me. I'd assumed she was a freshman because of her size, but the skin above her chest was speckled with sunspots, and deep lines cut between her eyebrows when she scowled.

"EVERYBODY IN LINES! GO, GO, GO!" The girl clapped her hands and crossed the floor to face us. Behind her a long row of mirrors reflected the windows that looked down at the quad. It was late afternoon. The sun bounced off a mirror and blinded me with gold. I took a spot in the back row and whispered to the boy beside me, "That TA sucks."

He shook his head. I was relieved to see that, like me, he was wearing loose shorts instead of leggings or tights. "Amy's our teacher," he whispered back.

"ALEXANDER!" the girl yelled.

"Yes?"

"STOP TALKING!"

"Sorry, Amy."

"AND WEAR TIGHTER CLOTHES NEXT TIME! I NEED TO SEE YOUR BODY!"

The warm-up was grueling. After we completed a merciless round of push-up/butt-spin hybrids called Kill Me Nows, Amy released us to get water and we ran to the walls.

I recognized a girl from the chemistry lab and said hi. "So when do we get to dance?" I asked her.

She rolled her eyes before lowering her bottle. "I know, right? It's been like this for a week."

"Like what?"

"Amy's classes get harder when she's in a bad mood. Last March she didn't get a grant she wanted, and she made us pay for it." The girl took another glug and shrugged as she swallowed. "To be fair, my butt looked amazing by May."

During the next part of class we went through a combination. Everyone else knew it, so I stood behind the others and watched.

"Hooey! Late Girl!"

"Chelsea," I shouted back. "My name is Chelsea."

"Your name is Goodbye unless you run the routine."

"I don't know it."

"Yes, you do." Amy clapped her hands and said to the class, "Again!" I stepped into the back line and she called out, "Late Girl, I'm watching you."

We danced without music and used the sound of Amy's instructions to keep time. The choreography began with a loping run, then a double pirouette and a slide onto the floor, hip first. Then up on our knees, then squatting like monsters, backs arched, tongues out. Contract, release, contract. None of these moves seemed to have names. As we danced, Amy chanted:

Right-left-RIGHT, left-right-LEFT!

Ba-da-da DADA-dum. Yes! Better.

Kylie, catch up!

Wha-ta-RA, wha-ta-RA.

Goopy . . . goopier, Alex!

When I stopped worrying about falling behind, I realized my body knew what to do. Dancing this dance felt like falling from a great height—easier if you didn't struggle. I got out of the way and let it happen.

When the combination ended, we did it again. This time I stopped trying to count the beats in my head and instead followed the inconsistent rhythms of Amy's voice. My limbs anticipated the changes before they occurred. I flooded forward in a rush, then hesitated, then popped and zinged and crashed.

After three more runs of the routine, I expected we'd try it with music, but Amy just frowned and stretched and held her hands behind her lower back.

"Get in your lines."

She weaved through her students like a farmer assessing his stalks of corn. Meanwhile, we heaved with breath and dripped with sweat.

"Good form, Lucy. Zane, work on your core, that will help with turns."

When Amy got to me, I didn't look at her. I stared straight ahead like a cadet.

"You knew the routine." She said it like an accusation.

"Yes, but. I didn't know I knew it."

"You didn't trust your body. It remembered everything, didn't it?"

I didn't respond. I didn't need to. My body had provided the answer.

"You're not winded," she said. "Is the routine too easy for you, Late Girl?"

I enjoyed a small smirk. Maybe it *was* too easy. Maybe I was some kind of modern-dancing genius.

The change occurred before my brain understood it. My knees bent and I was looking at the ceiling. Amy had pushed me backward and then caught me in the next moment. I was in her arms, my weight far from center. Helpless.

"Ha," Amy said, but it was more of an exhalation than a sentiment. Her hand supported my neck and her thigh held my glutes. Right away, I knew she was the stronger dancer. So much control in her muscles, I could sense the intelligence flowing through them.

My body imitated hers. Guided by her hands, I flew up to standing, then spun around. When Amy snaked the back of her hand against my spine and tilted her head into my shoulder, I did the same to her. We were woven together. My ponytail fell onto her neck. I was taller than her, but she was accustomed to being the smaller partner. Using her butt to scoop under my butt, she lifted me in the air and walked slowly in a circle.

Shh, ha! She set me down with a bounce. I pulled away, but Amy had anticipated this. She grasped my wrist and pulled so we were each suspended on one foot, our new center of gravity a shared and invisible point between us.

We held this position until the moment was over. Or rather, I held it until Amy told me it was over by sending waves of energy through her hand. The class applauded.

Amy didn't look at me afterward. She clapped her hands twice. "Get in groups." I felt bereft when she turned away. Invisible again.

At the end of each class we had to meet in small groups to create original choreography. I joined Alex, the boxing shorts boy, and two girls. They said our midterm exam would be an original routine that we would perform together. When I asked what their choreography looked like, the girls got up and executed a jazzy combo that wouldn't have been out of place at a basketball halftime show. With a stoic expression, Alex stood behind them and leaned forward onto the balls of his feet. Slowly, he lifted his left hand.

"Tragic," said one of the girls when they were done.

"You should come up with something," said the other girl. "Like that thing you did with Amy."

I stood and used Alex as my partner, but when I took his hand it felt like a dead fish. I pulled at his elbow and set his arm in the space between us. I tried butting my leg up against his, but Alex's body remained locked to me. My movements grew more and more awkward, until I wasn't inside my body anymore. I was in Roman's body, making the girls laugh, sticking out my butt and stumbling over my tummy.

"Time," Amy called. She switched off the sound system. "See y'all Wednesday."

Before she could leave, I jogged over. Time to get that B-plus.

"I don't think you know," I began, "but I was in an accident and it damaged my brain?"

Amy was squatting in front of the speakers and fiddling with the dials. "That's funny," she said. "How do you know it was an accident if you damaged your brain?"

She flicked her hair back and looked up at me with unmistakable dislike. She had round eyes that were probably gray, but they looked colorless in the afternoon sun.

"It was an accident," I said. "I didn't run in front of a car on purpose."

"You didn't?"

As I tried to recall the details of that night, my sore shoulder began to ache. I rubbed at it and heard the echo of my name. *Chelsea.* Someone had called out to me before I ran away. Away from something, into the street.

"It doesn't matter," I said to Amy while shaking my head. "I just thought you should know what happened."

"I know what happened," she said. "Do you?"

"Yes," I said. "I made a terrible mistake."

Amy seemed surprised to hear this. She stood, looking interested. I wanted to keep her interest.

"My boyfriend's car was totaled," I said. "I feel really bad."

"Oh," she said. "Poor you."

Suddenly I felt embarrassed. Beyond embarrassed. Guilty.

"I know I could have hurt people," I said. "Believe me, if I could do it again—"

"You really don't remember?"

I shook my head.

"But you knew the routine."

"That was just muscle memory. Or whatever."

Amy seemed unhappy with this answer at first, but then she nodded.

"Brain damage. Got it."

"Listen," I said. "I hope my absence won't affect my grade."

Amy glared at me.

"You'll get what you deserve," she said, and walked toward the door.

————

I kept picturing Amy's face, which was all curves. The shape of it was a circle, and her cheeks were two raised circles, and her lips made a small, puffed-out cupid's bow. My face was all edges. I had a pointed fairy nose like my mom's, a sharp chin, diagonal cheekbones, and a right-angled jaw.

When I was younger I'd looked at the ballerinas on Roman's wall and thought they were perfect. I wanted my body to be thin and hard, all length and muscle, and I wanted my movements to be soft. But I'd grown into the opposite thing, a duck instead of a swan.

Now whenever I saw an attractive woman who didn't resemble me, I felt ugly in her presence, as if her beauty negated mine. But when I ruminated on Amy's looks, my own features increased in value. I had this face, this body, these thighs and cheeks and hands. And the more I thought about them next to Amy, the more I liked this face, this body, these thighs and cheeks and hands. I remembered the way we'd moved together during class and imagined what we must have looked like.

By the end of my seminar on Middle Eastern politics, I felt so undeniably beautiful that after class, I hurried to the bathroom and masturbated in one of the stalls. Not about Amy, I told myself, but about me.

I woke up sore and stiff on Wednesday. Most of the pain was located in the spots targeted by Monday's hideous warm-up, but I knew some of it was from the extracurricular exercises I'd been doing under the covers. On my way to Howards Hall I texted Simon to invite him over for spaghetti and something I called "physical therapy." He called me immediately, sounding excited and a little choked up.

I was still on the phone with him when I walked into Rehearsal Room B. Amy buzzed over, notebook in hand.

"It's Late Girl."

"Not today," I answered blithely. All that orgasming had made me feel as distant as a saint.

"No phones in the studio," Amy said. "You'll get it back after class." She held out her hand expectantly.

I said goodbye to Simon and gave her my phone without any argument.

"You seem good," Amy observed. "Something different?"

I shrugged. "I'm feeling better."

She puckered her lips in disapproval. "You're lucky to be here."

"I know," I started to say, but she interrupted me.

"If you're all better, take the front line."

I did as she suggested and wedged myself between two girls who exchanged a tense glance before making room for me. Being in the front line terrified me, but it also made me feel alive in a way that hadn't happened since Roman. I told myself I was older now. Tougher. I could handle the attention. Even if it came in the form of criticism, I wanted to be seen.

We learned new phrases of the routine that day. *Sliver sliver POP! Back turn splash, hit-down-kick.* In between runs I studied the mechanics of Amy's body. Her center of gravity was generally low, caught between her hips, but for certain moves—turns, jumps, inversions—she let it rise into her solar plexus. In motion, Amy was beautiful. She knew her instrument so well that she could extend it beyond the borders of her cells, into the ether. She could, with a flick of her head, change the temperature of the room or make you see something that wasn't there. Out of nothing she conjured partners, walls, obstacles, gravity. I wanted to put my body near hers again so it could be transformed.

"Yes," she said as we ran through the combination. The word was a secret she didn't want to reveal, but the goodness of my body drew it out of her. "Yes, Late Girl. Yes."

After that day I took the center spot in the front line as if it were mine. I had never been this bold in ballet. As a child I was so afraid of failing, I didn't understand that fear could make me a better dancer. But there in front of Amy, terror met desire, and my body excelled.

———

For several weeks Simon reaped the benefits of my return to dance. By this I mean we fucked. A lot. I loved having sex because it gave me another way to use my excellent, living body, which was maturing into a lean and pliable weapon. Simon's body, while nice, was immaterial to my body's pleasure. During love-making I grabbed my own ass, cupped my breasts together, bent backward until my tummy became a bridge. I made a lot of noise and didn't care if my suitemates heard us through the walls, not even after Simon and I emerged one afternoon and saw Lauren sitting in the common room on the love seat, grinning down madly at an open copy of *The Heart is a Lonely Hunter.*

Despite the excellence of my body in the bedroom, I could not squeeze another compliment out of Amy. One afternoon I was marking some tricky footwork instead of listening to her instructions, and she shoved me so hard I fell over.

As I felt myself falling, the memory of the accident moved through me. I could see the slow-motion lights spinning above me and hear tires braking against the pavement. And with the infusion of memory came new information: I hadn't been running away from something. I had been running toward something.

My hands stung when they smacked the wooden floor.

"You're not balanced," Amy observed.

On days we didn't have class, I practiced the routines so much I dreamed about them, and Simon complained of getting kicked in the shins at night. As a student of Roman's, I had wanted to be a dancer because I could not imagine being anything else. Now I could imagine being anything, but I wanted to be a dancer.

———

My choreography group fell apart right before our midterm exam. Due to aesthetic differences, we decided to each create a solo based on the theme of secrets. We would perform them together and hope we didn't run over each other.

The day of the exam I felt ill. I hadn't settled on any choreography because my moves felt fake and pretentious. When it was our turn to perform, Alex started the music he'd chosen, a watery excerpt from *Music for Airports*, and did his slow-hand thing. Then a hip-hop song came on, and the girls did a series of pep-squad kicks and spins. Then me. The class sat around me in a semicircle with Amy at the center. Because I hadn't chosen any music, you could hear my feet padding across the floor. I had hoped that my body would know what to do, that instinct and fear would give me something to say. But I had waited too long to make a decision.

Jerkily, I danced a snippet of Petipa's *Sleeping Beauty* that Roman had taught me years ago. *Passé relevé, passé relevé, pas de bourré couru.* The shame felt like lead in my veins, and my limbs drooped and mumbled. I criticized my own performance as if I were sitting in the audience. Nothing was fully extended. There was no musicality in my phrasing.

When I finished, the other group members enacted their routines in their own bubbles of space. I moved through my stolen phrases again and watched Amy, whose face remained a mask. After my group sat down and endured a critique by our peers, she dismissed the class. I ran over to her but said nothing. I needed her to tell me the truth.

"I'm sorry," I said.

"For what?"

Hadn't she been watching? If Amy had been watching, she would have seen my body lie. But Amy was looking in her bag.

"That wasn't my choreography."

"Duh."

I felt uncomfortable. Invisible. My body instinctively resorted to its old gesture from Roman's class, stretching out one leg to flex and point the toes.

"It's no big deal," Amy said. She began to move past me. "I'll just give you a zero."

"NO." My pointed toe caught her between the legs. It had been an automatic motion, a closed gate to keep her from leaving. But when we looked down, there it was. My foot on her crotch.

Amy could have brushed the foot away. She could have walked right through it. But she stopped and looked at it instead.

"I want an A." Though I didn't tell them to do it, my toes began kneading the fabric of Amy's yoga pants. Trying and failing to grasp the light material. "Or at least a B-plus."

It was a charged moment, thick with possible outcomes. My inner thigh began to ache, and my toes were starting to cramp, but I let the foot remain where it was.

"You're a punk," she said quietly. She reached down and held the offending foot in her hand, then bent her face over it, as if she wanted to talk to it privately. When she gave the foot a gentle shove, it floated back to the ground.

"What will you do?" she asked.

I blinked at her.

"If I let you retake the exam. What can I expect?"

"Not ballet," I assured her. "I'll make something new."

"Nothing's new to me, Late Girl. I know all your moves." Amy lifted her brow so imperceptibly that after she left, I wondered if I'd imagined it.

———

That weekend Simon surprised me with tickets to see a modern dance troupe perform in the city. I wore a daring top with an open neckline that descended almost to my navel. The shirt made Simon uncomfortable. He did not want people looking at my body as if it were an object.

"But my body *is* an object," I told him. "When I dance, it's planes and angles. Negative space and spheres." That's all the V of flesh was. A shape and a color. Without the interpretation of other people's eyes, my body could mean anything.

I enjoyed the first half of the show, but Simon did not. He wriggled in his seat like a toddler and unwrapped multiple packets of gum. I had to tell him to put away his phone. At intermission we filed into the lobby with the rest of the audience. It was a beautiful old theater, with velvet drapes and crystal chandeliers above a wide staircase.

We found a place to stand in front of a poster. In thick red letters, the word AWESOME stretched beneath the dancers' feet.

"You guys!" called a familiar voice. Lauren, my suitemate, was coming over.

"What a coincidence!" Simon said, also with enthusiasm. Simon and Lauren nodded at each other and chirped, "Coincidence, coincidence."

I understood it wasn't a coincidence. Simon understood it, too. Lauren was in love with him. He seemed embarrassed by this fact, but also pleased. Because I wanted to see how they would react, I asked Lauren to go with Simon to get us drinks at the bar. Her face nearly ruptured with excitement as they walked away together, and I saw Simon wiggle his eyebrows to make her laugh. A moment later, I felt a tap on my shoulder.

"Nice shirt." Amy smirked.

"Nice hair," I said. In class she'd been wearing it under a bandanna, but now it was lifted and hardened with some sort of product.

"What do you think?"

"Of the dancers? Good."

Amy made a face, and I laughed.

"I know them," she said, spanking her program across her forearm. "I danced with them for years. They're a bunch of assholes."

A regal woman in the bathroom line was staring at us. She looked at her watch, which had a diamond band that matched the chandeliers, and then she abandoned her spot and came over.

"Amy!" Kissing both cheeks. "I thought you'd gone to Europe."

"No, I'm still teaching. This is one of my students."

The woman looked at me appraisingly. Her gaze landed on the exposed flesh of my chest, and she glanced at Amy with an expression I couldn't read. A mix of admiration and disapproval, maybe. A warning and a wink. My heart beat faster in response.

"Amy, haven't you taught her anything? This girl is a ballerina. Look at that turnout."

We all looked down at my feet. The toes faced away from each other and my hips were open and ready.

"Like a little duck," the woman added.

"I'm working on it," Amy said. "Rome wasn't torn down in a day."

Just then, Simon returned with the drinks.

"Lauren had to pee," he said too loudly.

"This is my boyfriend," I said to no one in particular. I took a plastic cup and held it in front of my chest.

"This is Regina Weil," Amy said of the older woman. "She was a colleague of mine in New York."

I'd heard of the Regina Weil Company. It was known for putting dancers in unusual spaces, like taping them to subway walls or tying them to ropes beneath a Manhattan pier.

"We have plenty of ex-ballerinas," Regina said to me. "I take them in like refugees."

"Congratulations on the MacArthur," Amy said. "You deserve it."

"MacArthur!" Simon repeated. "Isn't that the genius grant?"

"Yes," Amy said.

Regina lifted her chin and looked away. She hummed, as if talking about her own genius bored her. "Yes, well. What's next, that's all I care about."

"Spoken like a true innovator," Simon said.

"What choice do I have?" Regina glared at Amy. "The next generation is nipping at my heels."

"Yeah, right," Amy said. "You must have heard I didn't get Lincoln Center."

"Or the NEA," Regina added. "Such a pity."

Amy didn't say anything. I could tell the word "pity" had enraged her.

"You'd better go to the bathroom now," I said to Regina. The words sounded rude even to me. Why had I said them? My emotions were a dark and windless cave.

"Yes, well. Nice to meet you," Regina said to Simon. And then, to Amy: "I'm sure she's a lovely dancer."

"She's spectacular," Amy said, and the cave inside me filled with blazing light.

When Regina was gone, Simon extended his hand to Amy. "You must be Chelsea's teacher."

"Guilty. And what do you think of the show?"

"So great," he said. "We can't get enough of it."

"Actually." I looked down into my drink. A carpet of bubbles clung to the bottom. As I watched, a few released themselves up to the surface where they self-immolated and became air. "I'm not feeling well," I said to my cup.

"Oh no, babe. That's terrible."

"Do you need a ride home?" Amy asked.

Simon opened his mouth.

"Yes," I said. Yes, Amy. Yes.

"Babe," Simon protested. "I can take you home."

"Don't be silly," Amy said. "You're enjoying the show."

"You can sit with Lauren," I told him. "We'll all meet up at your place."

When I kissed him on the mouth, I felt Amy watching, and a subtle heat bloomed between my legs.

———

In the car we barely spoke. I didn't ask questions because I didn't want to say something stupid and break whatever spell had put me there, alone in a car next to Amy.

I hadn't told her where I lived, or where Simon lived, if we were still pretending I was going there. I hoped we would go to Amy's, that I would get to enter her house and sit on her furniture and smell her detergent, but Amy parked the car in an empty lot on campus. Into the silence, she jingled a ring of keys.

"Time to get that B-plus."

It was a cold, damp night. As we walked to Howards Hall, the campus lights drained the color from our skin and turned the asphalt's soggy leaves into streaks of orange paint. I followed Amy to a side entrance of the building, through a door I hadn't known existed. A metal staircase led us up to Rehearsal Room B.

The studio was locked. Amy had the key. She crossed to the collection of supplies by the mirrors. My hand groped for the light switch, but Amy told me to stop.

"I have something better," she said, and turned on a flashlight. She tried to shine its beam on me, but I was too far away.

"Come," she instructed, and I did. Because the light was in my eyes, I couldn't see her face. "That's enough." The beam sat on my chest. Amy moved it south, over my tummy and thighs.

"Turn around," she said, and I turned. Shadows stretched and contracted on the wooden floor as she moved closer.

She stood behind me. "Go on," she said. "Show me."

Roman used to say that the body never lies, but I don't think this is true. The body is an incompetent liar. If someone is watching it closely, the body will give you away.

While Amy watched me closely, I asked my body to remember what the rest of me couldn't. The reenactment felt careful and slow at first. My performance was just that: a performance. But then I stuck out one foot, flexing and pointing my toes, and I realized this movement was true. I had done this.

I went through the motions until they felt right. I'd been drinking at French House. Draining Solo cups and throwing back shots.

For Amy, my body did this.

I'd run up and down the sidewalk in town. Pushing past bouncers, shouting into bars.

For Amy, my body did this.

I'd taken out my phone. So drunk I could barely open my texts. I jabbed at the thing in my hands. Typed: *I miss you. I'm sorry. Come here.*

And because I'd asked her to, Amy did this.

I opened my eyes and looked at her. She had been there. She had left the bar to see me. And I?

I had kissed her.

Tried to kiss her.

Threw my body against hers. Felt her pushing me away. Saw her running across the street. Not knowing I would follow.

"I thought you remembered," Amy said. "I thought you wanted to forget."

My purse sat on the floor of the studio. I approached it slowly because a bomb was sitting inside. I went through my old texts and saw an unfamiliar number.

The number said:

I can still taste you

What would your little boyfriend think

God your cunt

I know it's fast but

Sorry

Listen

What you said after class

Just tell me how you feel because

I know how I feel and

Right

Got it

Don't call me

Please

Delete this

"Chelsea," Amy said, and the sound made me shiver.

"What happened to Late Girl?"

Amy's mouth relaxed and her eyes went soft. I recognized this face even though I couldn't remember the last time I'd seen it. This was how she looked when she allowed herself to look at me.

"Late Girl may be late," she said, "but she's here."

I moved to the light. To Amy. And then my body did the most honest thing a body can do. It gave her this mouth, this tummy, these thighs and cheeks and hands. Wanting, as always, to please its teacher.

March 6, 2009

He gets up and goes behind the sofa. A hand falls over my eyes, callused and warm, and I hear a voice say:

One-two-three go! One-two-three go!

Jason played sports as a kid. If he could roll my trauma into a tight little ball, he would hurl it at my face to cure me of my fear. At his last *go*, I spring from the sofa and slide across the floor like a goalie.

Jason would be a good T-Ball coach. He is patient. He is kind. He tells me what I'm doing, because he thinks I do not know. I am evading. Ev-a-what-now? I play dumb. Who's that over there? Yikes. Zoinks. Never look here.

Just do it, he says. Three-two-one go.

It would be easier if I were standing on my head. If I were holding a wet and squirming cat, I'd have something physical to work against, but a Jennifer Convertibles sofa is too benign. I'd prefer a hospital. Do they let you rent out the OR if you have a good, bloody reason?

Jason cracks his knuckles. The knuckles say: Enough of this bullshit. The knuckles say: Don't make me beat this out of you. But Jason is a kind man. He would never say those things with his mouth.

No. Wait. This statement is unfair. No knuckle of Jason's would ever say these things. Jason is simply enacting a habit. A ritual of air and bone.

As he bends to check the time on his wrist, Jason's long nose almost touches the smooth glass face of the watch. The nose lifts and looks at my nose. It waits. Now we're in a play and I'm acting like a person with a nose, a normal person sitting with her nose on the sofa. But the performance is unconvincing. I'm not on the sofa, I'm out the door. I'm down the street banging my head on the hood of a parked car. When Jason says my name, I don't know which of his eyes to look at.

———

He thinks we should go all in. The kit. The caboodle. Some people buy a house or get a joint bank account; his form of commitment is to know what happened. I don't remember much. He asks again—No really, what happened? He wants my life to be a piece of string. Thin, taut, navigable. Look here, my life is bunched into his hand. My life is in his pocket.

I trust Jason. I do. But the problem is not a problem of trust. It is a lack of evidence. Some people frame their memories and hang them on the wall, others submit them as headshots or distribute them via Christmas newsletters. My memories are a stack of dirty Polaroids in a drawer. When I reach for an image, the clocks run backward and the photos fade to white in my hands.

In the small studio apartment that is full of our things, Jason asks me to sit down. He says those sticky words, *your past*, and my mind dries out like a desert. Prairie dogs with question-mark heads pop up and disappear. I can't wrangle a fact, not one. A scruffy head emerges from the ground. I have it in my sights. Do rifles have crosshairs? I have it in my crosshairs. Those shining black eyes, those rattlesnake eyes. I lower my gun and let the thing go.

Jason presses his fingers together like a psychiatrist. What am I feeling now? And now? He doesn't want to push me. But remember—we're as old as we've ever been. How old do I want to be when I open the cage and let myself out? Should we wait until I'm dead?

I wiggle my butt on the sofa. I wish I had to go to the bathroom. Nobody makes you say things if you have to go to the bathroom.

Just tell it simply, he says. Like a fable.

There isn't any moral, I say. Except that everyone is awful.

That's good, he says. People should know about that.

I am quiet, staring at the crevice where two cushions meet. Then I say:

Line.

Jason knows what this means, because Jason is an actor. On this very sofa I've been a bitchy wife, an ex-con, a pregnant teen, and innumerable flawed gentlemen from Shakespeare. It's easy. He gives me a name, and the words that come after the name are mine. But now there is nothing, no blinking colon to tell me what to say.

Jason starts to tap his left thigh, which I know from experience is starkly white beneath the dark-blue jeans. He says, Okay, not now, I get it. But you can't stay in there forever.

He asks to set a date. I tell him I like dates.

But only when they're purple.

———

We met at the planetarium. I was just a program girl then, learning how to do the shows. He came every day that week,[1] and on Thursday the girl who did the talking went to Mexico and I took her spot at the mike. I was nervous. The pointer shook in my hand. I drew a fuzzy red star in the sky. When the lights came up, Jason asked me to go for a drink. Still riding on adrenaline,[2] I said yes.

He wasn't a stalker. He was developing a show about space. He bought me a Tom Collins[3] and offered suggestions for how to control my nerves before star talks: 1. Take big, slow breaths; 2. Shake it out before your entrance; 3. Pick a point above the audience and focus on it.

He was an actor, and he was serious, and that made me think he was a serious actor. Chicago is full of actors—the bouncy, flirty types—and it was a relief to meet one who didn't invite me to a one-man show in his parents' basement.

But that serious stare of his, cold and bright like a lighthouse beam, longed to inspect my leaky little dinghy. Let's talk about your past, he'd say, lingering over the word as if it indicated a land of

---

1 Creepy

2 Terror

3 Gross

chocolates and toffee—Yum yum, my past! After he moved in, I found a leather notebook under his side of the mattress, in which he'd written, INABILITY TO SHARE = LACK OF COMMITMENT? I told him to quit therapizing me. He wondered if something happened when I was a kid. Shouldn't I tell him—shouldn't I *want* to tell him—if something had happened when I was a kid?

———

Dear Jason:

I will give you 10 allusions for 1 linear narrative.

I will give you 27 moments for 1 cohesive timeline.

I will give you 84 blowjobs if we never have to talk about this again.

———

If I don't talk, will Jason leave me?

Jason, leave me!

I'd like to see him try. I'm a mess in my head but I clean up nice. You should have seen me on New Year's Eve. That dress! Dancing like I don't know what. While Jason the wall-tree scrunched behind furniture, unable to do anything but be himself (shy, snide, overly tall). At parties he fades, he flips the switch to neutral, but with people I don't care about I'm electric, I'm a tennis player on coke, a puppy on caffeine, bebopping and strange. Men line up in xylophone rows and I play them: tinka-tinka tonk. Another shot from the bar, and I am looking good. Jason wears glasses. He looks better in the glasses than he does without them. Without them his face is a plate of dough. And I love him! Me! He is going to leave me!

After he goes, stupid things will make me cry: diet soda, sports equipment, Texas. Last night I walked home in the slush with grocery bags cutting into my hands. A neighbor came out of her house with a snowboard. She was tall and pretty. Her coat was a green ski jacket that shouldn't look good on anyone. If Jason leaves me, I will hate her.

And there are jokes that will be lost, like drowned clowns. A raised eyebrow can make him cough, laugh-and-cough, caloff. When Jason leaves, my life will be an empty auditorium, with gum wrappers and bent programs in his place.

Does this sound cruel? I don't mean any of it, not deeply. I don't mean anything deeply, which is exactly why Jason will leave me. But how can I mean anything with this anchor on my foot? Nothing means. It hurts.

JASON: You're backing away. You were doing good for a minute, but then you balked.

ME: Like a donkey.

JASON: Like a hoof-footed animal. Yes.

For him, the past is contained. It is a lake he can row out on without getting lost. Mine is an ocean that breaks at the continents of family and home, eroding the shore. I take out a pen and draw him a map. It looks like a spaghetti stain.

Hey, I say. I'm Chef Boyardee.

Jason says nothing. Those cool blue eyes, crinkled at the corners. How can we be right for each other? If my children have those eyes, I'll never know what they're thinking.

ME: The problem is a problem of distance. I can tell you about that fuzzy shape on the horizon, but I can't tell you about this thing that's crushing my foot. What else is there to say? It's big. I can't get around it.

JASON: Pretend you're a sailor. Pull up the anchor and circumnavigate the globe.

I close my eyes and imagine a warm salt breeze. We are pioneers. A sudden glacier on the starboard bow? No problem. We mount the thing and have a picnic.

I open my eyes. Jason is still there.

ME: That scenario is totally unreasonable.

JASON: It's your metaphor. I'm just trying to help.

We agree upon a date: March 6, 2009.

———

A friend of mine told me about the time she was raped. Not raped, exactly. Fingered while she was half asleep, camping in the woods. Raped? Raped. I tell her she can define the word how she likes. Likes? Liked. She doesn't like rape. Rape is a fantasy for some but a nerve for her. I put my hand on top of her hand to show that we're the same.

But we're not.

I can't help myself, I think an unkind thought. It's unkind because trauma is trauma, finger-fucking is fucking, and we're all in this together. The done-wrong girls. The victimistas.

But I suck my lips between my teeth to keep from shouting out: Is that all you've got, sister? IS THAT ALL THAT YOU'VE GOT?

Women are trained not to step on each other's sadness. Your friend's pain is the most painful pain in the world. You say things like, My sadness turns pale and runs out the door when it sees your sadness. Your sadness will eat the room, it will devour the door and the radiator, my god! But you are just being polite.

Those of us who have been broken, whose pantyhose arms are sewn up the seams, we keep quiet with our well-adjusted smiles. There is no threat of unexpected happiness sneaking in through a window and taking us by surprise. Our sadness drinks from a deep well. Any time I'm close to feeling good, I just drop the bucket and pull up some more. Do you have a sad story? Go ahead. My story is better and worse than yours.

———

I agree to tell him on March 6, 2009. When I make this deal, it is March 6, 2008. There are lots of reasons to believe we won't make it: the war abroad, the war at home. Jason wants to teach in South America or join the Peace Corps. I talk about going back to school. But now it's January 24, 2009, and we haven't moved an inch toward our imaginary goals.

There's still time, I think. People are hit by buses. Why not me?

———

Because I've never told this story before, I feel the need to practice. After Jason leaves for work, I stand in the living room and take deep breaths. I find a point on the wall. Oops. Forgot to shake it out. I take big breaths and try to shake it out. I choose a point on the wall that's half a foot taller than Jason. He says it's easier if you don't look them in the eyes.

I still do the show at the planetarium. I've gotten pretty good at it, even throwing in a few watery jokes of my own. My co-workers[4] all left recently, three last August and one in December. The new people are teenagers. They look and act like cousins, with the same thin fingers tugging at the same brown hair, asking me to sign things in the same soft voice. When they are late for work, their dewy eyes tremble with fear. They refuse to believe there was a time when I didn't do the show. I separate one from the herd—Amber, who seems nice—and try to train her. She has trouble with the winter constellations. Cepheus is the king and Cassiopeia is the queen. Triangulum is the triangle. It isn't that hard to remember.

I tell Amber I used to hate public speaking. She gives me a look like I'm lying. I tell her the trick is to make it a story. If she gets caught up in the story, she'll forget that she's the one telling it.

My voice shakes, she says. And I don't know which shoulder is Bellatrix and which is Betelgeuse.

Neither do they, I say.

———

In ninth grade I fell in love. I liked it, of course. In that town you needed to drive to get someplace good. The person I fell in love with had been driving forever. I'd always felt older than my friends, more mature, and now here was the proof—a man in my room.

4　Friends

That summer my life cracked down the middle, split into before and after. I wasn't fourteen. I was an old woman beaten down by love, and I was grateful to the man for making me this way, because being fourteen had sucked. It was way worse than being an old woman beaten down by love. It was worse than almost anything.

Then a strange thing happened. I kept getting older. One kiss from him put a year on my lips. Soon I was ancient. My skin withered and my legs grew sore, and I started to learn there was no age old enough for the things I had to do.

I left him eventually, or rather, he let me go. Since then I've watched my friends grow up and get older. But not me. I'm just stalled here, a bicentennial lover, waiting for them to catch up.

———

Six years lie murky beneath the surface and four are completely drowned, bloated underwater. An object floats up from the wreckage. I row out to retrieve it, whatever it is. A clock radio, a rock with the word LOVE on it, a homemade crossbow. I try to sink the thing. If it doesn't go down, I take it to the Salvation Army. Mom says to get a receipt. Dad can claim it on his taxes.

Ten years of my life fit into eleven cardboard boxes. I sift through the contents. It's stuff nobody else wants, stuff nobody else hates. Why did I think this story was important?

———

February 2009. Jason starts preparing. I find internet printouts about supporting loved ones and counseling and *Psychology Today* articles about thriving in long-term relationships. I throw everything in the trash. Five minutes later I'm digging out the paper and hauling it to the recycling bin. I may be a monster, but I still have a conscience.

The anchor weighs heavy on our minds. Sex is not so good. Sex is awful. Sex is okay, but is *that* how it's going to be from now on? One night I wear silky lingerie. It makes him sad, or something. He touches my bare shoulders. His face looks crinkled, tired.

The next day I come home and find a teddy bear on my pillow, dressed in a slutty getup of satin and lace. Under its butt is a note from Jason: I'M BEAR-Y SORRY! I cry huge, sloppy tears. I'm a sucker for puns.

———

Symbolism, catechism. My father's house had one too many rooms. There were four beds and only two children. Temptation, calculation.[5] There was also a crow's nest, a basement, and a den. I blame the architect. I plan a mean letter.

———

Jason is familiar with the structure of drama. It appeals to me, too. I would rather stage a fictive world for my unhappiness than look him in the face when I say: This is what happened, it happened to me. I don't want to see his reaction, up close, so tight, each flinch and nod recorded for later analysis. I move around the room, trying to get reception: Do you hate me now? And now? How about now? It's a shame our studio is too small for a proscenium stage.

———

5 Exploration, adulation, lubrication, situation. Education, persuasion, narration.

MOTHER. *Early fifties. Small, prone to anger and excitement.*

FATHER. *Mid-fifties. Large, just wants everyone to be happy.*

SISTER. *Nineteen. Small, defiant, silent.*

BROTHER. *Eighteen. Large, charismatic.*

DAUGHTER. *Fourteen. Larger than her sister. Quiet, sensitive, nervous.*

THE TREES are outside. Together they form THE WOODS, which meet THE BACKYARD. THE HOUSE is set back from the other houses and there is a steep HILL where the kids play sometimes in WINTER, and once they were playing KING OF THE MOUNTAIN and it was an excuse for THE DAUGHTER to touch THE BOYS when she barreled into them and what a thrill it was to hug those arms beneath THE COLD JACKETS, to press against their BOY-SMELL under the guise of violence. We fell down the mountain but nobody got hurt.

FATHER: (*Leaves the room.*)

MOTHER: (*Exhales smoke.*) Well, somebody's got to be the bad one.

SISTER: You can't read with the lights off.

MOTHER: Everybody knows. Even the sofa knows.

THE SOFA: Fuck you.

MOTHER: Honey, your sister's a liar.

SISTER: You can't read with the lights off. (*To the audience.*) I say this twice. I'm hitting you— him—with something.

BROTHER: I think she's throwing up. Did you get my note?

DAUGHTER: He kissed me here, here, and here.

MOTHER: The men touched him in the dark. He was just a little kid.

BROTHER: Look under the rock that says *love*.

DAUGHTER: I wrote about it in my journal.

THE ROCK: Love.

DAUGHTER: The one with the polka dots.

THE BEANBAGS: Well, she's done it.

(*Long pause.*)

BEANBAG 1: Aaaaaaaaaanal sex.

BEANBAG 2: Aaaaaaaaaaand it's awesome.

THE BEANBAGS: Totally. Totally.

BEANBAG 1: And she can still walk.

BEANBAG 2: Walk, well, sort of. Whoops!

DAUGHTER: (*Slips, pratfalls, sobs.*)

THE BEANBAGS: (*Chortle.*)

THE FIREPLACE: My mother always said, the way a man treats a dog is the way he'll treat you.

MOTHER: What happened?

SISTER: (*Doesn't speak.*)

MOTHER: Were you making kissy faces?

SISTER: (*Doesn't speak for years.*)

DAUGHTER: I'm either fifteen or sixteen. I am getting older but not—bada ching!—wiser.

MOTHER: Did she see you making kissy faces?

FATHER: (*Leaves the room.*)

BROTHER: (*Leaves for good.*)

DAUGHTER: I am the oldest person I know. My sister is thin as a sheet. Aren't we lucky to have such a big house where we never have to see each other? I will shut the windows and keep this to myself. I'm not worried. I'm not worried. I am the strongest person I know.

———

Nobody wants to eat next to a dead body, or read a book next to a dead body, or sleep with a dead body on the bedside table. Nobody wants to see that, smell that. In the world of home decor, the only thing worse than a dead body is a zombie body, one that used to be dead but is now alive. So I ask myself as March 6, 2009, approaches: Which are the salient details, the ones that will recall the body without reincarnating it?

———

I listened to the walls. Four years I listened.[6] Did I sleep? Like, ever? What about school, what about breakfast? I don't remember. The days were swallowed by the nights. In bed, I listened for the sound of feet on the carpet.

Jason wants to know about my dad. They met twice. On both occasions, I almost bailed. Jason gets all perky when I mention him now. He thinks a portion of the curtain is about to lift. What I don't tell him is that my father is just a sideshow in the trauma-lama circus, not the main attraction. Whatever. Let him be distracted. I do a tap dance of worry at the lip of the

---

6 Possibly just two, but there are four I can't remember.

stage: Let's go out of town, let's have lots of sex, you can meet him next time!

Yikes. Zoinks. Never look here.

———

It's not an ultimatum. Jason has drawn zero lines in the sand, but I see them all the same. As March 6, 2009 approaches, the lines move closer. They make a box around my feet. Which one do I cross? Tell him = I Stay. Don't tell = I Go. There are other lines. Ones that Jason doesn't believe in, but I do. Tell him = Watch Him Recoil. Tell him = Know for Certain I Deserve to Be Alone.

Jason has started substitute teaching and is usually asleep by the time I get home, but tonight he and his bare chest are waiting. I come in wearing my glasses. His long nose points to the center of a novel. The blue eyes above the nose dart up, startled, as if I were a stranger. You look different, he says, closing the book. Really different.

I take off the frames and dangle them from my lips. They are glasses, baby. Glasses. How different will I look when the anchor has been lifted? Facts can color a person. For example:

JASON: Is your hair different?

ME: No, I'm just evil.

JASON: Oh. It makes you look different. It makes me look at you differently.

———

March 6, 2009. We have cleared our schedules. Jason fills the Brita and brings it to the sofa. There are also paper towels. I don't know what he plans to do with those. Maybe we'll have a hostage situation. There will be bargaining, threats, and I will release one tear for each of his demands.

One. Two. Three. Go.

He sits down and gives me a gentle look. I say I hate sincerity. It's like a window with no curtains.

I don't want to lose you, he says.

If Jason leaves me, will I find someone else? When I think of this other man, I picture him wearing a slightly wrinkled suit. Other than that, I can't imagine who this righter person might be, or what color hair he has, or what he will do when I try to push him away.

Okay, I say. Okay. But I'm not going to pounce. I'm going in slowly, so I can get out before the metal snaps on my foot.[7]

I'm not going anywhere, he says.

In the beginning, I say.

He nods.

In the beginning was the world.

And?

And the world was Pennsylvania.

And?

That's supposed to be funny. Did you think it was funny?

And?

I need to know if it's funny. I'm thinking of taking this act on the road.

---

7 In the woods you see these animals sometimes, dead animals, with tiny mouths full of their own fur. If the trap is good enough, they choke on the fur and never reach the bone.

He slips his hand beneath mine and closes his eyes. I stack his fingers in my palm and squeeze, like he's a wet cat I don't want to get away.

And?

And the world was a house, I say. Wooden, blue, and large.

The Birds in Trafalgar Square

After my mother died, I had more money than ever before. She would have told me to spend it, spend it. In her will—the terms of her surrender—she left me all the good things and gave the difficult postmortem work to an assortment of hired men. My mother and the men had thought of everything; there was not a single unpaid bill for me to file. "Go on vacation," her accountant told me. "You can honor her memory by having some fun."

We rarely traveled, especially after the surgeries began, but before I was born she'd seen much of Europe on my father's arm. "All cities are fun if you're rich," she told me, "but each city requires you to spend money in a different way. *Par example*, Paris is meant to be savored, but London tastes better when you swallow it whole."

I arrived in London intending to honor her memory, not by having fun but by being rich. I stayed at an extravagant hotel and endured high tea and bought new clothes that needed to be dry cleaned. I went to the Royal Albert Hall and sat within spitting distance of pop stars whose music I barely liked. I did a helicopter tour and a boat tour and an icon wine tasting in a six-hundred-year-old crypt. I went to the Dorchester and Claridge's and ate gold shavings that didn't have a taste.

Doing these things felt desperate and embarrassing, like in high school when I'd wanted a boy to notice me and then acted like an exaggerated version of myself to get his attention. Paying to be treated like a VIP wasn't the same thing as being a VIP—they might even be opposites. I thought about calling my father. The inheritance money had come from my mother but originated with my father, so spending it was a way of connecting them, even posthumously. I thought about going home, but no semblance of home remained.

After doing the things in London my mother would have loved, I began to consider the things she would have hated. Getting a job seemed appropriate, but without a work visa I would need to be paid under the table. According to the bartender at my five-star hotel, uneducated young foreigners like myself had two options. I thought stripping sounded more interesting than pulling pints, so I decided to try it.

———

There were plenty of strip clubs in London, but none of them wanted to hire an American girl who didn't have an NI number. I phoned Spearmint Rhino, Stringfellows, and Sophisticats, then went in person to Secrets Hammersmith, Holborn, and Euston. I'd heard that an illegal American had gotten a job at Secrets Holborn, but the manager took one look at me and decided I wasn't worth the risk. After that I tried the strip pubs—the Flying

Scotsman, Ye Olde Axe, and the Griffin. Unlike the clubs, the strip pubs offered a more structured environment in which a girl danced onstage and then went around the room with a pint glass. Unless she was truly ugly or the men were truly cheap, everyone put a pound in the glass. It was a brilliant system because you barely had to speak and rejection was impossible, but the pubs were small and afraid of losing their licenses. I finally found a strip pub/club combo called Metropolis. The housemother told me to come back with two dresses on Tuesday night, and I did.

Metropolis was in Bethnal Green, between the Indian restaurant row and the boxing arena at York Hall. My first night started off slow. If the girls had been wearing different clothes, you might have mistaken us for customers at the DMV. I stood at the bar for over an hour before a man approached, a shy Indian fellow who asked for a dance and followed me through the swinging doors that didn't have a lock. The doors simulated privacy, but the bouncers could easily look over them, and Cheryl the house mum had shown me where the emergency button was hidden on the wall.

"I haven't seen you before," said the quiet man. I told him it was my first day at Metropolis, but that I'd stripped before in Texas. In reality I had never been to Texas, but the man seemed to think I'd grown up there.

"Lonestar," he said. "Two-step, Austin, Denver."

"That's right!" An exuberant twang snuck into my voice. "You sure do know geography."

I slid off the top of the dress so it pooled at my waist and rolled my hips in a circle. I didn't know if I should look at the man or the wall. I chose the wall. The man's eyes kept flicking between my breasts and my face, and when the dress fell to my ankles, the distance they traveled grew wider.

"Keep going," he said. "Keep going, keep going."

His nerves put me at ease. I took a step closer and felt the heat from his body. I put my hands where he wasn't allowed to put his.

"Keep going."

But I quickly ran out of tricks. When the man said, "Okay," I began to get dressed.

"I like you," he said as I struggled to tie my straps. "You're what the French call 'oh natural.' "

"Thank you."

"You remind me of my ex-wife."

"Thank you." I asked for fifty pounds, which probably reminded him of his ex-wife, too.

———

I found a flat on the east edge of Shoreditch. The building was crumbling and the residents shuffled through the corridors, but the flat was furnished and not too far from work. The Tube took me out in the evening, and two buses got me back in the morning.

Metropolis's main floor was large and open, with perpetual soccer on the television behind the bar and a stage in the center of the room. The second floor was quieter, with a bar stuck in the corner and rows of private rooms, each outfitted with a silver pole. The third floor was reserved for fantasies: slutty croupiers, soapy bathers, beach volleyball players who stood on a sad patch of sand. We weren't meant to go above the first floor without a client, but it was a place to cool off when a man behaved badly. I was on the second floor, drinking a Stella that cost almost as much as a dance, when Cheryl came over.

"Get a glass," she said, pointing at my beer. I had thought drinking from the bottle would make me approachable. I thought it could be my shtick: like one of the guys, but naked.

I poured the beer into a pint glass and turned away in a sulk. Just then, a confused heap tumbled from a private room and quickly righted itself, smoothing its skirts and ties. The jumble separated into three men and two ladies. The girls wore their bleached hair long and had a tremor in their faces that reminded me of rabbits. The last man locked eyes with me as he walked past.

"Hey," he said.

"Hey," I said.

He followed his friends to the stairs. When he turned back to me, the motion seemed intelligent, like a clever dog pointing at a bird. He paused at the top of the stairs and waved.

"What are you doing?"

He sounded like someone I knew. Not a specific person, but like anyone I might know.

"Nothing," I said, and followed him.

Downstairs a pretty redhead was onstage, walking in tired circles around a pole. Sometimes Metropolis felt like the island of lost toys, and the girls were sad dolls who'd been discarded by their childhood selves. Other times, it felt as ordinary and uncomplicated as an airport lounge.

"American," the good-looking man said when I approached. I nodded. "What are you doing here?"

"I don't know." An honest answer, for once. "What are you doing here?"

"Me? I'm with the band."

He pointed at the speakers above us.

I liked him. I'd never liked a man in the club before, and it completely confused me. I felt there had to be a rule about showing genuine interest in a customer—fake interest, yes, real interest, no. His eyes were framed by pretty lashes and were a warm brown, maybe hazel. He leaned into my ear to shout over the music. "You're a good singer, right? I can tell."

"Yes," I said. "Rock and roll."

A friend from his work had just gotten engaged, he said, so they'd brought him there to celebrate. I asked the man if he wanted to celebrate with me, and he said all right, and I led him through the swinging doors. He sat on the leather and I put my legs around his knee.

"You're cute." I felt myself blushing. But what was that? Strippers don't blush.

"I bet you say that to all the guys."

"I've never said that to anyone," I said, then added, "here."

Telling the truth felt illicit, arousing. I released the top of my dress and lifted one breast in each hand, squeezing them together. I put a shoulder on the wall behind him, spooning his front with my back, and rolled my torso until my dress slid down my hips and fell to the floor like water. I'd been practicing this move at home and felt pleased at its execution, but it was almost the end of the night and I could smell my own sweat. It smelled vaguely like my father, a musky, back-of-the-closet smell. I stepped out of the dress and moved away from the wall, away from the man, and tugged at my lavender G-string.

"Nice pants," said the man. I looked down. "Not trousers," he said. "Pants."

Cheryl, who must have been passing just then, looked at us over the top of the doors. "You take too long to get your clothes off," she said to me. "This man is very lucky." She smiled at him, but I could tell she didn't think he was lucky at all. "Half a song," she said, which was how long we were supposed to take.

The man was already standing.

"Wait," I said. "I'm supposed to show you everything."

"Next time." He handed me a tenner and walked away, and I went down to the dressing room to remove my dress for the sixth time that night. It was an important moment in my career as a stripper: the first night I broke even. Every other time I'd lost money because we had to cough up fifty quid for the house fee. It didn't feel good to pay for the privilege of standing around for eight hours in high heels, being unpopular. But I told myself I was paying my dues. The best girls had regulars, and the best regulars were the ones who took you upstairs, where your time was more valuable.

I walked out of the club wearing my jeans and peacoat. The man and his friends were there waiting for a car.

"She's a nice bird," one of the men was saying, "but I wouldn't want to fuck her."

The good-looking guy asked if I needed a ride.

I hesitated. We weren't supposed to talk to customers outside the club. If we gave our time away for free, there was no incentive to pay for it. "I'm taking the bus," I said, and the men laughed in response. "I am," I said, "right there." They looked past me, as if doubting the existence of the bus stop. I turned and started down the street. A girl from the club was already waiting there, but we didn't speak or even look at each other.

The men got into a minicab. I pretended not to notice. Later that night, from the comfort of my tiny flat, it seemed so simple—he likes you, get in the car!—but I didn't want to break the rules. And anyway, if the good-looking guy wanted to find me, he knew where to look.

———

I am not a good singer, but I do like music. When I was ten my mother and I started a band called Fraught with Pith—she was Fraught and I was Pith—and we played shows for Jackie, our depressed beagle, until I quit to focus on pre-algebra. After the divorce my father offered to pay for private music lessons, but I felt too protective of my mother to say yes.

When I was a child I had prayed for my parents to get divorced; I thought it would save my mother's sanity. Her jealousy turned feral when my father went abroad for work, and he would come home to find she'd gotten a new nose, or reupholstered the furniture in electric-blue satin, or shipped me off to boarding school in France. Each attempt to get his attention was eventually reversed—I only went to L'Ermitage for one semester—except for the surgeries, which stuck. When he left us for the last time, she was no longer beautiful, but tight, and when she died her face was more canvas than skin. Mirth, fear, regret, and boredom all looked like the same emotion in the fleshy wash of pigments she applied each morning from her hospital bed.

After the divorce, my father relocated to Belgium. My mother still felt married and resented his absence. When she died, he sent flowers to the funeral—six boxes of cheap carnations. Was this a message? We both knew she preferred reluctant and tender things, like the potted hibiscus that produced a single blossom every other year. But then I realized the carnations were probably selected by his secretary. My father trades money, yen for krónur, that sort of thing. This is an important job. Choosing funeral flowers is less important, almost as trivial as being my only living parent. I began putting the secretary's number on forms as my emergency contact, and when I dropped out of college and moved to London, it was the secretary I decided not to tell.

My mother would have hated the stripping, but I think she would have understood it. Stripping was clear and impartial. It told me how much I was worth, and I know she wondered about this, too. Her own value was so hard to pin down. In her late forties she could make my teenage boyfriends choke on their sodas just by coming in from the garden in dirty overalls and a straw hat. But the ideal face, the ideal body, remained out of reach. As we both grew older I could hear the spite in her voice when she said the word *pretty*, as if she'd been forced to eat a mouthful of orange rind when she'd expected to bite into an apple.

I wanted to be worth a lot at Metropolis, so I practiced. I learned how to arch my back and bend my knees to make my ass look higher and tighter. That was what my mother had tried to do to her face, make it higher and tighter. I learned to hold in my stomach all the time, even at the grocery store, even on the four A.M. bus to Earl's Court. I tried to guess each man's fantasy and become that thing. I started leaving work with a little money in my pocket. Not nearly enough to live, but enough to feel I was improving.

———

After I'd been at Metropolis for six weeks, my father sent me an email. He'd noticed that the funds in my personal account were running low. Should he go ahead and transfer some of my mother's savings? Did I need his help?

I had less than a thousand pounds. Yes, there was plenty of money sitting in my mother's American bank account. I didn't want it. I wanted to be the kind of dancer who got invited to the top floor.

And yet I felt pleased about my father's email. He hadn't contacted me after the funeral. To get a message like this felt like a reward. I wondered what my mother would have done. Reply? Retreat? I told my father I would catch a quick flight to Brussels if he took me out to lunch.

The immigration officer at the airport wanted to know what my plans were in Belgium. He wasn't smiling, but his eyes crinkled pleasantly, and I got the feeling it was a genuine question rather than an interrogation. I couldn't think of anything other than the name of the restaurant. "Actually I'm a food critic," I said. "I'm here to review the Comme Chez Soi."

The man's eyebrows sprang up, filling the bald arches left by his receding hairline. "Really? What a career!"

My father's secretary had booked me one night at a hotel north of the city center. It was adequate and small, the kind of place my mother would have called *n'importe quoi*, or "whatever." I arrived there early. It was a cold, bright day, so I decided to walk to the restaurant. On the way I bought a ten-pack of Gauloises and smoked them, one after the other, and threw out the empty container near the Anneessens metro. When I think of the things I saw that day—Saint Gudula, the Grote Markt, the Mont des Arts—I remember those Gauloises, the way my throat clogged up and the taste of burnt spit on my tongue. I wouldn't have admitted it then, but I was nervous to see him. To be seen by him.

I spotted his face in the restaurant window, through a shadow of branches that danced across the glass. In his youth he had been a handsome man, square-jawed and intense, but now his colors had faded and his eyes had sunk too far in his skull. I rarely looked at him closely because his face was a lot like mine—not beautiful, but strong. Despite the resemblance, I hoped my twenty-year-old body and the maturity I'd gained from stripping would make me unfamiliar, but he recognized me immediately and waved me to the table. He had already ordered a beer, which sat half-drunk in a glass as tall as a vase. I felt a rush of dislike when I looked at the beer, followed by a rush of guilt. Everyone in Europe drank alcohol during lunch. It was not a good reason to hate him.

My mother liked to repeat the same phrase whenever life went wrong for us. "It's not your father's fault," she said when a birthday card arrived late or not at all. "It's not your father's fault," she said when the infection from her second rhinoplasty made her head swell like a balloon. Her mantra left an impression on me, because if you keep hearing that all the bad things in life are not your father's fault, you start to wonder if they are.

The other men in the restaurant were my father's age, and without exception they sat with twentysomething women. Girls on the left, men on the right, with a single red poppy in between. I smiled at my father and took a sip of water. When I brought the glass down I caught him staring at my nails, which were dusty and uneven, the glue from the press-ons still visible.

"You're here." He smiled in a distant, pleasant way. "How long has it been?" Two years. But I pretended not to know. "Dear Lord, you look like a woman."

He seemed upset about this, so I picked up the menu and said, "Don't worry. It's just a woman-suit. I'm actually a kangaroo."

My father bantered with the sommelier. I studied the other women in the restaurant. They were thin and lovely, with clothes that dangled precariously off their bodies, as if breasts and shoulders and hips were not anatomical objects but geological ones. Cliff faces. Rock beds. I wondered what it took, what sacrifices a girl had to make, to become hard like that.

The sommelier left. My father talked about my college, which had been his college, too, while I secretly wondered how I could court the favor of the Comme Chez Soi women. My dress was an empire fit, one of the dry-clean-only outfits I'd bought with Mom's money. It had seemed chic when I packed it, but now I suspected I looked like a child playing dress-up. I wanted the women in the restaurant to take me to the bathroom and show me their secrets. They could re-part my hair or tie a scarf around my waist, and I would stand there, doll-like, until their manicured hands had fixed me.

Lunch arrived, a clockwork of twin plates: quail eggs, sea bass with basil, and chocolate mousse with bourbon vanilla. When the wine had been poured and the bottle set into a bucket of ice, my father asked about my life. I pretended the lunch was an interview and answered his questions politely, trying to put a positive spin on any sign of weakness. As I spoke, he leaned forward intimately, a little drunk perhaps, like an overeager boyfriend. Each detail I threw him made him swoon with interest. A lame joke that should have received a chuckle won a roar, and with each sigh or smile I deemed him false, false, falser. His behavior might have made some other girl happy, but I was intent on maintaining the balance of our emotional divide: he must always feel guilty, and I must always feel nothing.

My father ate voraciously, slurping the buttery eggs and using a napkin to wipe the grease from his lips. Several times he had trouble hearing me, and I became angry, though the source of the anger confused me. Was it that he couldn't hear me, or that he wasn't listening?

"Sorry, hon. Your dad is getting old."

He took a small, flesh-colored bean from his pocket and put it in his ear. "I hate to wear it. But I can still taste things properly, as Chef Lionel will attest." He speared a slice of creamed fish and twirled his fork extravagantly before putting the fish in his mouth.

The little bean unnerved me. It seemed like proof of something. He must have been alive all those times he'd been away, alive and losing his hearing. I was so disturbed by this thought that I didn't notice when his gaze shifted to the back of the restaurant.

"Ah!" he said, dropping his napkin. "The most beautiful woman in the world."

He stood and lifted his arms. I twisted in my chair to see a dark-haired, olive-skinned woman with large, loose breasts that tumbled inside her shirt like a pair of puppies. She hurried across the room and flew into my father's arms.

He said, "Cari, darling, this is my daughter. Sit down. We'll get you the mousse."

"No," said the woman called Cari. "I did not mean to interrupt." She had an accent that made her words sound thick, like she had recently been eating mayonnaise. A waiter brought her a chair, and she sat in it, spouting apologies.

"Darling, I want you to meet her," my father cooed. "It's important. You're important."

She said something soft and fast in Spanish, placing her hand on my father's cheek. Then she turned to me. "He is a real sweetheart, your father. An old, snuggy teddy bear!"

I must have looked horrified, but my father just laughed. "Cari is from Colombia," he said. "You'll never guess how we met."

"We met on THE INTERNET!" Cari screamed. The other women looked up from their meals and frowned, but Cari was laughing too hard to notice. "My parents, they love him. Even though he's old."

Cari—short for Caridad—launched into the story of her courtship with my father, pausing to act out the most dramatic moments. He had pursued her for months online before flying her in to visit. Cari missed her family, of course, but meeting a man like that—so charming, so generous—was what she'd always dreamed.

"And now I live here," she said finally. "In exciting Europe."

"We had to get married quickly, of course," my father said calmly. "For the paperwork."

"Of course," I said. "That's why you didn't invite me."

Cari reached through the dirty glasses and took my hand. A cage of gold bangles sat awkwardly around her wrist. On one of her fingers, a large diamond winked at me. "I am sorry to hear about your mother," she said softly. "I don't know what I would do if I lost mine. She is my heart."

I couldn't look at her. Instead, I looked at the diamond. I wondered exactly how much it had cost.

"Really?" I said to the diamond. "Is that what you told her when you left?"

In the edge of my vision I saw Cari glance at my father, who gave her an encouraging nod. "When we get married for real," she said in a silky voice, "I want you to be my best maid of honor."

"Thank you," I said. "Excuse me." I stood, and Cari recoiled, as if my rage had rolled across the table and slapped her. "Bathroom," I said, and left.

By the time I returned, things had gotten jolly. My father and Cari were eating his mousse and giggling while they licked the spoons. I sat down stiffly and started to eat.

"So tell me," my father said, motioning for a third glass to be brought to the table. "What made you decide on London? A boy, perhaps?"

I'd prepared for this. Meeting my father's gaze, I described how a speaker had come to my economics class and talked about the importance of international experience in today's marketplace. After a visit to my college's career center, I found a work-abroad program and applied for a job with the marketing department of a dance club. Metropolis, had he heard of it?

"No," he said, "But I haven't been inside a club in thirty years." His expression softened, and he leaned back in his chair, looking at me fondly. "And you set it up on your own? What a little go-getter."

I smiled across the table. We had achieved a weirdly simpatico moment, in which he was proud of my lie, and so was I.

"When I was your age," he said, "I didn't know what I wanted to do."

"Neither did I," said Cari. "Until I met *mi esposo.*"

She leaned over to kiss him on the lips. Cari looked so young. How could she touch him? Did she know about the bean?

My father drained his glass and looked at his watch. "Listen, I'm stuck in meetings for the rest of the day, but why don't you two go shopping? My treat."

Cari squealed and squeezed his leg. "Waterloo?"

"Waterloo?" I asked, thinking of the terminal in London.

Cari took my father's credit card with one hand and flapped the other dismissively. "It's the best. Couture. You'll see."

Outside the restaurant my father and I shared an awkward hug and made plans to have dinner the next day, but we both knew these plans were half-hearted. The next morning I would phone his secretary to cancel, and she would reply that my father had unexpectedly been called out of town, but that he hoped I'd send him a picture of the dress.

———

The dress was a Versace. I had never owned anything remotely like it. Cari picked it out.

"Don't you just die to see such a thing?" She pulled it off the rack and held it out. I had to admit, it glittered. Not like the tacky disco-ball outfits I'd worn as a child, but like moonlight scattered across the ocean. Still, I hesitated.

"Don't be crazy. Do you have a boyfriend?" I shook my head, embarrassed at the price of the dress, which I'd just found on a tiny tag. "Well," she huffed, "do you want one?"

Cari had seemed pretty enough in the Comme Chez Soi, but now I saw a weak chin and sharp nose that was too large for her lips. Her neck was too short, her forehead too high, and a careful layer of makeup hid a smattering of acne that rolled across her cheeks. Here was a girl who knew how to play things right. I believed she would do well at Metropolis.

A saleswoman with tall hair came over and removed the dress from Cari's hands.

"It will look stunning on you," she said in perfect, unaccented English.

"Not me," said Cari. "Her!"

The saleswoman looked at me for the first time. Her face held no expression and her words came out clipped and efficient. "What is the occasion?"

I couldn't answer. The dress was too risqué for anything formal, but too beautiful for anything normal.

"She's in the music industry," Cari said quickly. "She is going to—what? The premiere of a record?"

"The British Music Awards," I said. "I'm a singer."

"Yes," said the saleswoman, regarding the dress critically and fluffing it out. "This will do. Follow me."

We went back to the changing area. The dress was a little large on top, but otherwise it fit perfectly. There was no mirror in my stall, so I had to go out to Cari and the saleswoman to see how I looked. The sitting room had mirrors in every direction. Cari and the saleswoman stopped chatting when they saw me, and Cari stood, clasping her hands.

"I hate you!" she said. "You're too beautiful!"

I stopped in the center of the room and saw myself, not as I truly was, but how I could be.

"The transformative power of Versace," said the saleswoman, coming up behind me and pinching the fabric. "We'll take the bust in, of course."

"You must own this dress," said Cari. "No man will resist it."

I looked at my profile and wondered if this was true. The dress was the color of snow and had a scooped neck that almost reached my nipples. The material was so soft that I couldn't stop touching it. Was I irresistible? There was only one way to find out.

———

I took the train back to London for two reasons: to pass through the Chunnel, and because there would be more room in the carriage to hang the Versace. When I got back to Shoreditch I wanted to see how it looked in my own little flat, in my own rented mirror, so I zipped it up and twirled. The dress looked like money. Bright white money.

And so did I.

I wore it that night to Metropolis. The dress did all the work. It greeted people and drew them closer. It caught their attention and reflected what they wanted. By the end of the night I'd given twelve dances and spent two hours in a private room with a group of financial planners and a slender Bulgarian. The Versace didn't come off easily, but that turned out to be a good thing. I pulled the zipper down slowly and the men stared at the triangle of flesh, watching it grow bigger. By the time I was naked a full minute had passed. I turned to face them and got on my knees, giving a slow rise until someone's nose was between my breasts. Then I got dressed. I felt confident putting the Versace back on, even though the tightness of the fabric should have made this awkward. Sometimes I asked the men to help with the zipper, which they were more than happy to do.

An hour before last call the good-looking guy came into the club. I didn't approach him but made sure he saw me before I went upstairs. Within minutes he came up beside me, and I told him it would be twenty, not ten, because he'd been away so long.

"Absence tax," I said.

He didn't argue, but followed me into a private room and sat on one of the benches. I looked at the mirror on the ceiling. Up there, I looked like someone else entirely. I did my little show with the white dress, but let it last longer, and when I was down to my G-string I turned to the man and asked if he wanted to see everything.

"Fifty," I said. We both knew this wasn't how it worked. He stared at me for a moment, then reached in his wallet. I took the note in my teeth.

"I like you," I said, putting the bill in my garter. "I like you so much."

I pushed my G-string down and stepped over to the man. I thought he would put his hands on me, and if he did I thought I would let him, but he just sat there like he was supposed to. I felt like breaking all the rules, and when I realized this might be a sexy thing to say, I went ahead and said it. The guy looked interested and asked what I had in mind. But I didn't know.

I put my knees around his legs and let my ass fall into his lap. His hands cupped my cheeks but didn't squeeze. What next? If I kissed him, that would be too much; there would be nothing left to give. I pushed my breasts up to his mouth. I felt his breath against my nipples, but neither of us moved closer.

After a moment I slid off the bench. I wanted to apologize, but if I did, all the power I held would disappear. The man didn't look sorry when I picked up the dress and put it back on, though he did ask me to join him downstairs where his friends were waiting at the bar. I knew I should say no—*I am hard to get, pay more for me, sir*—but instead I followed him, holding onto the handrail, knowing that with each step my currency lost value.

At the bar, the man bought me a drink. Fifteen quid. It made me feel a little better.

"You don't know the birds?" one of his friends was saying. "It's illegal to feed them."

"What?" said a northern girl. "Pigeons?"

"It's Livingstone. He wants to round them up and kill them. With poison."

"It's true," said a Russian with long white legs that dissolved under a silver dress. "I live very close to Trafalgar Square, three years. You don't see them anymore."

"We should save them," said a busty Croatian. "Take them to the country and free them."

"Euck," said the northerner. "I hate bloody pigeons."

"I'll take you to see them," said a large, ruddy man. He said this to the Russian, who fed a practiced boredom to his uncooked steak of a face.

"I might go see these pigeons," she said. "But I don't think you know much about them."

The man leaned in and said something to her hair. The other girls in the circle were looking around, counting the men. As always, the numbers were uneven and not in our favor.

"I know where they are," the ruddy man said. "They won't disappoint you."

"At this hour?" A woman in leopard print laughed. "They'll be asleep."

"Nah," said the man. "These birds are up."

It was the end of the night. The women without suitors leaned heavily on the bar, letting their shoulders fall inward like butterflies shutting their wings. The ruddy-faced man said that he and his mates were going to see the birds, and anyone who felt like it could come along. The Russian and the Croatian were interested, but said we'd need to sneak out to avoid the bouncers.

"Like at camp," I said, but no one understood. The good-looking man asked if I wanted to see the birds. I didn't know what I wanted, so I said yes.

———

When I asked why she sliced up her beautiful face, my mother explained it like this: "You can't buy happiness, but you can buy attention. If you're a woman, these things are almost interchangeable."

She scheduled the final surgery during my fall break so I could drive her home and keep her bedside stocked with liquids. The complications that led to her death wouldn't become complications until weeks later, when I was back at school, but on the afternoon of the surgery I was at the hospital, waiting for her to be wheeled into the bland recovery room—a "whatever" room. She came to me wrapped like a hasty present. Eyes and chin covered with bandages. The skin behind the fabric was yellow and waxy, and her voice was loosened with drugs. Puffy and slow, she twisted her head and looked at me with her non-eyes and said, "Am I beautiful?"

It was a joke. One she'd been saving for me. But I didn't want to give her the satisfaction of a laugh.

My mother didn't like being done. She liked looking in the mirror and finding the raised scars the surgeons had hidden above her hairline. She liked to trace the raised beds of skin with her fingertips. She liked the process of planning and executing her next transformation.

The named goal was always beauty, but the actual goal was something else, something off to the side: the effort that beauty required. If one day she'd woken up beautiful and adored, she wouldn't have been happy. There would have been nothing for her to do then, like the time I caught her in the garden in the middle of June, surrounded by peak blossoms. She'd spent the first half of the year on her knees, wrist-deep in rock and dirt. When all that work finally paid off in a heady rush of scent and color, she sat on her stone bench and looked around in displeasure, stewing in joyless abundance.

She wanted me to be different. A new kind of woman: confident, happy, smart. And beautiful, which I think to her meant satisfied, complete. "Don't give away your power," she warned. "Know when to walk away." She didn't have to explain this further. I knew the right time to walk away was after you'd gotten his attention.

———

Trafalgar Square at four in the morning was still Trafalgar Square, bright and surprisingly busy. It was cold, though. I shivered in my peacoat and saw the lower edges of my dress sparkle in the streetlights.

The ruddy-faced man led our group of six around the fountain and across the street. The Russian girl kept her arm connected to our leader, and the busty Croatian walked beside the third man, whose silence implied he was capable of anything. I walked next to the good-looking guy and made the obligatory joke about Nelson's Column. As we left the square and turned down an alley, I held my coat closed to ward off puddles that might splatter the hem of the Versace. Our group passed through a cloud of steam that rose from the grill of a sausage cart, and the smell of cooked onions made everyone hungry.

The first alley led to another alley, and then another. Eventually we stopped at a derelict pub that had once been called the Gardeners Arms, but which now was not called anything. It was dark. I blinked hard to clear my vision, but didn't see anything special about the place. No pigeons, no other birds. Then we heard a scraping noise and everyone turned.

Three women stood in the shadows at the far end of the brick wall. One smoked a cigarette, one picked at her hair, and the third tapped at her phone with zombie-like boredom. Two wore mini-skirts in garish, highlighter shades of green, pink, and yellow, while the third wore a blue dress tight as a bandage. It was the clothes that told me they were prostitutes, those bright curves glowing like neon signs in the dark. Their shoes were even higher and thinner than the ones I wore at Metropolis, and above that their spindly legs teetered and bowed and their black hair fell like spilled ink across their faces.

The men from the club were laughing. Even the good-looking guy. He seemed embarrassed, pink-faced, nervous, but he was laughing, too, with his back all hunched and his neck a quick flash of white like a fin in dark water. All three men kept their hands balled inside their jeans, and they moved like windup toys, first buzzing away from the women and then buzzing back, their shadows shortening and lengthening across the cobblestone.

"Idiots," said the Russian quietly. She started moving down the street, then stopped at the corner and lit a cigarette. The Croatian and I followed her.

"I don't get it," said the Croatian. "Why are they laughing?"

"They think it's funny." The Russian blew a warm stream of smoke into the air and winced down at the ash falling from her fingers. "They think we're the same."

"No, they don't." I looked back at the good-looking guy, who giggled with horror as the ruddy man tugged at his pocket.

"Wrong," said the Russian. "*You* don't. I don't. They do."

We pretended not to watch while the ruddy-faced man pulled something out. The other men got quiet and the ruddy man said, "Feed the birds, yeah?" and threw what he had. A flash of gold hit the side of the building and bounced into the road. A piece of silver danced. The accompanying sound was sweet and tinkly. Glockenspiel, I thought. Wind chimes.

The prostitutes looked at the noise and shuffled away, just a yard or two, to stay out of range. They did not look at us.

The men also ignored us. They had thrown all their coins and were now shoving the good-looking guy in the direction of the women.

"They don't know," I said. "How it looks to us." The Russian shrugged and offered me a cigarette. I took it and added, "It's criminal." But I didn't really think the men were that bad. I was thinking about Metropolis.

The Croatian pulled out a mobile and chirped, "I'm calling a minicab. Want to share a minicab?"

The Russian turned to me and blinked. "Where do you live?"

"Shoreditch."

Her head twisted slightly, like a hawk getting a better look at its prey.

"American, yes?"

I nodded. The Russian glanced down at the flaps of my coat, which had blown open in the wind.

"Nice dress," she said, and turned away.

I had forgotten I was wearing the Versace. I wished I wasn't. My teeth clenched down on the cigarette.

"A car's on its way," said the Croatian. I almost said I'd split the ride with her, but something stopped me. Silence. The men weren't laughing anymore. I turned and saw the ruddy-faced man looking down at us. Though I couldn't see his eyes, he seemed to be considering something. I knew that soon he'd lead the men back to us, and we would have to deal with them.

"Get home safe," I told the girls, and walked around the corner. I didn't look back until I'd made it to where none of them could see me. I heard traffic up the hill and climbed toward the sound, reaching the Strand just as I finished the Russian's cigarette. I'd smoked it all the way down to the filter.

The Strand wasn't busy at that hour. I was lucky to hail a black cab. Inside, the light was yellow and soft, and the seat accepted my weight like a giant hand. The cabbie talked just how I wanted him to talk, like a kind grandpa with a gentle cockney accent.

"Where to, miss?"

I told him the address.

"American!" he said. "On holiday?" As we pulled into the street, the cabbie's blue eyes regarded me in the rearview mirror. "What's a pretty girl like you doing out so late? You've got to be careful around here."

I mumbled, "Not that pretty."

"Of course you are. A pretty girl in a foreign city. Who wouldn't want to snatch you up?"

We drove along the river and then turned north, moving past glowing storefronts and the identical trees of well-tended parks. I leaned back against the leather and held my jacket at the throat. There was a smudge on my skirt, big as a fist and gray like fireplace ash.

"My dress," I said.

"It's nice," said the cabbie. "Where'd you find that?"

After a while I said, "Oh, it isn't mine," and the cabbie, well trained in the art of conversation, let it go.

The traffic light changed and we began to roll forward. I looked out at the parked cars, and a weird reversal happened where it felt like the city was moving through me instead of me moving through it.

I decided that tomorrow or the next day I would go to an internet café and buy a plane ticket. I would return to America where they would let me be a sophomore. But first we had to get through the city, past Harrods and a darkened kebab shop, past Waterstones and Barclays and all the museums I hadn't visited. London seemed sad to me then. Each blurry brick building felt like a loss, and I wondered at the maze of it—all these empty things we had to pass, just to get me to my door.

Billy M

Not that I wanted to think about Billy M, but in Knoxville I stopped for gas and saw his name on the cover of the *S—— Review*. I threw the magazine on the passenger seat and drove until a crawl of traffic on I-81 gave me time to read the poems. None were about me.

I'd heard most of these poems last year in San Diego. Billy M had read them to me slowly, lingering on the smutty details: the coarse horsehair on an older woman's tummy; the grinning tilt of a young girl's ass. I flipped through the pages until my eye caught on the word *nipple*.

O valorous nipple, which incites me to
Rapture
Our twin tongues mixing, marking
Forging a coat of arms
To ward off the
Six o'clock
Alarms

I imagined the sort of people who liked the poem. I pictured them jerking off in a dark corner of the library, surrounded by Lowell and Yeats and Whoever. The smell of the books' paper, the thickness of the pages, turning them on. I thought about that and got a little hot. I thought about Billy M sleeping with other women, and I got even hotter. But I did not want to be a victim of arousal. Why should a guy like Billy M get to have all the fun? So. I lifted myself off the leather to get a good angle. I was a girl, sure, but I could also be a hunter.

By now the traffic had smoothed out. Ten miles passed at sixty miles per hour, and Billy M's pages flapped in the wind. It took longer than usual, but I got there, fingers quick against the cool teeth of the zipper. I called out his name, and a voice beside me said:

"Oh, look! My poems."

Billy M sat in the passenger seat, holding the *S—— Review*.

"Hey," he said. "What are you doing?" He looked at my hand, which was down my pants. "Are you driving? Driving and—that—at the same time?"

"No," I said. "What?" I scratched myself. "I have an itch." I removed the offending hand, rubbed it on my jeans, then put it on the wheel. "What are you doing in my car?" I said. "I left you on the beach."

He looked out the window. "This doesn't look like California."

"That's because it's West Virginia."

"Oh. What's in West Virginia?"

"None of your beeswax," I said.

Two weeks ago Billy M threw an apple at my head and called me a cunt. Clearly, the details of my life no longer fell under the realm of his beeswax.

Billy M tore open the pockets of his board shorts. I glanced over and saw sand spill onto the floor of my car. "No wallet," he said. "I must have left it at the beach."

"Look," I said, "I'm flattered that you missed me. But it's not appropriate for you to be here. I'll drop you at the next bus station." I pressed hard on the gas to show I was serious. How, for the previous eleven days, had I failed to notice a six-foot-two-inch man hiding in my car?

"No cell phone, either," he said, hands skating over the shiny surface of his rashguard. "And just for the record, I don't think I missed you."

"Then why did you get into my car?"

"I didn't," he said. "The last thing I remember is—"

It was getting dark. Up ahead, I saw a sign for a town. Seven miles at eighty miles per hour equaled five more minutes with Billy M.

"You're pissed," he said.

"I'm not pissed. I'm confused."

"No," he said. "You're pissed. I can tell."

I gripped the wheel. In thirty seconds, four minutes would be left.

"Is this some kind of apology?" I asked. "Are you sorry for being an asshole?"

He shrugged. "Is a duck sorry for being a duck?"

It was just the type of thing Billy M would say.

"You knew about the girls from the beginning," he said. "I told you how it was."

"People change," I said. "The best ones do."

"Sure," he said. "They become worse."

He put on his seat belt.

"Don't get too cozy," I said. "We're almost there."

He clicked the belt into its holder and said, "Remember that tea cozy? At the house in Long Beach?"

I hesitated, just for a second. "Nope. Must've been somebody else."

The last time we had sex, I pulled the sheet over my head and he kissed me through the fabric. Mouth cotton mouth. Hand cotton breast. There must have been some original time when we liked the way it felt to look at each other. But I guess we wanted to feel like strangers again.

Billy M leaned across the stick shift and poked me in the shoulder.

"Aren't you from Delaware?"

I flicked on the turn signal.

"Is that where we're going?"

I took the exit and slowed for the Stop sign at the end of the ramp. Both directions looked dark. I went left.

"Seventy percent of turns made are right turns," said Billy M.

"Ninety percent of statistics are made up on the spot," I said.

"Ah," he said. "It's just like old times. We're Abbott and Costello. Conan and Andy."

"Fucking Whore and Asshole."

"Exactly. That's exactly what I meant."

There were no buildings, only pastures with cows. I turned around and drove the other way.

"This isn't a town," Billy M said. "Where are the houses?"

I stopped at the crest of a hill and got out of the car. Billy M got out, too, and called across the hood.

"Are we there yet?"

"You are," I said, and jumped back inside. I locked the doors, but I wasn't so fast with the windows. Billy M managed to get half a forearm through before I could roll them up.

"That's the bitch I know and love," he said.

I revved the engine. "Why are you here?"

"I don't remember."

"Try."

"I was at the beach."

"And?"

"And then I wasn't."

"You were here."

"Yes."

"You got into my car."

"No."

"You were surfing."

"Yes."

"Did you see me?"

"Yes."

"You saw me get into my car."

"I saw you get into your car."

"I told you I was leaving. I was leaving for good."

"Yes."

"But you didn't care."

"I cared." Billy M waved with his trapped hand. "I care now."

"Not good enough," I said. "Everyone cares when they're stuck."

I lowered the window half an inch and the ribbon of his arm slipped out of sight. When I heard his sneakers scrape against the gravel, I released the clutch and floored it. I sort of wanted to feel a sick bump, but there was no bump. The car was halfway down the hill before I looked in the rearview mirror. All I could see was the dust I'd left behind.

———

I drove east toward Delaware. In my peripheral vision I kept seeing white blurs of imaginary deer, so when a motel appeared I parked in the lot and went inside. The lobby was empty. I rang the bell.

"There you are!"

It was Billy M.

"I got us a room." He held up the key. "Last one in gets the bathtub."

I'd been driving for miles since I left him behind. A hundred at least.

He peeled off his shirt and walked down the hall. "Man," he said. "I'm beat." I was annoyed to see Billy M's chest looked good. Why couldn't my brain hallucinate a flabby Billy M instead?

He unlocked a door and I followed him in. The room consisted of a single bed, a chair, and a television. "Enjoy the tub," he said, flopping onto the bed.

"A hundred miles is pretty far," I said. "Did you hitch?"

He patted the mattress. "I think we should give it a go. Let's pretend the bed is the only rock in a river of lava. Look out! Your feet are melting."

I took out my phone and dialed his number, but the call went to voice mail. I looked straight at Billy M and said into my phone, "If you're not with me right now, call me."

He smirked. "Well, that's not confusing at all."

I hung up the phone and threw it at him.

"Do you remember dying?" I said.

"No," he said. "Do you?"

———

While Billy M slept I stood in front of the bathroom mirror and performed all the rituals of exorcism I knew. I said his name and spun three times. I got his poems from the car and read them aloud. I read them backward. I read them backward while stomping my feet. I put my ass on the cold tile floor of the bathroom and said his name when I came. I awoke the next morning with a wet face and a mouth full of bath-mat fur. Billy M was singing in the shower.

"Good morning, starshine." He popped his head around the curtain and grinned. "Welcome to another beautiful day in purgatory!"

I should have known Billy M would be enthusiastically dead. When the editor of a prominent magazine stood him up at a bar, Billy M had come home happy. He said he didn't mind getting stood up because it meant he'd been invited in the first place. And wasn't it nice, being invited?

"You're supposed to put the curtain on the inside," I said. "I'm drowning down here."

"If you're drowning, you aren't dead," he said. "Good news!"

Billy M stepped out of the shower. From my vantage point on the bath mat, it was clear his toenails needed to be clipped.

He dripped and asked, "Do you have any toothpaste?"

I closed my eyes. "In my bag."

Billy M left the room. I shut the door and locked it.

"Hey!" He came back and knocked on the door. "Weh am I thuppose to thit?"

Billy M banged around the motel room looking for a receptacle worthy of his saliva. He must have found one, because the knocking resumed with increased fervor.

"You'd better come out," he said. "The bathroom is a cave of ice. Careful! Your eyelashes are freezing."

I tried to think of times when I could have died. There were lots. I'd been driving for days. "I think one of us is a ghost," I said. "I think it's you."

"Well," he said. "You know what that means."

"What?"

"No condoms."

I went to the mirror, said my name three times, and spun around. I closed my eyes and opened them, but I was still there.

"Guess what?" I said through the door. "I'm feeling solipsistic."

The first time we ever slept together, Billy M had asked me how I felt. The answer was "Slutty," but I didn't say "Slutty." He touched my mouth in the dark.

"I can't see your face," he'd said. He put his fingers against my lips to read my expression. "Do you feel happy? Do you feel sad?"

"Do I feel proud?" I said. "Do I feel stunned?"

I had work the next day and needed to sleep, but Billy M kept me awake with adjectives.

"Do you feel incompetent? Do you feel duped?"

Daylight eventually came through the window. He could see my face. Still, we'd tried to think of better words.

"Do I feel obstinate?"

"Do you feel maligned?"

"Garrulous?"

"Petulant?"

"Fond?"

When we finally got up, I didn't feel slutty anymore. I felt hungry. And a new feeling, too, one I hadn't been brave enough to say—hopeful.

———

I opened the bathroom door. Billy M was gone. I sat on the bed until the room got dark, and I stayed awake most of the night, listening for the crunch of the key in the lock.

In the morning I put on my ski jacket, brushed the frost off my car, and drove back to the interstate. I flicked at the radio, but got only fuzz. The sun was up. I drove so the sun stayed behind me. I drove until a green sign welcomed me to Ohio, and another thanked me for visiting.

The signs in Indiana proved equally hospitable, as did the signs in Illinois. I counted the time in my head.

Seventeen hundred miles at sixty miles per hour means twenty-eight hours to go. If I didn't stop, I could be there tomorrow.

Seventeen hundred miles at ninety miles per hour means nineteen hours to go. If I drove even faster, I could be there today. Time zones would blow through me, and I would beat the sun.

Seventeen hundred miles at seventeen hundred miles per hour means only one hour to go. Me and my car and all my stuff, we could be there by lunchtime. Pulling up into a sandy stall. The sound of flip-flops, the gulls and the heat. Shading my eyes against the smell of sardines. Searching the swell for a brown-backed man.

The world outside the car was a blur of green and white, but inside, the wheel and I were steady. The pages of Billy M's poems didn't move. I saw the word *waiting*. I saw the word *pull*. The finger of the speedometer wobbled in warning, but I had done the math. If I wanted to get there yesterday I'd have to really push it. And I wanted to be there yesterday. I wanted to really push it.

Great Romantics

U li agreed with her grandmother. She would play the Rachmaninoff for the famous teacher in Princeton. After all, Rachmaninoff was frequently performed by the winners of the regional piano competitions Uli attended each year—winners who were often Asian girls like her.

Well. Kind of like her. Uli was only half Japanese, but Grandma Kitty assured her this was a good thing. Uli could play Rachmaninoff with the cold precision of an Asian girl and the overflowing heart of an Irish-English-German romantic. But Kitty also acknowledged that certain aspects of Uli's mixed background were problematic. The winning pianists came from Philadelphia and Pittsburgh instead of the corn-and-cow center of the state, they had been playing the piano since the age of three or four, and they studied with very good teachers. This last difference was the one Kitty could rectify, and she believed that if she did, her granddaughter would become a great musician.

They drove to New Jersey on a Thursday, skipping school to visit the famous teacher in the parlor of her brownstone. The parlor had a better piano than Kitty's living room did, a Yamaha that looked old but sounded bright and clean. Uli slid her skirted bottom against the bench and set her hands on the keys. The black ones were dull from the years they'd spent under other children's oily fingers. She rolled out a few scales to test the instrument's tenor and resistance.

When the teacher nodded, Uli began the Rachmaninoff. The room filled with sudden, wrenching life. Notes stampeded off a cliff and were caught by a tempestuous sea. Kitty and the famous teacher disappeared beneath the waves, and Uli rolled up and down, trying to stay afloat.

She was fifteen. So far, her experience with romance had been limited to music. She recognized her own confused desire— her desire to be desired—in the brooding ache of a Liszt rhapsody and the dreaminess of a Schubert sonata. She didn't understand teenage boys or the girls who dated them, but when she played she understood how love and the longing for love could trap itself in an eternal melody. Someday, the music told her, when she was older and more beautiful, she would be swept away by a feeling that would eclipse her classmates' silly backseat fumblings.

Uli was sailing, soaring. But the famous teacher stopped her at the sixteenth measure.

"The piece is not a porno," she said sternly. "It is a striptease."

"Oh." Uli looked down at the keys. How had they betrayed her so quickly?

"My granddaughter is a good, quiet girl," Kitty said. "She is unfamiliar with pornography."

"Hmm." The teacher looked doubtfully at Uli's hands, which had automatically returned to the piece's opening position. "When did you start playing?"

"Eight," Uli whispered. But this was a lie. She'd been nine and a half when her father brought her to live at Kitty's house.

The teacher looked to her grandmother. "So late!"

"She came to me at eight," Kitty said. "She began lessons right away."

"You didn't mention this before. I'm not fond of wasting my time."

Kitty was already sitting straight as a rod, so all she could do was lift her chin higher. "She's an excellent student. Tell my granddaughter what you want her to do, and she'll do it."

Yes, Uli thought. She was good at following instructions. Perhaps that was her greatest talent—not music, but dutiful compliance. This is why Kitty loved her. Kitty knew exactly how things ought to be done, and Uli knew how to obey.

The teacher snapped her chin toward Uli. "Don't gush. Only geniuses are allowed to gush. Are you a genius?"

"No."

"A prodigy?"

"No."

The teacher's expression softened, and she leaned forward, blocking the yellow light from the Tiffany lamp. Uli watched a long shadow spill across the octaves like a stain.

"Tell me something small and true."

Uli hesitated. She took her hands off the keys and set them in her lap. She was a good, quiet girl, like Kitty said.

"The same piece, or . . . ?"

The teacher leaned back, put two fingers to her lips, one from each hand, and folded the remainder in a knot below her chin. Uli wondered if this gesture had a special meaning in the secret societies of music she would never be asked to join.

"Forget what you practiced. Just play something true."

Uli looked dumbly at the keys. Set her fingers above them. White faces slick on her dry skin. The second hand of her grandmother's watch ticked against the silence. It made a noise that sounded like *Tsk. Tsk.*

She realized she'd been holding her breath, and as she exhaled, she looked up at the famous teacher's face. It was all right to do this now because she knew she'd never see it again. The teacher had a nose like a beak and waxy skin marked by broken capillaries. She wore a lot of makeup, especially around her eyes, and her hair was dyed an unnatural shade of glimmerless black. A thin white scar wound from just below her left ear to her collarbone.

Uli stared at that scar and played a single note. A middle D. The woman tightened her lips with displeasure.

"All right," Kitty said. "I'm sorry we wasted your time."

———

The next day Uli returned to school. "Bad shrimp," she said to her English teacher, a man who loved early American literature and the latest high school gossip.

"So your family won't be relocating, then?" he smirked. "To Princeton?"

Uli's cheeks flushed and she shook her head. That had never been the plan, but so what? It didn't matter now.

The teacher reclined in his chair. "You missed a pop quiz on *The Awakening.*"

"I can take it now."

But the teacher, repulsed by her eagerness, waved her away. "After class."

She gave him her late homework, a dozen facts about Kate Chopin she'd copied from the textbook, and retreated to her desk. The girl assigned to sit behind her, a know-it-all called Susie, poked Uli's shoulder blade with a pen.

"Are you going to the Bens' tonight?"

"No."

The Bens were two boys in the junior class. Because their last names were Harding and Howe, they often stood side by side and so were fated from childhood to become mortal enemies or best friends. They chose the latter, and now they were sixteen and popular and held parties at the Howe family river lot.

"Why not?"

"I have to practice piano."

"On a Friday night?"

Uli was about to reply with a snotty *Yes, on a Friday night*, when she realized it might not be true.

Each day for the past five years she'd spent two hours after school practicing the music Mrs. Abramson had assigned at their last lesson. Then Uli switched to homework, which she tried to complete quickly so she could spend the remainder of the evening playing for fun. "Fun" meant going through Kitty's collection of sheet music and dropping the discarded pieces on the floor until they swamped the piano bench. She could sight-read almost anything, and this made the feeling of playing in the evenings very different from the afternoons. Rather than practicing or performing, it was like putting in a cassette tape and dancing to whatever came out of the speaker. The music cleaned her insides the way a rush of water cleared a clogged pipe. All her thoughts and feelings flew down the drain and disappeared.

Kitty wouldn't allow Uli's practice to be interrupted, so each night after dinner Uli's grandpa went out to Maurey's Tavern or Franco's to watch TV and have a few drinks. Meanwhile, Kitty cleaned the kitchen and did the dishes before retiring to her room. At ten o'clock Uli dropped the fallboard over the keys and collected the rivers of sheet music before going to bed. There were never any chores for her to do, no responsibilities but school and piano. She was fifteen and did not know how to chop a carrot or load the dishwasher. Beyond grade school, she'd never been to a party.

"I'm going at seven," Susie said. "I could pick you up in my car."

"Your parents will let you go?"

Susie frowned and flicked the tail of her purple headscarf around her neck. "What, your parents won't?"

"Grandparents," Uli corrected her.

"Muslims aren't always strict," Susie said, her voice suddenly caustic. "That's just a stereotype."

Uli opened her mouth to apologize but heard herself saying instead, "I'd like to go with you, Susie. But I may need to do something for my grandmother."

"Like what? Chores?" Susie shrugged. "Just do them later."

Yesterday they'd driven out of Princeton in silence. At home Kitty said she had a terrible headache and told Uli to order pizza for dinner. Normally they ate a home-cooked meal on the dining room table that had been carved by Kitty's forefathers, but that night Uli and her grandfather ate at the coffee table, parked in front of a Steelers game.

Grandpa had sat beside her on the sofa, merrily licking the grease from his fingertips and forgetting to ask about Princeton. When Uli reminded him, he didn't ask how the audition had gone but asked her what she'd played. Rachmaninoff, she said, and explained that he was a late Romantic, perhaps the last of the great Romantics, whereas Beethoven was early and Chopin and Liszt fit in between.

After Grandpa left to watch the second half of the game at Franco's, Uli wrapped the remainder of the pizza in foil and went to her room to finish *The Awakening*. She didn't practice piano that night, and Kitty didn't tell her to do it, either. But at ten o'clock, as Uli was brushing her teeth and washing her face, Kitty knocked on the bathroom door and placed a small silver box on the lip of the sink, saying, "I thought you would like this." Without waiting for her to open the gift, Kitty padded along the cream carpet of the hallway and shut her bedroom door. Inside the box, a gold bracelet rested on a bed of pink silk. A grand piano charm dangled from the chain, and a small, real diamond was embedded in the open lid.

Uli had closed the box and placed it at the back of her closet. The bracelet was obviously expensive, but she knew she'd never wear it.

"You're right," Uli said to Susie. "I can totally go to the party. Want to meet at Wendy's?"

———

Susie waved through the windshield as she pulled into Wendy's, and Uli lifted her Frosty in greeting. Two hours earlier she'd left a note on the refrigerator for Kitty: WENT TO GET PIZZA WITH SUSIE, A GIRL FROM SCHOOL. She'd intended to deliver this half-lie to her grandmother verbally, in person, but at five o'clock the house was still empty. Uli grabbed her jacket and portable CD player for the walk into town. Then, right before she left, she pushed another handwritten note into the cork message board, tacking it directly below the first: BACK BY MIDNIGHT.

Any other teenager might have left a similar note and it would mean nothing, but Kitty would see it and go insane. "Midnight" was an hour so outrageous, so outside the bounds of what Uli had ever done, she might as well have written FUCK YOU, GRANDMA!

"Nice car," Uli said to Susie as she opened the door.

"It's my dad's. Wait, we need ice."

The girls crossed over the concrete strip to the gas station and hauled four chunky bags to the trunk.

"Put them on the jackets," Susie instructed. "My dad will freak if we mess up the upholstery."

They got in the car and buckled their seat belts. Something about the act of simultaneous buckling made Uli feel sophisticated and responsible, like a real adult. When Susie put her hands on the wheel, Uli saw she'd redone her nails in a pale, glossy rose. She was also wearing makeup, and her shimmery headscarf perfectly matched her nails.

"You look pretty," Uli said. "I mean, you always do, but."

Susie flicked her head self-consciously. "Thanks. You too."

Uli wore dark jeans, and under her jacket, a long-sleeved tee that read HANGING 10. The 0 was a cartoon wave drawn in a flower-power style. She'd gotten it at the thrift store two summers ago while visiting her sister and mom in Hawaiʻi. Kitty did not let her wear the shirt to school.

"Your hair," Susie said. "Did you curl it?"

Uli shook her head, and the relaxed waves brushed against her cheeks. "A little," she admitted.

They turned onto Lincoln and drove past the grammar school and the playground.

"I really like Ben," Susie said, sighing a little.

"Ben Howe?"

Susie nodded.

"But you're Muslim."

"So?"

"So you have to marry a Muslim." When Susie didn't say anything, she added, "Don't you?"

"I just like him is all. I'm allowed to like him. Is that okay with you?"

"I guess. Ben Howe is cute."

"He's nice, too."

They turned onto Bloomingrove Road, which would take them past the campgrounds to the junction with 973. Uli's grandfather had taken her out this way to go fishing a few times, before her life was usurped by piano.

"I do need to marry a Muslim," Susie admitted. "But it's not like I want to marry Ben."

"What are the parties like?"

"Fun. Lame. Depends."

"Do you drink?"

"Alcohol?" Susie shook her head. "My dad would freak. He drinks Coronas, though."

"Isn't that . . ." Uli searched for the word. "Illegal?"

"Haram. But my family's not that strict. Like, I don't always wear a headscarf."

"I know. I mean, I noticed."

Susie bit her lower lip, then released it. "You're Japanese, right?"

"Yeah."

"On your mom's side or your dad's side?"

"Mom's side," Uli said, and at the same time Susie also said, "Mom's side." Uli was confused, so she laughed.

"Let me guess. You eat rice and own a kimono, but you don't speak any Japanese?"

"My mom's in Hawai'i," Uli said. "I eat rice when I'm there, or at the Chinese buffet with my grandpa. I don't own a kimono."

"I thought we'd be friends," Susie said, "because we're both different."

Uli's heart beat faster. Was she different? Different like Susie?

"Oh." She could not say yes or no because neither answer would be right. Instead she thought of the strangeness of the word *oh*, like the "oh" in *zero*, which was both a curling wave on her shirt and a circle that contained the concept of absence.

"My mom hit a deer up here." Susie slowed as they took a big curve in the road. "It ran into the trees, but for sure it died."

"Oh. Can I roll down the window?"

Susie did it herself using the fancy buttons in her father's fancy car. The wind hurled itself against the open window in blasts and sucks and Uli leaned into it, loving the cool hand smacking her face, waking her up.

———

The hunting lights from a parked truck speared the darkness. A small group had gathered near a cooler on the truck's open bed, and a clutch of the girls' peers stood farther down the bank, silhouetted against a campfire.

Susie asked Uli to take the ice bags out of the trunk and then quickly abandoned her, running off toward the fire. Uli put the bags next to Susie's back tire and wiped her hands on her jeans. She wondered how weird it would be if she continued to walk down the dirt road alone. It would be nice to let the dark sink around her, to hear her sneakers kicking up rocks and to smell the river rocks and pinesap. But Susie would tell people she'd left, and then it would become a story—the one about that girl who went to a party and disappeared.

She decided to carry an ice bag and imagined what the truck kids would think. Look at Uli, such a helpful guest, let's invite her next time! The first person she recognized was Ben Harding, whose legs dangled off the tailgate and whose arms were wrapped around Cindy Lucas. From the casual way Ben snuggled his crotch against Cindy's spine, Uli understood that people her age were having sex now.

The other faces materialized out of the colorless dark. Don Strommer and Erin Newsome, who had their hands in the back pockets of each other's jeans, and Monica Kerensky and Nate Parker, their tennis-team arms interlinked.

"Hey," Erin said. "Look who's here."

Uli dropped the bag of wilting ice. The country song on the radio ended and another took its place.

"Is that beer?" Uli shouted and pointed at the red container. "Susie and I brought ice."

"Oh, thanks," said Ben Harding. "Susie's a smart girl."

"We always run out of ice," confirmed Erin.

"You want a beer?" Ben Harding released Cindy and scrambled on his knees to fish in the cooler. He extracted a cold can and tossed it to Uli, who somehow caught the thing and, feeling a rush of emotion, cried out, "Yay!"

"Ha-ha," Cindy laughed. "Yay, beer!" Her laughter morphed into a scream as she recoiled from Ben Harding's hand crawling beneath her sweatshirt. "Babe, that's coooold."

Another pause ensued, longer than the previous one. Did these people converse when Uli wasn't around? Or did they just grope each other to the smooth twang of Tim McGraw?

"Excuse me," she said. "I'm going to circulate." She regretted this sentence immediately and ran away from the truck. Down by the campfire, Susie's pink headscarf glowed like a radiant jellyfish in the sea of heads, and Ben Howe was telling a dirty joke.

". . . and while he's eating her out, the guy finds a piece of carrot and says, 'Shit! I'm going to be sick.' And the whore says, 'Funny, that's what the last guy said!' "

Susie groaned and smacked her forehead with her palm. The guys in the group laughed while the girls squealed in minor triads. A clear G-sharp emerged, and then, from the girls sitting on a blanket, a droopy E.

"I can't believe it," Ben Howe said. "Uli's here!"

"And she's drinking beer," said Josh Greenhill. "Wicked."

"We brought ice," Uli said. She flapped an arm to indicate where the ice could be found.

"Do you burn?" asked Josh. "Who's got the—oh, I have it."

Josh moved closer to Uli. In one palm sat a lighter and in the other, a glass pipe that fluttered in the orange light of the fire.

"I don't," Uli said, meaning that she didn't smoke, would never smoke, but then she heard herself saying, "know what to do."

"I'll show you," Josh said.

Two pep squad girls exchanged eye rolls. One of them was in her gym class—Mara. She had dark, perfectly straight bangs cut a quarter-inch above her brows. She also had lips that Uli envied, full as ripe fruit and painted the bloody maroon of cherry skins.

Josh told Uli to watch him first. He held the skinny end of the pipe to his lips and lit the ashy bowl, but the glow went out immediately. Josh insisted on refilling it.

"Don't worry. I'll make it fresh for you."

"Josh is coming down with yellow fever," said Mara. Everyone except for Susie and Josh laughed. Uli pretended she hadn't heard. She felt ridiculous holding the pipe to her lips and waiting for Josh to bring the lighter in. The cold, wet beer was still in her other hand. Her eyes crossed as she gazed down her nose at the yellow flame. Smoke rose from the bowl.

"Toke, toke," Josh chanted, his voice cracking a little.

Uli pulled away and coughed. She bent her body in half. It felt like she would never stop coughing.

"She's your problem now, Joshie," said Mara.

Josh asked, "How do you feel?"

Nose at her knees, she waved one hand in the air. Josh took the beer from her and cracked it open. "Drink," he said.

The beer was so cold and good on her throat, she hardly noticed its sourdough taste. "I'm fine," she said. Josh's face was too close to hers. He seemed really concerned.

"He popped your pot cherry," said Ben Howe. "Way to go, Joshie."

"I don't feel anything," she said.

"Sometimes you don't at first." Susie turned to Ben. "Got any more jokes?"

"Did you hear about the guy who's paralyzed on his left side? He's all right now."

Susie groaned, but Uli laughed.

"I get it," she said. "Don't you get it?"

"We get it," Mara said. "We're just not stoned."

"I'm not stoned." Uli stood up straighter and felt very tall.

"Ready for another?"

"No way." She put her hand on Josh's arm. "I'm fine."

"You said that already," said Susie.

"This is boring," said Mara. "Let's go swimming."

In two days it would be May, still too early for night swimming, but a week of sunshine had warmed the shallow creek bed to a temperature that was not intolerable. Mara seemed more interested in taking her top off than actually getting in the water, and she and one of the other cheerleaders made a big show of stripping down to their underwear before wading in up to their calves. Their steps were slow and deliberate over the slick creek stones, and their white bras turned an eerie moon blue as they inched away from the fire.

The others watched from the grass, but then Ben Howe tore off his pants and ran out. The girls, delighted, swore at him. Ben kept sloshing forward until he reached the deepest part of the creek, where the water swallowed his thighs. The other boys and some of the girls stood hollering from the rocky bank.

"You're an idiot, Ben Howe!" Susie yelled.

"Nice boxers!" yelled Josh, grinning at Uli.

Uli noticed that Josh had cute hair. Curls. They bounced when he laughed.

Ben Howe shouted back, "Hey, look! I'm Edna What's-Her-Name!"

"Pontellier," Uli said, but only Josh and Susie heard her.

"Pontellier!" Susie shouted to Ben, cupping her hands into a megaphone.

"It's too hard to be a woman," Ben yelled. "I want to die!"

The girls in their underwear waved their arms as if Ben were in danger. Then Mara slipped and ended up squatting in the river. She laughed like this was the funniest thing to ever happen to a person.

The scene ended when Ben chased the cheerleaders out of the water and onto the rocky bank, where they hopped and dripped and yelped about being cold. Two boys' hoodies were donated to their cause, and while the girls zipped these up to their chins, they didn't put on their pants right away, instead choosing to stand by the fire to "dry off."

Ben Howe, wrapped in a blanket like some kind of victim, stood next to Mara and looked down at her body. Uli looked too and saw that Mara's pink panties were soaked clean through. A shadowy mound of pubic hair appeared in the frosted window of fabric, but Mara didn't seem to care.

"Hey," Josh said, appearing next to Uli. "Want to go for a walk?"

She followed him through a break in the bushes into the next lot, where a shingled cabin with dark windows faced the water.

"We shouldn't be here," Uli said.

"It's okay."

"Someone could shoot us. They'll think we're deer."

"You don't know much about hunting, do you?"

"No," Uli agreed. "I don't like hunters."

Josh started walking up the bank to the cabin and said, "It's not cruel or nothin'. If we don't do it, they die of starvation. Hey!" Josh stood above her. "Come here a minute." He sat on the cabin's stairs and patted the wide step. Uli sat down beside him and pretended to be cold so that Josh would put his arm around her. "We all had a mandatory class about it in third grade. Hunter's Safety Ed."

"I came at the end of third grade."

"From California, right?" He pulled her closer. "That's so cool. I'd love to live in California. My family went last summer. I met some great people. Like my cousins, and . . . it's different there, you know?"

"My mom lives in Hawaiʻi," she offered.

"That," Josh said, "is amazing."

She wanted him to kiss her then. The chance of it rose and fell like an arpeggio under her fingers.

"Look." Josh stood up. The space he left in his wake felt cool and airy. Uli watched him move to the cabin wall.

"Don't!" she warned. But he didn't listen.

Josh removed a hunting cap from a peg and thrust it on his head so the earflaps dangled. Then he swaggered back to Uli, pretending to be bowlegged, and pointed his hands at her like he was aiming a rifle.

"Wulp," he said in a thick backwoods drawl. "You'd best git runnin'."

When she came to live in Pennsylvania—after her father left her there—Uli's grandfather would take her out to breakfast at the Old Caboose Diner while Kitty went to church. Their favorite booth was the one in the middle of the diner because it had a good view of the train set that ran around the ceiling in loops.

After a few months, living with her grandparents began to feel normal. Uli understood that she wouldn't be returning to California and her parents wouldn't be moving to Pennsylvania. Her mother had a new baby in Hawaiʻi, and her father was overseeing a big construction project in Santa Rosa. Nobody explained to her that this big project was so big it would last a decade. Maybe they didn't know.

One Sunday, which turned out to be their last Sunday at the Old Caboose, Uli's grandfather went up to the counter and left her alone at the table. It was 1988. Uli was nine years old.

"I don't know," said a man in a booth by the window. He wore a camouflage cap on his head. "Must be some kind of Chink."

There were two of them, large men with large hands gripping mugs of coffee. They wore green clothing like the cartoon men in G.I. Joe commercials. Uli felt their eyes on her but pretended not to notice.

"Hey!" Josh stood above her. A look of concern played on his face. "I was only joking." He removed the hunting cap and sat on the porch step. She looked away when he bumped her shoulder.

"You didn't go to Madison Middle," Josh said.

"No. East River."

"Why?"

"Better music program."

"You play piano, right? I hear you're really good."

Was she good? Josh would think so. Kitty and the church choir and Mrs. Abramson thought so. But they were people who didn't count. At home in the top drawer of her desk she kept an old catalogue for Juilliard. She'd been looking at it for years, but it was only right then, sitting on the step with Josh, that she knew she should throw it away.

"My grandmother wants me to be a concert pianist."

Josh nodded. "My grandmother wants me to be a physical therapist."

"Oh." She paused, then asked, "Why does she want you to be a physical therapist?" At the same time Josh said something, too, and they both laughed.

"What?"

"It's dumb," he said, "I'm being dumb." He bowed his head, and the gesture charmed her. She liked being the one who wasn't embarrassed for once.

"Tell me!"

"I just . . ." He met her gaze. "I'd like to know what you are."

Inside, Uli's heart bloomed like a flower and closed like a fist.

"My ex-girlfriend is Filipino," he said. "She lives in San Diego. I thought maybe you were Filipino, too."

"I'm Japanese. Half Japanese."

"Wow. That's so cool."

Josh's face was in front of hers. She understood he was going to kiss her, and then he did kiss her, sucking hard on her upper lip until a central bit of lip-flesh entered his mouth. She wondered what to call that part of herself. A lip-dip. A semi-detached bud.

Uli pulled away and forced out a cough to cover the whimper her body was trying to release. Later, when she rewound this moment and played it over and over, she would decide that this had been her way of mourning all the other first kisses she'd hoped for, which now could not exist.

"You're really pretty," he said.

"You're really nice."

Josh tilted his head, and this gesture annoyed Uli. She thought he'd probably tilted his head at lots of girls. Practiced the head tilt over and over the way she'd practiced the Rachmaninoff.

He said, "What are you thinking about, Uli?"

She shook her head. She was thinking about the hunting cap. About the girl in the diner who was using her fork to cut her pancake into triangles.

"It's a plague." The second hunter spoke louder than normal. Each word rang in her head. "It's an influx."

"Naw," said the man in the cap. "I like those type of girls. They never say nothing." She felt his gaze across the aisle. "Hey," he said. "Hey!"

Uli didn't look up.

"See what I mean?"

Her grandfather returned to the table, and the hunters called him over to talk. Asked him, "What is she?" Just like that. "What is she?" Grandpa said, "She's my granddaughter," and the men laughed and said some things. The one in the hunting cap pointed his finger at Uli and made a click with his tongue and his teeth. "Bang," he said. After that, Grandpa hurried her out of the diner so quickly he forgot to leave a tip. He always left a nice tip, and for a long time Uli thought his embarrassment over this mistake was the reason they started going to Denny's.

Years later, she asked her grandfather if he remembered the hunters.

"Dick and Wayne," he said.

It took a moment for her to understand that these were the men's names.

"Went to school with Dick. And I'm close with Wayne's brother." Grandpa put his hand on her shoulder. Light, pianissimo. His touch was always like that. "The thing is, being different gives you an understanding. Dick and Wayne, they don't have that. You're lucky that you do."

On the moonlit deck of the cabin, Josh continued to stare with that puppyish head tilt. He'd asked what she was thinking about, but he didn't really want to know.

He was still waiting for an answer. She said, "Being Japanese, I guess?"

"It's rad," Josh said. "I mean, I like it."

"Thanks." But it felt weird to accept a compliment about that.

"Maybe you'll go to Japan someday," Josh said. "Maybe we'll go—"

"I need to get home."

Josh looked surprised at first, then mad. They threaded their way through the bushes and didn't talk. Uli anticipated some unwanted attention when they returned to the campfire, another "Way to go, Joshie," but nobody noticed them except for Susie, who approached with a flat expression.

"We should probably take off," she said, and Uli didn't argue.

Once they were in her father's car and back on paved roads, Susie proclaimed that Ben Howe was super conceited. "He's not even that good-looking."

"He's funny," Uli said. "People enjoy that."

Susie raised her eyebrows. "Josh is funny," she said. "Do you like him?"

"He kissed me."

"No way!" Susie smacked the leather dashboard. "So how was it?"

"The kiss? I don't know."

"That's okay," Susie said, as if she'd known all along it must have been bad. "I'm sure you're aware of this, but Josh is a total Asia-phile."

"Oh. Yellow fever." Mara had called it that. Uli didn't know which part was worse—that Josh didn't really like her, or that Mara was right.

"It's not his fault. Most girls around here look exactly the same. It's still a compliment or whatever."

It was eleven nineteen when Susie dropped her at her grandparent's house. The light in the living room was on, which meant they'd waited up for her. Oh no.

But the front door was unlocked, and inside the house it was quiet. She went to the master bedroom and listened through the door for Grandpa's snoring. Nothing. She went to the refrigerator and saw her two notes tacked to the corkboard. After considering for a moment, Uli took them down and folded them into tight, Chiclet-sized packages that she dropped in the trash. Then she went to the bathroom to brush her teeth. She made sure to wash her face thoroughly to remove any trace of pot and campfire smoke. Then she turned off the lights and locked the front door. She could almost pretend this was her house, that she lived here alone.

She went to bed. She couldn't believe her luck.

———

The next morning she slept late. She made two packets of instant oatmeal and dumped extra brown sugar on top before taking her bowl to the sofa to watch Saturday-morning TV. During a noisy commercial, Kitty came home. Uli hugged the warm bowl to her chest as if this would hide it. Then she saw her grandmother's clothes, which were wrinkled, and her face, which was like some other woman's face.

"Grandpa had a heart attack," Kitty said.

She entered the room, holding her hands in front of her as if she were judging the heat of a stovetop. For the first time in Uli's life, Kitty looked old. She touched the back of the sofa, then guided herself around it and sank into the cushions. She hadn't removed her coat and the front door was still open. Sunlight streamed in the doorway, along with a fat and buzzing fly.

"Oh my god." Uli put down the oatmeal and inched over to her grandmother. She wondered if she ought to turn off the Animaniacs, who were singing on the television.

"The doctors did everything they could. They prepared him for surgery, but he passed away this morning. I was with him."

Uli waited a long time before saying, "Did he suffer?"

Kitty put a hand at the base of her throat and looked at her with sudden recognition.

"No. Thank god."

This was the moment when they should have hugged, but instead Uli turned off the television and Kitty ran her hands along the dark tweed of her skirt. Uli looked at the skirt and realized Kitty had been out somewhere when it happened, maybe with friends, maybe at lunch. The message from the hospital must have been waiting when Uli got home. She darted to the answering machine. The light was flashing red.

"I'd like you to play Chopin at the funeral. The one with the grace notes." Kitty lifted her hands in the air and moved her fingers. She began to sing, faintly. "Da-da-da . . . da-da . . ."

"Nocturne in C-sharp Minor," Uli said, desperate to make her grandmother stop.

"I called." Kitty let her hands fall through the imaginary keys. "I called and called."

"I went to get pizza with Susie." Uli went to the trash bin and pulled out the two notes. "See?"

"It was a heart attack. I have to call your father."

Uli lowered the notes into the trash, burying them under a coffee filter, and said, "Oh, Grandma. I can do it."

But she immediately regretted the offer. How could she tell her father that his own father had died? Would he even care that she had lost her grandpa, a gentle man who loved the morning paper and Egg McMuffins, a joyful man who cheered for the neighborhood dogs Kitty chased from their yard?

What could she say to him? What if he cried?

"No. You should practice." Kitty rose unsteadily from the sofa and moved to the beige telephone on the wall. "Practice, practice, practice." An old punch line to an old joke.

Uli was good at following instructions. She went to the wall of sheet music, where Chopin's nocturnes were sprinkled between Mozart's sonatas. She found the correct piece and opened it. Kitty was right. Grandpa had liked this one.

She arranged the music on the mahogany stand and began to play a bit slower than the required tempo. The room filled with the tender progression of the right notes in the right order. At the same time, she could taste her own guilt. It stung the back of her throat. She did not believe her grandfather's death had been a punishment. But she might have been at the hospital. She might have said goodbye. He had been so kind to her.

She stopped to wipe her face against her shirt and began the piece again. For the rest of her life, she would play the piano with greater dedication. There had to be a reason for her grandfather's death, or if not quite a reason, a domino effect that led to something good. She would do it for him. She would have a career. And when she became a real musician, if people asked what she was or where she came from, she would play them something small and true.

Sister Fat

He told me he was famous. I had never heard the word in English.

"Fey. Mess," he said.

"A. Moose," I replied.

The boy scratched his sandy beard and searched for a synonym in his childish Tokyo-ben. "Chomei. Yūmei. Yubi—ah, ah—Yubikitasu?"

"Oh," I said. "You are *ubiquitous*! I am ubiquitous, too."

The boy laughed and switched back to his native English. "C'mon. If you've never left the island, you can't be famous."

Well, this was a stupid thing to say. Fuji-san never leaves Honshu, yet Mount Fuji is known worldwide!

"A fool's mouth is wasted in speech," I said, and pointed to a distant tree shrouded with mist. "Now let's suck face in the root cave."

We walked to the island's eastern edge, where the waves spat mist and the rocks moaned. I squatted, grabbing a limb of heavy pine and telling the boy to follow. He looked down at the wet cliffs with a longing I'd seen once before.

To disrupt his depression I asked, "In America, am I on TV a lot?"

"You?" He shook his head three times: No, no, no. "You have to be filmed before you can appear on television." Then in Japanese, he added, "Stupid cow."

"Eat shit," I said. "You don't know a thing about a thing."

The boy assumed he was my first American, but no. A wrinkled doctor who smelled like the pith of an orange had taken pictures of me. I performed several different poses. He promised to put them on Hollywood TV. Surely the yellow-haired boy had seen them by now?

I jammed my fingers between two rocks and followed the crack to the mouth of a cave. The yellow-haired boy came down quick and easy as a waterfall. When he reached the ledge, I pulled him inside.

"Neat," he said, touching a slimy root above our heads. "Do you think it will fall?"

I offered to lie down if it would make him feel better.

"Distribute the weight," I said, rolling onto my back. My bottom enveloped the loose stones and my dress snuck above my knees.

"Like an elevator," he said, snuggling next to me. "When it drops."

His breath was powerful. Minty. Callused fingers explored my belly rolls. When his hand got to my breasts he whistled through his teeth. Nipples the size of starfish, that's what Mother says. An ass to rival the moon. The boy squeezed my shoulder and ground against my thigh.

"It's like you're all tits," he said. "Tits, tits, tits."

The blond boy did not taste like custard as I'd hoped, but he had an oatmeal color to his privates that I found pleasing. His nose cast a profound shadow, but then, that is the American way of doing noses. If I looked at it from the correct angle, I could convince myself this would be an okay nose for my unborn child.

The boy climbed on top and rubbed until his bamboo became a jellyfish. I made sure to scoop up all the goodies and stuff them inside my own dark cave. After this transaction was complete, he slid to my side and patted my shoulder fondly, as if it were a well-behaved dog.

"I know we just met," he said, "but I think I want you to kill me."

I sucked at my lips and considered this. Men had asked me to do bad things to them before. Hitting mostly, but also smothering, choking, and insulting. Murder would not be impossible. In my imagination, I had performed the act on Mother many times. Surely a stranger would be easy! But the snap of his bones—that sound could haunt my dreams, just like the *whoomp-whoomp*.

"How would you want it?" I asked.

"Here," he said, waving his arm. "Like this."

Simple. The rocks would do most of the work, and the ocean would clean up after. "Okay," I said. "We can make a deal. But I need something in return."

"Is it money? I have shitloads of money."

I asked him how much is a shitload. He said it was a lot.

But as Father says: What is a dead man's handshake worth? Very little, unless he wears expensive rings.

"I need all the money first, and documents for travel." After some thought, I added in English, "And one helicopter, please."

The boy lit a cigarette. "How do you know the word 'helicopter' but not the word 'famous'? "

I smiled coolly. "You would like to imagine how."

I took the cigarette from his mouth and inhaled half of it in a single drag. My lungs are the largest in my family, except for Sister Mermaid.

"I can get you anything," the boy said. "I have, like, three different phones."

"Very nice," I said, pushing one of these phones away. "But listen. I cannot kill you until I give my father a present. The present is a baby."

I watched the boy's head retract into his shoulders like an eel in the reef.

"Father needs a friend," I explained. "After I disappear in the helicopter, who will make him laugh? A baby, that's who." The boy seemed to relax, so I continued. "Father cannot make children since Mother broke his *chinchin*. And you will be a perfect father. Being dead, you will not interfere."

The boy looked unsure.

"Come on," I said. "Die now, or die later after lots of sex. Same thing in the end."

I offered my hand and he took it. "Fine," he said. "One week with full access to my junk. After that, you kill me." We rocked our hands and bowed. Then the boy lifted my skirt and licked for ten or fifteen minutes.

"You are not making it easier to kill you," I said. "But whatever."

After my pleasure was complete the boy wanted to revisit his bamboo, but I needed to prepare for that evening's performance. I reached in the pocket of my dress and gave him a coupon for a box of popcorn. "If you come for the show, you will witness how *A Moose* I am."

"Sorry," he said. "I don't like crowds."

"It is not a crowd, *Hisou*. Just a boatload. You will come! Our popcorn is good, but do not drink the tea. OK, now I say bai bai!" Before he could protest I waved heartily, as if trying to communicate with a monkey in a cage, and started up the cliff.

―――――

For nine generations we have lived on this island, ever since Baba Fujikoto's little pine boat blew off course and sank into the sea. There is nothing to do here but kill birds and count blades of grass, so Baba Fujikoto and his wife had a good time with each other and made ten babies. These ten babies also had nothing to do, so they also had a good time with each other, and this pattern continued until my family outnumbered both the birds and the blades. Isolation spared us from war and disease, but in time, we began to look different from other Japanese. It was Baba Fujikoto's grandson, Hirokoto, who saw the commercial potential in his children's deformity. When a ship of sailors landed during a storm, Hirokoto charged them two bu each to behold our amazing bodies. Then the typhoid came. Our numbers diminished, and now people come to see the rare chorui bird more than our strangeness.

As I walked back to camp I saw the captain, a man the color of cooked beef who smiles too broadly and too often. He was arguing with passengers who wanted to know why the boat would be docked for another three hours—the answer, of course, is that we pay him to stay so the passengers become our audience.

When I was halfway home, Father ran to greet me.

"Mother is in a mood," he said. "Did you do Mister Blue Jeans? How much did you get?"

"Nothing yet. But he has a very small phone."

"Good! My little Aijou."

Aijou has a double meaning of "sorrow" and "beloved daughter." It is my pet name because I am Father's favorite child. Oh, how it would hurt him to know I was plotting my escape! I could not have explained it. My life was good enough. I was the star of the show. But just like Brother Angel, I believed my destiny lay beyond the island. Yes, it would be hard to leave behind a soft, warm baby, but in America I would have many admirers. You could even buy a baby there, if you were ubiquitous enough.

Father kissed my shoulder, which is the highest part of me he can reach, and I felt him slip five apricot kernels into my hand. "Mother will bring the yams soon, so eat quickly."

Each day, Mother fed us fermented yams to prevent our future babies. She did not want her daughters to be impregnated by a tourist who would produce normal-looking children with normal-boring bodies. But since Brother Angel flew away, there are no brothers left. Our family line will end. Father hated lying to Mother, but he really wanted a nice fresh baby, so each day he gave us apricot kernels to contradict her yams and help us get pregnant.

I ducked inside my tent to eat the conception kernels, snapping their wrinkled shells between my molars and chewing their bitter bits into powder. Most people would find the taste intolerable, but I am used to eating foul things.

I was removing a stubborn chunk of kernel from my teeth when Mother broke through the flaps of my tent.

"There she is—Princess Fancy Pants. What? You think I have time to mash your stupid sex juice?" She held out the bowl of yams, which I accepted reluctantly. Okaasan squatted and watched with snake eyes while I ate.

"Your fat stomach requires five yams more than Sister Mermaid."

"Sister Mermaid is shorter than Father. She's like a large dog."

Mother pounced across the mat and slapped me so hard I nearly dropped the bowl. "Get off your high horse!" She threw back her jaw and whinnied. Mother is not a pretty woman, but she has a double-hinged mouth that I have always admired. When I was little, I would beg her to open her face. Now she used the trick to taunt me, snapping her jaw and lifting her hands like hooves. "I saw you with that albino. Off giving it away for free?"

"It was an investment." I scooped out the last of the yams and held out the bowl. "He is coming to the show."

Mother leaned forward and opened her mouth. Deep at the back of her throat I saw the nautilus of brown teeth that led down her gullet. "Fool," she breathed. "We don't make money from the show. The profit comes after, and your bed price is falling."

She was right. Less demand. Fewer offers. My womanhood could now be purchased for the price of a ferry ride, and my sisters' sex was cheaper than the plastic snacks the tourists brought from their convenience stores.

"In my day," Mother continued, "the show was artistic. But now it is slop tossed to pigs."

"You explain it so well, Okaasan." I bowed. "Thank you."

She grunted and reset her jaw with both hands, clamping her teeth so they crunched. "I don't know where it all goes," she grumbled as she left. "You're looking so thin."

After her shadow on the wall disappeared, I ate Father's final kernel and tapped my nose three times for good luck. If all went well, Father would soon have a friend and I would be flying away to America.

———

Since Brother Angel left us, the show has been the same: first Zou, the Elephant; then Ikkakujuu and Sai, the Twins; Ningyo, the Mermaid; and me, Futtota, the Fat.

I searched the gathering crowd but saw no sign of the boy I'd begun calling Hisou. After he saw my act, would he still want to die? Unlikely. Maybe he would go to Hollywood with me, and I would teach him what it means to be A Moose.

Onstage, Sister Elephant was being led in circles by a miniature monkey. The monkey, Kiki-Kuku, was older than Sister Elephant. She called it Okaasan—Mother—when she thought no one was around.

A popcorn box flew out from the crowd and hit my sister's shoulder. Zou blinked as if in a dream. A better performer might have used the disruption to her advantage, but Sister Elephant had very little talent. Just a pair of elongated earlobes, one of Mother's dirty teeth at the back of her throat, and a problem with urination. Like Father's, most of Zou's deformities were internal.

The crowd laughed as Kiki-Kuku jumped on my sister's head and held up her ears, stretching them as wide as its hairy arms would go. It pumped up and down, creating a small wind with the flapping lobes, while behind the curtain Gramma Bat played a silly tune on a pipe. The pipe was pure gold and had been given to her by a Malaysian prince, back when Gramma Bat was the one who closed the show.

The twins entered next. They are not very interesting, but men seem to like them. Their act is a song-and-dance routine called "Tea for Two and Two for You." It is a big joke when Sai takes a sip of tea and Ikkakujuu spits it out. Really she has had the tea in her mouth the whole time. The only bit that requires skill is when the twins lock horns and stand with their feet against a wall. Sai had been gaining weight, however, and the move looked shaky that night. After they dismounted I noticed Sai hobbling a little, but perhaps that was an injury from the previous evening's sale. Because the twins have sharp horns jutting from their foreheads, customers often choose to take them from behind.

Sister Mermaid entered. Time to take my place backstage. I moved through the dark trees as Ningyo's scales flashed onstage in the torchlight. The crowd clapped politely, not knowing the scales were only plastic, brought to us by the captain and sewn by Ningyo herself onto her webbed skin. The webbing, at least, was a real talent, as was the six-and-a-half minutes she spent upside down with her head submerged in a fishbowl. While Father led the crowd in counting down the seconds, people paid extra to come onstage and touch the translucent rainbow of skin that stretched between her legs.

I stepped behind the stage curtain and bumped into Mother.

"Slut," she said.

I held out my arms.

"Lazy," she said, attacking my robe. She pulled the fabric away and sprayed the back of my naked body with a can of lemon cleanser. "Here," she said, putting the can in my hand. "Do the front yourself, Skinny Butt."

Shivering and damp, I lifted each breast and sprayed, then arched my back and sprayed my rolls, rubbing the sticky cleaner between them. I reached around to spray my ass and thighs but left my chitsu alone. For some things, a natural smell is best.

On the other side of the curtain, Father raised his conch and played a long, low note. Silence followed. A white sheet billowed in the salty wind. My backside flared with heat as Okaasan, Obaba, and Zou lit the torches behind me. The audience murmured at the sight of my huge shadow cast onto the sheet. I must have looked like a monster. A terrible thing . . . *Ubiquitous!* I parted the curtain and took the stage. The lights were bright, and I could not see my future victim in the crowd. It did not matter. He would see me.

I raised one arm and jiggled. There was a time when this would have received applause, but audiences are not what they were. People today have seen all sorts of things on their little phones. They do not want to see the magic right in front of them.

My routine is not beautiful like Brother Angel's. It is strong. I stomp my foot against the ground to wake the mighty Sakura.

I sweep my arm low to cut down all living things that aspire to heaven. I am not a great dancer, but the moves are great moves. I speak to Earth, and Earth responds. When she sings with her molten throat, she calls me Aijou, like Father.

I lifted my second arm and jiggled, but again, no response. Determined to win their hearts, I spun on one heel and bent over, squeezing a cheek in each hand. Someone called out, "Hey Fatty!" and a plastic bottle bounced off my thigh. Inside, I laughed. They did not know my magnitude.

I picked up the bottle and put it under my left breast. The bottle did not drop, and a small number applauded. Yes! But one audience man got up to leave. My confidence faltered. People had wept hot tears when my brother, Enjeru, danced.

I remember the span of his wings, which were not wings at all but solid bone, gray and slightly charred. It was my job to clean them, first patting with a sponge and then sanding down the edges until they looked smooth as buttermilk. The wings branched out from him like antlers, but the bones were fragile and often got infected. Each morning I spread a cool mixture of tea and honey on the sores while he slept. Despite this attention, Brother Angel became depressed. By the time I was asked to lie with him, he had stopped eating. Yet the weaker he became, the more the audience loved him. Mother said if he hadn't been an angel, he could have been a dancer. It is the one thing we agree upon.

My choreography ends with a series of jumps on a wooden platform, and because Hisou was in the crowd, I attacked it with extra vigor. Sweat bounced off my body like hard rain thudding on a rock. My feet bellowed through the floor, and the people joined in—clap!—clap!—clap! But we were stopped by a scream. At first I assumed it must be sickness from the rotten tea Father sells, but another voice cried out, and another. Several women fainted. Others stared into the darkness and pointed with long white fingers at a shadowy man. For a moment I held the wild, squirming thought that Brother Angel had come back, but then the man stepped backward, and his face caught the flame-light. It was Hisou.

He stood at the edge of the tree line, watching my performance from afar. But people lifted their phones to capture him. The cameras flashed, and in one silver moment I saw Hisou's face. Grinning in terror.

With a single mind, the people decided to consume him. The quiet sea of bodies gathered into a wave, and the wave grew tall and rushed toward poor Hisou, who stood there, fixed to the ground like the mighty Sakura. A thrilled screech rose from the mouths at the front of the wave. Hisou shut his eyes and held out his arms to give them a big American hug.

Then he was gone. Swallowed. I knew I could not hesitate if I wanted to save him.

Using my bulk to part the crowd, I smushed and smashed all those who dared to get between me and Hisou. He had disappeared entirely, but I suspected the truth lay under a pile of women. I peeled them away like wet leaves until I saw his pale skin glowing like a star against the dark grass. As I lifted him up, people tried to cling to his clothes. I batted them away and slung Hisou over my shoulders. Father lit an entire box of firecrackers. The explosions made the crowd scatter. I could smell the Sakura burning and looked back to see its uppermost branches dotted with flames.

Hisou lay across my arms in a stupor. When we entered my tent, he whimpered and clung to me. I covered him with a blanket and patted his head.

"So this is A Moose," I said. "I thought it would be sweet. But it is bitter like the kernels."

We huddled on my mat and listened to the chaos of the fire settle into normal sounds of frogs and wind. Eventually my family gathered outside to clean the smoke from their skin and tell stories about the thing that had just happened. After every detail of the riot had been tucked into the past, Father began to sing an old song about the island.

"*We are what you'll never see. We go where you can never be.*" His voice was thin and full of years. I wondered how much time remained for him. For us.

"*We, oh we.*" I joined in softly and held Hisou's hand. "*We are alone and free, in a magical land across the sea.*"

———

"Bright and shine," Mother said in English. "What, you sleepy beds? Up-up-up." I opened my eyes to a strange sight—Okaasan's teeth, shining through a smile. "Obaba make what-you-say. Number one food today." Mother squatted and bounced her ass up and down. I recoiled, afraid she might pounce like a tiger. "Silly Aijou," she said in Japanese. "Get your friend to come out. We have much to discuss." Then, as if not knowing what else to do, she clapped her hands once and backed out of the tent.

"She never calls me Aijou," I said. "Only Futtota, the Fat."

Hisou rolled over. He was naked and thin as a willow, and when he opened his eyes, they were morning-sea blue and rimmed with salt. "Today you will kill me," he said.

"No. I need to gather your seed. We have agreed to this."

The boy's face folded like paper origami. I snuck my shoulders around his thin bird ones and moved him like the wind moves the reeds.

Now I understood. Hisou was haunted by the terrible beast called A Moose. But I was not afraid. My thick legs would wrap around the beast and tame it. Just think of last night! I had saved us all.

When Hisou quieted I dressed him in a robe—blue silk, a gift from a British ornithologist—and an old pair of slippers. It pleased me that we shared the same size foot. My toes were brown and small. His were hairy and pink. But our shoes did not know the difference.

After he was dressed, Hisou scratched at his growing stubble. The gesture seemed so familiar that I kissed him on the cheek. He looked surprised, and I explained, "You could be my sister in those clothes." Then we went outside.

The twins and Ningyo sat to the side of the fire, washing their costumes in a large iron pot. Zou was helping Father lay out plates of fried fish. Mother waved us over to the best seats beside the fire and said in English, "Come-come, good-good!"

"He speaks Japanese better than you speak English," I told her.

For a moment I thought Mother would strike me, but she laughed instead.

"Silly Aijou! I just polite. He good guest. He VIP!"

Father removed the fish pan from the fire and came to say hello.

"I am Ushi-Jin," he said, bowing to Hisou, "the Human Cow."

"Father has two stomachs," I said proudly. "And we suspect, more than one heart."

"I have six hearts," said Father. "One for each of my children."

It became oddly quiet while Hisou counted the faces around him.

"You see only five of my children," Father explained, "because Brother Angel is no longer with us."

"I'm sorry," said Hisou. "I know what it's like to lose someone."

"Please," Mother said. "Take-take. Sit good!"

Hisou sat on a log. I started walking to the garbage tent. Mother stopped me by clicking her tongue.

"Eat with us, Aijou."

I turned around. Her hands were folded neatly in her lap, but she blinked rapidly. Nervously.

I had not eaten a hot meal with my family since I took the name Futtota. Inside the garbage tent, I ate anything: bruised fruit from the tourists, stale popcorn and buns, old egg stew. I did not mind. One can enjoy anything if it draws her closer to her fate.

At Mother's insistence, I sat beside the fire. The chopsticks felt slick and strange in my hands, but soon I was a slave to the breakfast, lost in its layers of good smells. There was fresh fish and more! Eggs cooked in pork fat, fried bread, crisp-skinned pears. I'd forgotten how good warm food felt on my tongue. It was like kissing and then swallowing the lips of your lover. Okaasan's larder must be empty now, I realized. And what, what? My sisters had not been invited to the table. It was all for me and Hisou.

I was loading my third plate when Mother laid out her plan, switching to Japanese for the words she did not know.

"You have to agree, young man, it's a very good deal. Five girls to sleep with any time you please, and I will give you almost all the profit, sixty percent. Meanwhile, we pay for all production costs. The overhead, the marketing. My family will feed you, give you the best tent. Life here will be humble, but you will be the star. In time we will build flush toilets and a stadium. And we can offer protection! How about ten armed guards? Then you can really relax. No more sobbing like last night."

"That's very kind," said Hisou, "but I don't want to perform anymore."

Mother and Father went silent. Hisou unthinkingly took a large sip of the foul tea, and, like Ikkakujuu, kept it in his mouth.

"Hisou wants to die," I explained. "I am going to kill him."

Mother turned pale.

"Don't worry," I said. "He's going to pay me a lot."

Everyone looked to Hisou.

Cleverly, he raised the empty cup to his lips and returned the sour tea to its chipped home. "Yes, Aijou has agreed to be my murderer. We have it all planned out."

"You will stay," Mother said. Her eyes trembled with fury. "Work here one or two years, then we can kill you, no problem." Sometimes when she becomes excited, Okaasan's jaw will flip open on its own and does not close until she calms down. Out of politeness Father and I busied ourselves with food, but Hisou had never seen Mother's trick before. His gaze landed on the slimy circle of teeth that decorated the back of her throat. She struggled and pushed at her head. I stood and bowed to my parents.

"Thank you for breakfast. We will leave you now."

All at once Mother's jaw snapped shut, and Hisou was released from its spell. He leaped up, banging his knee on the table, and hurried after me.

We returned to the cliffs. I followed not so fast as his waterfall, but more like a round tear plopping down a child's cheek. I swung into the cave and stumbled. Hisou fell too, grabbing my wrists, and then there was tasting and sucking. The sea sparkled under the morning sun.

"That time was pretty good," I said when he was done. "You are slippery as a fish."

Hisou lit a cigarette. I wrapped my robe around my shoulders because the wind had come again.

"Sorry about Mother. She got worse after Brother Angel left."

Hisou remained naked, his flesh so white it looked like snow melting on the rocks.

"That deal she offered—does that happen a lot?"

"Never." I played with the belt of my robe. "You are considering it, maybe?"

He blew a thick cloud of smoke that hovered between us like a real thing. Then a gust of sea spray broke it apart. "You saw those people. They wanted to cut me up and take me home in pieces."

How could I say what I felt? That Hisou, this pale stranger, was more like a brother than Enjeru had been. And what of Father? What of the baby?

"Hey," said Hisou. "You okay?"

I looked down. The light was dim, but I saw a dark spot staining the silk between my legs, and when I touched the spot it felt warm. I tasted my fingers. Blood. A week of sex would not be enough.

But so what? There were babies in America. Perhaps I could send one to Father. Or perhaps I would not care about my family after I became more powerful. As Father says: Do the stars worry about broken telescopes?

"If I do the murder now," I said to Hisou, "can you make me famous like you?"

He smashed his cigarette against a rock.

"Yes. My manager, Richard, will help you. His number is in all of my phones."

"What will he do?"

"Richard's a suit. He does everything."

A suit. I knew this word.

Before Brother Angel flew away, a Shanghai businessman came to the island. He spent three nights in Enjeru's tent, and every morning I cleaned his outfit, three beautiful, complicated cloths of silver that he called a suit.

After the businessman departed, I started getting fat. It was because of the extra food Father snuck to give me a talent, but Mother misinterpreted my bulk. I must be pregnant! Enjeru would have a son! I let Okaasan believe in the fake baby. I let Enjeru believe in it, too, and this is why Mother hates me to this day. It was my growing body—my growing lie—that gave my brother permission to leave us.

I never told anyone, not even Father, but Enjeru asked me to go with him. I laughed in his face. No one had ever left our family before.

"You and me and the baby," he said. "Together."

"You leave first," I joked. "Hurry up and go."

A few days later I was washing dishes when a strange wind blew straight down into my tub of water. Then the wind changed and blew sideways, yanking a cloth from my hands. I looked up and saw a giant bug with a mechanical halo. The wind grew louder and made a *whoomp-whoomp* sound as the bug sank onto our field. Suddenly Enjeru burst from his tent. He ran right up to the bug and climbed inside its stomach. Mother ran and shouted, "Son, my son!" I stumbled after Okaasan and we stood together as the wind stole words from our mouths. The bug rose up. My brother's face perched in the sky like a bird, and then a second arm leaned out. It was the silver suit from Shanghai! He lifted his hand in farewell, and Brother Angel and the man flew away.

Later, I asked Mother what was this awful thing. "Helicopter," she said. The word was not Japanese. It snapped like kindling in her mouth.

"I want a helicopter," I said to Hisou. "And one shitload of your American dollars."

"Done," he said. "Just let me call Richard." He moved to the mouth of the cave, and I observed his white bottom. Each cheek was dimpled at the side like a colorless bean. His spine stuck out grotesquely, knob by bony knob. To think of the child we might have had, with its chicken legs and pimple elbows! But Father would have loved it all the same.

Hisou closed his phone. "A chopper will be here in an hour."

"And the money? The ticket?"

He waved his hand vaguely. "Richard will take care of that."

We looked at each other. I thought: I am the last thing this man will see in this world. The thought made me proud.

"Do it," he said. "I'm ready."

I reached out to him. But my arms moved with a dreamy slowness, as if Hisou and I were underwater. Blood slid between my thighs. The gush of it made me weep.

"No," I said. "You come on the helicopter. You wear a silver suit. And wave at my mother goodbye."

Hisou closed his eyes and walked to the edge of the cave. I watched him lean toward death, trying to get there on his own. But he could not.

"Whatever," he said cruelly. "I was lying, anyway." Hisou tore at the pocket of his jeans, looking for a cigarette.

"What is the lie?"

"You," he said. "In America, there are people who are fatter. People with more fucked-up families. You? Famous? Never."

I smashed my foot down, and the roots trembled above our heads. "How would you know?"

He produced a hollow smile. "Because I am on a billion screens. Strangers want to die for me. But you?" Hisou laughed. Laughed! "People will only die for you," he said, "if you sit on them."

It did not take me long to cross the cave and throw my body against his. Driven by instinct, his hand groped the wall, but the wall dripped rocks. Our bodies bounced when we hit the ground. He began to slide down the cliff. I held my arm against his wrist, and it was this weight that stopped him from dropping. His legs kicked. Beneath us, water sang.

Hisou looked up at me. "Let go." His face was a baby's face, made blank by too much pain. "Please," he said. "Aijou."

And it was this word—*sorrow*—my father's love in this strange boy's mouth—that helped me do it. With much regret, I gave my friend the ending he wanted.

———

Mother waited at the tents.

"Idiot Christmas!" She grabbed my ear. "Where is he, slug-breath?"

She sank her teeth in. I knew not to struggle if I wanted to keep my ear.

"Please!" Father repeatedly slapped Okaasan's back. "Tell her, Aijou!"

I dropped to the ground and buried my face in the mud. Hisou had told me Richard would come in an hour. While I waited, Father and Mother argued and sometimes Mother hit me. Then a distant *whoomp-whoomp* rattled the island like thunder, and I allowed myself to smile.

"He is coming," I said. "Don't look up, Mother!"

She brought her hands to her face.

"Enjeru," she said. "My son."

The helicopter landed in the field, and our costumes went flying in the wind. Still, I lay on the ground. At the edge of camp I saw my sisters. They held each other close, wiped the hair from each other's eyes. Mother rushed forward and fell back, indecisive as the tide. Father held her elbow and shouted in her ear. I knew they were too weak to stop me.

I pushed at the ground but could not stand. I tried lifting my legs but could not roll back onto my knees. The wind from the helicopter made a firm ceiling above my head. *Futtota*, I thought. Our names are our fates.

A man stepped out of the helicopter. He wore a smooth jacket and sunglasses and shouted in English.

"Up," he said, offering his hand. "Up-up-up!"

If he helped me, I could leave. "Come on," he said. I understood his English perfectly, but I did not reach out. The man was a stranger, purple and mean. He wore a torn T-shirt instead of a suit. And he thought I was stupid. Ugly. I lay there with my nose in the mud while he yelled obscenities and kicked me with his boot. I tried to obey, but sadness overtook me.

I looked to Father. His parted lips moved against the wind. And while the sound of the helicopter was great, I could hear his voice so clearly. *Please. Aijou.*

I do not know how long I lay there, but the *whoomp-whoomp* got louder and softer. I cried into the mud. After the birds began to sing again, I felt a small hand at the center of my back. Father. He helped me to my feet. "Poor Aijou," he said kindly. But I no longer felt warmed by his pity. He walked me to my tent, one of the few things that remained standing in the rubble.

"I know you are sad," he said. "But remember: One bad meal must not keep you from eating." I nodded, hoping he would go away. "Things will improve," he said, kissing my shoulder. "You will see how they do."

Father bowed in farewell and went to help the others repair the damage. The twins ran from tree to tree, collecting lost clothing and hanging it on their horns. Ningyo dove into the water to chase a tent that was drifting out to sea, and Zou slowly gathered wood and brought it to Father. Even Mother worked. She squatted and sorted through the blown ashes, looking for lost treasure.

I opened my hand. Five apricot kernels sat in my palm, put there by Father during his kiss. Each wrinkled brown seed was a tiny egg. The eggs would grow bigger if I let them. But no. I closed my hand into a fist and crushed the kernels into powder, then lifted my fingers and gave my children to the air, felt all five of them fly up and disappear. When I had nothing left, I crossed the field and joined what remained of my family.

Our Country Daughter

My daughter wants to be a country singer. She makes this announcement during our Xbox game of *Overcooked! 2*. I don't know music, especially not country music, and the only name I can think of is Taylor Swift. I take a chance.

"You mean like Taylor Swift?"

Maddy wings popcorn into her mouth. "She's not *country-country* anymore. But yeah."

"Cool." Then carefully—casually!—I ask, "Which of her songs? Do you like her new stuff?"

Maddy grabs the controller and unpauses our game. Pink and blue lights explode across her face. "Seriously, Melon. I need your tomatoes."

Melon is not my name, but it's what Maddy calls me. The woman whose genes she shares? She gets to be Mom. THE MOM. My name is Ellen, so to Maddy I'm Melon. Not exactly a parent. More like a fruit.

"Melon! Come on."

I ignore my own virtual kitchen and toss my daughter tomatoes, cheese, and mushrooms. I want her to have everything she needs so her little chef-hat dude can make his pizza.

After Maddy trudges to bed, I do a search for country singers and find pictures of girls in Moulin Rouge nighties and leather boots that rise up their thighs. I see someone twerking in assless chaps. Is this the inspiration for Maddy's new career path?

I love my daughter, but I don't know her very well. And even though I was born and raised in the South, I'm not a fan of anything country. But Maddy is. Maddy is. In the deep lake of my worries that night, I swim around a single island of thought: What if my daughter becomes a country singer? All the things I want for her, and all the things I've done—what if they just don't matter?

———

Maddy lives with my ex-wife, Alison; Allie's husband, Kevin; Kevin's daughter from a previous marriage; and the twins Allie and Kevin had six years ago. This blended family lives in a three-story house where the Haw and Deep Rivers merge and become the Cape Fear. Because of the rural spot my ex selected for her/our family, I rent a small house halfway between their home and my job.

I don't like where I live. It's a quaint town that's home to a college known for having a pretty campus, fake classes for athletes, and gun violence. I work for a medical company that manufactures a special sealant used in brain surgery. Yes, it's as riveting as it sounds. People around here are generally impressed when I name my employer, and I can tell from the fancy glass in the lobby there's plenty of money floating around the place, but I and my team of IT nerds are hidden in the bowels of the building, in a windowless, freezing room where they store the servers and malfunctioning laptops. My job isn't amazing, but it's enough, and I'm grateful for that.

I get Maddy every other weekend. Lately we don't do much together because she wants to stay home and "veg." Once I bought tickets to a touring production of *Mean Girls*, the musical. She sulked during the drive into Raleigh, so we ended up getting Chick-fil-A and calling it a night.

She likes going shopping, but I often get reprimanded after these excursions. According to Allie, thirteen is too young to wear lipstick, regardless of the color. And what was I thinking, letting her buy stockings with a line up the back? I don't understand. Maddy's ripped jeans seem much worse than the tights Allie is waving under my nose. "Honestly, Ellen. Can you please get a clue?"

It's Sunday night. I'm standing on Allie's front stoop, letting her dig into me. She's talking in that pinched voice I know intimately and hate like crazy. Is hate the most intense form of intimacy? Is it a kind of love?

Her eyes are bright with anger, and she's kind of smiling. Behind her, open shopping bags sprawl on the living room rug. Maddy is showing her haul to her stepsister, an enthusiastically average girl who gets to wear eye shadow and lipstick because she's two years older than Maddy. "From now on," Allie tells me, "concealer and lip tint only."

I think, What the heck is lip tint? But I don't ask. I nod, and leave, and drive back home in darkness.

———

Maddy says everyone likes country music now. There's no stigma attached. She actually says "stigma," which makes me think maybe her Catholic school isn't so bad, even though it has a four-out-of-ten rating on Greatschools.org. A few years before Maddy started there, the biology teacher got some heat for teaching Creationism to his students. In the end, the teacher retired. But still.

I grew up in a forgotten, in-between town like Maddy's. You can smell the wrongness of these places from the highway, a scent not unlike the chemical-shit stench of a Monsanto soy field on a breezy day. My town is downriver from Maddy's, and like hers, it's surrounded by orange grass and lakes ringed with algae that poisons people's dogs. You can call it economic stratification, or you can call it the heartland. Point is, I know these places well.

Maybe it goes back to the power plant. Kids grow up thinking their parents must be stupid for living within spitting distance of it, so the kids become mean. I didn't want to get mean. I wanted to get out, and this made me a magnet for violence. All through high school I walked in a ring of hate. Freshman year, I got smacked, sucker-punched, shoved into walls. Even the teachers openly disliked me. Being gay didn't help, but if I'm honest that wasn't the problem. The problem was me. As my granddaddy said, I "talked uppidy." In high school I kept my head down and waited. I swore once I left I'd never come back.

But things happened, like they always do. My mom got sick during senior year, and I ended up going to NC State. Then Alison happened, and Maddy. I know I've got nothing to complain about, not really. My daughter is healthy. I live in a quaint college town and work in a soon-to-be gentrified town, and I have enough gas money that twice a month I can drive along the river and rescue my daughter from the Carolina wilds.

———

Sometimes I think, with some aggravation, that Alison got everything she wanted. She's the center of a big family now. The Mom in Chief. She has a respectable career testing radiation levels in the water. She goes to the gym and is skinny. When Allie calls Maddy's cell, a word pops up: **SUPERMOM**.

And yet my daughter is entirely willing to throw her mother under the bus when we're waiting in the checkout line at Sephora.

Mom doesn't listen to me. Mom is too busy for me. All Mom cares about is the twins.

I crave these reports of Alison's failure, and Maddy knows it. She criticizes her mother to get my attention, but when I ask her to elaborate, she just shrugs.

"Your mom is very focused," I say, trying to be noble. "No one is perfect."

Maddy picks up a tube of something pink and sparkly.

"Can I get this?"

I look at the label. ALL-OVER BODY SHIMMER. Where does this fall on the slut scale?

"Would your mom let you?"

Sighing sadly, Maddy puts down the shimmer. "She thinks I'm going to be raped."

"Maddy!"

She shrugs. It's her signature move these days. So small and brief, it could be a nervous tic.

"She won't let me go to the mall. Because: rape."

I inspect my daughter closely. She's the middle child now, hungry for attention, and she's always been a bit of a fantasist. Allie might have prevented her from going to the mall on one occasion, and Maddy has whipped this fact into proof of her unending oppression. But I want to believe my daughter. Not only because doing so would make Allie the bad guy, but because if I intervene on Maddy's behalf, I'm helping. I'm necessary.

"That seems strict," I say. "I'll talk to her." Then—fuck it—I buy her the body shimmer. Okay, I'm obviously the spare mom. But maybe I can be the fun mom, too?

The checkout girl drops the tiny tube into a giant plastic bag.

"Don't put that stuff on your chest," I say to Maddy.

"Melon!"

I look up at the checkout girl, who smiles like she totally gets how hard it is to be a parent. In the next second, she turns to Maddy and rolls her eyes like I'm the dumbest piece of shit she's ever seen.

————

Over bowls of cheddar-broccoli soup at Panera, Maddy says there's an open mic night at a café. She wants to sing a country song. She wants her friend Daryl to film it.

"Is Daryl a girl or a boy?"

"Don't be so binary," Maddy says. I may be an *L*, but Maddy is much better at the *GBTQ+* part.

"Binary? I'll show you binary!" I brandish two trembling fists at Maddy. "To the moon, Alice! Bang, zoom." Maddy shakes her head and says violence isn't funny.

It turns out Daryl is a girl from Maddy's church who also wants to be a country singer. She's too chicken to sing at open mic night, though. Maddy releases this information while slumped over her bowl of soup, her shoulders almost kissing her ears. She's talking to me, sort of, while scrolling on her phone. When I get up to refill my water I sneak a peek at her screen. Instagram. It's mesmerizing, the way she filters through so much data. Maddy doesn't read, but scans, scrolls, taps, swipes, evades ads, taps, scrolls, scans. Some lizard part of her brain is thoroughly engaged. The rest of her is hidden. Latent. Dreaming.

If only Instagram were an Olympic sport. If only scrolling were a viable skill. What future employment will Maddy and her friends have, with this overdeveloped lizard cortex pumping and thumping, demanding fresh content as if it were oxygen?

When I return to the table, Maddy reveals that Daryl has Air Force 1s. According to Maddy, these are the best shoes in the world.

"Hers have a white-girl crease, though."

"A what?"

Maddy bends over her legs and, with a finger, draws a line across her toes.

"You get it when your shoes are old."

I have so many questions. Like: Who said these shoes were cool, is it because they're expensive, how expensive are they, why does Daryl have them and you don't? But the one I ask out loud is, "Why do you call it a white-girl crease?"

Maddy shrugs.

"Are white girls more likely to have creased shoes than girls of other races?"

"No. It's just an insult."

" 'White girl' is an insult?"

"Yeah. Like, not actually being a white girl, but calling somebody one."

Jesus. What kind of social progress is that?

"It's not racist," Maddy says, and sighs preemptively.

Two years ago, Alison moved Maddy to the poorly rated Catholic school after some Black classmates shoved her while they were all waiting for the bus. When I asked Maddy about the incident, she said she felt weird because she was the only white girl in her class. Maddy may have felt weird, but this statement wasn't true. It wasn't even a stretched truth. I called her teacher, and she said the class was mixed. She also said Maddy and her friends had been feuding for days with the girls in the bus line. The shove hadn't come from nowhere.

When Alison approached me about the Catholic school, I refused to give her any money for it. So what if Maddy felt uncomfortable sometimes? I want my daughter to get tougher, to stay put and figure it out like I did. But Allie moved her anyway, and this year I coughed up half the tuition.

I say to Maddy now, "Do you have any Black friends?"

Maddy says, "Sure." Smirking, she adds, "Do you?"

"Sure." I think for a moment. "I play kickball with Carlos."

"Carlos?"

"He's what-do-you-call-it. Afro-Cuban? And I have Black friends at work."

Correction: one Black friend at work. Andre. He's definitely a friend. We went to that Beerfest food truck thing and met up with his girlfriend. His girlfriend . . . Abby? Abby and Andre. Do I know his last name?

"Melon. Stop."

"Stop what?"

"You don't have to name all your Black friends. I get it! You're woke."

Woke is good. Woke is radical. I know I'm not woke. I'm practically asleep. But I want my daughter to grow up to be less asleep than me. Is that so terrible?

"Hey," I say. "Why don't you turn off that thing for a sec? Give your eyes a break."

"But I need to look at something. You want me to look at the wall?"

"We could look at each other."

Maddy retreats further into herself and winces.

"Awkward," she says, and within seconds, she's gone. Something on her phone pleases her, and she produces a hollow smile.

"You're breaking my heart."

It's the most honest thing I've said to her in years. She doesn't notice.

———

I went with Maddy to church once. It was Christmas Eve, and they chose her to sing "O Holy Night," just her alone, a solo. I picked her up along with Alison and the twins, which was nice. Everybody in dresses. Even I wore a tie.

But on the way to church Maddy sat in the back seat sobbing because the song was too high, and everybody would think she was an awful singer. Some other girl was supposed to sing it, but that girl broke her leg. I didn't understand how a broken leg interfered with singing Christmas carols, but tensions were high in the car, and, at times like that, the spare mom needs to stay quiet.

I didn't sit by Maddy in the pew. I sat by Alison, and Alison was beside the twins, and Maddy was on the end, looking like she might throw up. I wanted to leap over the others and hold my daughter's hand. Even though I knew she didn't want me holding her hand, I would have done it. But too many people were keeping us apart.

It was the kind of church where they sang cheesy rock songs. A stringy-haired man with a heroin-movie face played electric guitar while a woman sang "There is But No One Like You, God!"—or maybe it was "No One Likes You but God!"—while Alison and the kids stood up and swayed with the congregation. I didn't want to reveal my lack of faith, but I didn't want to sway, either. I stayed seated and silently clapped my hands. Then the song was over and Maddy took the woman's place onstage. For the first time since I was twelve, I seriously considered praying.

My daughter gripped the mic stand like she hoped it would keep her afloat. She was trembling, right knee fluttering against the bottom of her skirt. I felt her eyes lock onto mine.

As I looked back at her, a primal thought flooded my brain: *Help Maddy.* I can't say exactly what happened next. I was standing up. Cupping my hands around my mouth. And into the echoing silence of that church, I shouted, "*YEAH, MADDY!*" The fear on my daughter's face was replaced with surprise, and then revulsion. I was embarrassing her, yes. But maybe I was also saving her?

"*C'MON, MADDY!*"

I hollered and cheered like Maddy was Dale Earnhardt winning Daytona after twenty years of trying. The faithful turned in their pews to stare, but I didn't look away. I just whooped and gave her a big, stupid, double thumbs-up.

Alison said, "*EL!*" and pulled me down beside her, where I performed a little wave and folded my hands in my lap. I had done it. The temperature in the room had changed completely. People weren't thinking about Maddy being nervous, they were thinking about me being an asshole.

The congregation tittered and turned back to Maddy, who had gained control of her feelings and marshaled them into aggression. I could see a thread of her jaw popping out and retreating into the softness of her cheek. Without a word she stomped down the center aisle, and as she passed she threw me this look, like, "Die, motherfucker." Allie sprang up and helped her escape. We all craned around to watch them scurry through the big double doors at the back.

The guitar player nodded like this was all part of God's plan and launched into "O Holy Night." He tapped his foot as he played, and while he didn't sing, exactly, he arched his neck upward for the high notes so we could see his Adam's apple. *Faaaaall on your kneeees!* Everybody was thinking it.

No one spoke on the ride home, and I didn't see Maddy for a month after that. I figured it was what their family needed to do. Make me the bad guy. Maddy would've been great that night if it hadn't been for me, her big bad Melon. And I was happy to be that guy for her. I was. I would take all the blame in the world if it helped my daughter sneak past the memories she wanted to forget.

––––––

The open mic night is six weeks away. I start going to pawn shops. At one place I find an acoustic mahogany with a shaded edge burst. I don't know if Maddy plays acoustic or electric, but I like the way this one feels in my arms. Holding the guitar helps me picture a future in which Maddy is not a country singer, but something else. She doesn't have to be a girlboss to make me happy, or an engineer elbowing her way into a field of tech bros. Maddy can be a secretary, a sales rep, a dental assistant—I can picture this kind of quiet life for her, where she's a person with a career and a family and is also someone who plays the guitar. "My spare mom got this for me when I was thirteen," she'll say to her friends when they come over for dinner, and she'll point to this gleaming beauty with pride.

I buy the guitar. On the drive home, I think maybe I'll teach myself to play so I can jam with my daughter. That's a good, sensible dream to harbor.

I leave the guitar on her bed with a red bow stuck to the neck. When she comes over the following weekend, she walks into her room, looks at it, and walks out.

"It's nice."

"It's for you."

"I know."

"Do you want to try it out?"

"Not right now."

My Southern manners, which were drilled into me by my mother, start to yip and niggle because Maddy hasn't thanked me for the present. *She doesn't need to thank us,* I tell my manners. *She's our daughter.*

"Please?" I say to Maddy.

She sighs and takes the guitar to the screened-in porch. I sit across from her and try not to look nervous. Can she even sing? I remember a breathy, off-pitch voice coming from the back seat, but that was years ago.

"It's not in tune."

"Can you tune it?"

"Wait. I have an app."

She taps at her phone and starts to tune the biggest string, but the sound of the note warbling up and down is so grating that I excuse myself to make lemonade tea. When I return, Maddy's running her thumb over the strings, and it doesn't sound half bad.

"I forgot to buy a pick," I say as I set down the drinks. "Sorry!"

"That's okay. I don't know how to use a pick yet."

She strums, strums.

"Play the open mic night song."

She grimaces. "I need to practice."

"Well, go on! Practice."

She straightens her shoulders—a move straight from the Allie playbook—and says in a bossy voice, "Okay, but don't pay attention to me. Do something else."

I choose a book from the coffee table and pretend to read it. Maddy's phone chokes out a twangy guitar riff. She mouths the words that appear on the little screen, her entire torso bent over the guitar like she wants to protect it.

"*This girlie's got a handgun . . . da-da-da . . . shootin' bourbon and bullets . . .*"

My heart beats faster, skipping between disapproval and delight. Allie would never let our daughter sing this song. Which means Allie must not know! Maddy hasn't played it for her yet. She's only played it for me.

And then my daughter sings, "*He slapped my ass . . . but I slapped him right back!*"

And I think: *Shit.*

———

The next evening I'm back on Allie's stoop.

"Have you heard it?"

"Heard what?"

"Maddy's song. Guns and ass-slaps."

Allie turns to yell something at the twins. She looks flushed and a little drunk.

"Sorry, it's crazy round here. Kevin just said he's taking us to Disney World."

264 | JESSIE REN MARSHALL

"Us? Who us?"

She flips her hair back and runs her fingers through it. That move used to drive me wild. She still looks good. Damn it.

"*Us*-us! The kids and me."

"Maddy, too?"

"Of course Maddy, too."

I hear one of the twins say, "It's not Disney World, it's Disney World in France!" Allie laughs and nods, then turns back to me.

"Le Disney," she says. "Everyone is nuts."

"Wait," I say. "It's not during the open mic night, is it?"

"Oh." Allie pulls her phone from the back pocket of her jeans and scrolls through her calendar. "It's not a big deal if we miss it."

"It's a big deal to Maddy."

Allie gives me a look that means: *I'm the mom and I know everything. You're the Melon and you know nothing.*

She puts her phone away. "You're in luck. We leave the weekend after that."

I nod and shift my weight back and forth. Allie slaps her forehead comically.

"Jeez Louise, do you want to come in?"

But she's looking away from me, into the warm light of her precious inner sanctum.

"That's okay," I say.

"Thanks for bringing Maddy home." She doesn't look at me as she closes the door.

———

I met Alison when she volunteered, via coffee-shop ride board, to drive me to Chicago. I had an internship there with a tech company, and Allie was going to spend Christmas with her sister.

Another girl rode with us from Raleigh to Dayton, but all I remember about her is that she snagged the front seat, so my first interactions with my future wife took place in the rearview mirror. Alison struck me as efficient and friendly, a little too skinny and a little too blonde.

"You a Blue Devil?" she asked.

"No, ma'am. Wolfpack."

"Major?"

"Comp sci with a business minor."

"Bet the guys are all over you."

"No," I said, "but some of the girls are."

I stared at the top of her head. The blonde was actually lots of different blondes, like kernels of corn speckled across a cob. She glanced at me in the mirror. There was a lot of dark liner around her eyes, making them look really blue.

"You in art school?" I guessed.

She shook her head. "I'm a free agent, kid."

The twenty-year-old version of Alison called people "kid" a lot. It was a goofy affectation, like she wanted to look like Ingrid Bergman but sound like Humphrey Bogart.

We stopped for a pee break. I offered to drive for a while, but she put a hand on my shoulder and shook her head.

"No way, kid. I like to be in control."

I spent the next stretch of highway wondering if she'd been flirting, and by the time we reached West Virginia, I decided that she had. We dropped off the anonymous girl in Ohio, and I moved up front. Within ten minutes Allie invited me to touch her jeans—*They're too tight, right?*—and to pet her camel-colored coat, which had tufts of gold fur at the collar and wrists.

It was late when we got to Chicago. Not snowing, but smelling of snow. Allie drove past her sister's place in Tri-Taylor to drop me at a Super 8. When I got out of the car, she offered her hand.

"Nice riding with you, kid."

I wasn't ready to let her go. Over the next month, I met her for drinks, museums, meals. Wooed my ass off, which I could tell she liked. Each time we got together Allie wore that camel-colored coat with the fur. We spilled beer on it, dropped ash in the pockets. Years later I found out she'd thrown the coat away. I was so upset I picked a fight about her buying the expensive dishwashing liquid and we didn't speak for days.

Like me, Allie didn't intend to live in North Carolina forever. She wanted to drink mezcal in Oaxaca and walk along the Great Wall. These confessions made my own pipe dreams seem possible. Under the covers, I told Allie things I'd never said out loud. About becoming a journalist. About going to war zones and revealing the best and worst of humanity. If my tech internship didn't evolve into a job, I could buy a one-way ticket to Darfur. Allie said, "I'd miss you, El," as she wrapped her limbs around me like a viper smothering its prey.

Allie gave up on the Great Wall and Oaxaca like they meant nothing to her, which I guess they did. Maybe falling for a woman, having a child with a woman, was enough of a departure. I held on longer, talking about the Middle East until Maddy was born. Then we moved back to North Carolina to be near Allie's parents, and just after Maddy's third birthday my marriage slid into quicksand. A lot of things got said in the quicksand. Things we couldn't take back.

I like to imagine our family would have lasted longer in another city, in another country, far from where we'd grown up. And even now, when I'm free from my marriage but still rooted in family, I wonder where I would have landed if I didn't have Maddy in my life and Allie in the rearview mirror.

———

A week before the open mic night, I take my daughter to buy a country singer outfit. She's walking ahead of me in the mall like I'm her chauffeur or a stalker. I jog to catch up, then keep pace beside her, casually, like we're at the mall together. Which, you know. We are.

"Do you have cowboy boots at home? Because I kind of think they're essential."

Maddy is silent.

"How about that vintage place downtown? Where you found that sick jumper?"

I feel a surge of shame at saying "sick jumper," but that's what Maddy called it. She even showed me a picture of Rihanna wearing something similar, although Rihanna's jumper had looked complicated and sexy because she didn't have a shirt on underneath.

In the middle of the mall, Maddy screams. Or not a scream, exactly, but she definitely emotes. The dress in the window is brown, and other than being a little too short on the mannequin, I don't see any red flags. We go inside the store. There's a horrible, youthful smell in the air, like Axe body spray mixed with overripe fruit. Maddy disappears into a changing room. When she returns, the brown dress is still on the hanger.

"*I love it*," she says. "Can I get it?"

She grabs my arm and wraps her own arms around it, like we're on a date and she wants to take things to the next level. Sometimes I am disgusted by how much Maddy is like Allie. They are both flirts who cajole and whine to get what they want. Right now, Maddy wants the dress. Or is it my attention? My attention in the form of a dress?

"Why didn't you show it to me?"

"Because it's perfect, and I don't want you to ruin it."

"How would I ruin it?"

"By saying you hate it."

"I won't hate it. But your mother—"

"You hate everything I like."

"That's not true. Maddy!"

Now she's over at the register, waiting in line. What does she think I am? A walking wallet?

In an act of defiance I go outside and buy a soft pretzel. Jalapeño, but no cheesy dipping sauce because according to the menu, the pretzel alone is six hundred calories. Knowing this makes every bite taste buttery and wrong. I throw a third of the pretzel away and return to the store, where Maddy is arguing with the salesclerk.

"I found this on the fifty-percent-off rack."

"Someone may have left it there," the salesgirl says, "but that's not where it belongs."

"Come on. That's false advertising!"

I know lying is wrong, but a part of me is glad that my daughter is resourceful. I never lied as a kid. Never cheated on a test, never copied a friend's homework. But as I get older, I'm more inclined to say screw it. No one's keeping track. Unless you're religious, then I guess God is keeping track.

Maddy is religious, but not when it comes to commerce. She huffs and glares at the salesgirl. Standing her ground.

My daughter is not like me, I think. And then a smaller voice pipes up: *Maybe that's okay?*

"Hello, sir."

The salesgirl says this like I'm a respectable gentleman. Maddy turns, and I watch her face soften.

I've gotten called "sir" before. It's fine. I am a cool daddy-o. I hand the salesgirl my credit card. After I buy my daughter the dress, I'm not just a gentleman, I'm a hero.

———

On those rare occasions when Maddy is kind to me, it's like traveling back in time. I remember the way she'd slip her sticky hand into mine when we crossed the street. How she'd beg me to play tea party even though I mixed up the names of her stuffed animals. I think of those long summer days when Maddy would sit in my office filling legal pads with drawings of ball gowns while I ran diagnostics on hard drives and listened to Federer taking back Wimbledon.

Sometimes, even now, she forgets that she hates me. We get home from the mall and watch three episodes of a vampire series. I make popcorn with butter and sugar, the way she likes it, and when the cute vampire leaps across the dining table to attack the evil vampire, Maddy screams and laughs until she snorts. She's still in there, I think. I don't say anything about it, though, because pointing out the magic might make it disappear.

———

In the buzzing heat of summer, rain tends to turn the creek near our old house into a heavy green passage. One time I sat in that river and held Maddy close to my chest, and when I nestled her in the crook of my arm, her eyes locked onto mine. She was fourteen weeks old. The water ran cool over my stomach. I felt the sun on my face and closed my eyes. If Allie had been there, watching us from the riverbank, I wouldn't have blinked. She wouldn't have allowed me to blink—that's how worried she was all the time.

I opened my eyes and saw Maddy's head go under. Not all the way. Just her little lips. Her little earlobes. The river wasn't deep or fast. She wasn't in danger. But of course, she was so little, she was always in danger. I lifted her up and checked for signs of damage. She looked back at me and smiled in the way only babies and enlightened monks can smile, like their entire bodies are vehicles of joy.

I didn't tell Allie, but I took Maddy to the river all summer, and the following spring the three of us went there together. By that time Maddy had developed a dubious expression, like she suspected her parents weren't doing things properly, and Allie had begun to loosen up. I took my daughter swimming, and what do you know, she was like a little fish. She remembered. Some part of her remembered. And when Allie cried out, "She's a natural!" Maddy and I smiled like we had a secret.

———

On the night of the open mic I go to the café. Maddy and her friends are already there, standing outside in a girlish huddle. Is it weird that I'm happy to see one of her friends is Black? As I get closer, I can see the girl's boxy white sneakers. She says her name is Daryl, and I laugh out loud at myself.

Maddy wears ripped jeans and a shirt that shows her midriff. I wonder what happened to the brown dress and feel surprised that Allie okayed this new outfit, but I guess it's a special night. A night of firsts.

"So who all's singin'?" I say.

The girls laugh like I'm a great comedian.

"Just me, Melon."

Maddy says "Melon" like *Melon* means "idiot," but in a loveable way. I'll take it.

I go inside and see Allie at a table with the twins. Or rather, Allie is sitting at the table and the twins are underneath it. My ex-wife clutches a small mug like she's afraid someone will pry it away. When she sees me, she smiles.

What is going on tonight?

I climb into the chair next to her, trying not to kick the children.

"I'm so nervous," Allie says. She looks pretty. Her hair is straightened, and she's in a fuzzy red cardigan.

"Me too. Where's Kevin?"

She looks at the door like she's expecting him but says, "Had to work late."

"Saving up for Euro Disney?"

"Something like that."

I could pry more, but I don't. I ask about the brown dress. What happened to it? Allie shakes her head.

"Oh, El. That dress was a disaster."

Before I can ask why, one of the twins pops up. "Can we get whipped cream?"

Allie looks at me as if I'm their co-parent. I smile back like an airhead. Not my problem.

"Ask your sister to help you," she says.

The twins screech with joy and rush outside. Allie and I sit in an affable silence. The café is crowded. A kid in a trucker cap sets up some microphones on a carpeted platform.

I say, "What song is Maddy doing?"

"I have no idea."

This makes me feel fantastic, but I pretend it doesn't.

"Do you think she can sing?"

Allie looks appalled at first, then laughs.

"Oh, man. I hope so."

"I want her to do well," I say. "But not too well. Is that bad?"

"You're the cool one. You tell me."

The cool one. Really?

"But you're Supermom! You know everything."

Allie leans closer and says, "I've been wearing the same bra for three days. I'm spiking my hot chocolate with whiskey. As long as Maddy doesn't do a striptease, this night is a win."

I hold out my hand, and she takes it. "You're doing great, Al."

"Al and El," she says. "I miss us sometimes."

Maddy and her crew go to the counter for drinks. The twins dart around their legs, high off the attention they're getting from the big girls. Maddy leans forward to talk to the server. A feathered earring flashes against her cheek.

"You pushed that girl out of your vagina," I say.

She spurts out a sip. "Don't remind me."

"No, look at her. She's a full human. She exists."

Allie's face crinkles into folded pads of worry. "I don't want her to make the same mistakes I made. I want her to be better than me."

"Oh," I say lightly. "She is."

Allie laughs. "Our country daughter is singing a country song. How the heck did we get here?"

I want to tell her that our mistakes must not have been that bad, because here we are, alive and looking at our daughter. But before I can say anything, Maddy rushes over to tell us she's the first performer on the list. She rocks on her heels, a tornado of energy and nerves. Allie's face reflects Maddy's. She's happy because Maddy is happy. I realize I'm smiling, too. My face is like their faces. What is going on tonight?

When the trucker hat kid says our daughter's name, she gets up on the platform and puts both hands on the microphone because both her hands are shaking. She says hi in this tight little squirrel voice, and her friends go wild. I don't have to shout "Go, Maddy!" to embarrass her. I can see that she's deeply embarrassed because we're all looking at her, but also, she wants us to look at her. Being stuck between these two feelings is what it's like to be thirteen. I remember that now.

The music starts up through the speakers. It's not the twangy guitar riffs of the slap-me-around song. It's an easy waltz tempo like a walk along a river. When Maddy sings, I can barely hear her at first because she's telling us a secret. I catch a few words. *Row, slow. Old sea, lonely.* It's a pretty song. A song that sounds like Maddy.

She gets to the end of the first verse, and her friends clap so loud, Trucker Hat turns up the music. The twins leap to their feet and do jumping jacks. "Maddy, Maddy!" She is their brightest star.

My daughter looks over our heads and laughs. Then she looks down, taking a moment for herself, and right then I can see another version of Maddy, one who is old enough to make her own choices. Maybe she'll be a dental assistant, or a journalist, or a mother. Maybe she'll live in this town for the rest of her life. Maybe she'll move away and I'll wish she had stayed. Regardless, she'll be a little messed up about it, because that's what choices do to a person.

This woman—my future, unknown daughter—will resemble me and Allie in ways she won't understand. And like us, she will run from where she came from and run back to the people she loves, again and again. As the years pass through her like a river through the fields, the pattern of this journey will make zigzag scars across her heart.

And in time, those scars might resemble the ones that reach across mine.

ACKNOWLEDGMENTS

My parents, Maile and Jeff Marshall, are the reason this book exists.

One: Because of them, I am here. And because I carried the knowledge of their love, I kept writing through obscurity, rejection, and doubt.

Two: They taught me to value stories and art. Thanks to my dad, I grew up with "the tape list," a database of the movies and TV shows in his massive VHS library. Having hours of on-demand entertainment might not seem like a big deal today, but in rural Pennsylvania in the eighties, it was extraordinary. Obsessively rewatching things like *The Last Unicorn*, the animated *Lord of the Rings*, and *Watership Down* helped to develop my aesthetic and gave me a healthy fear of harpies, orcs, and militant rabbits. In the other corner of my childhood, my mom was a painter who spent her life trying to make things beautiful, including me and my sister. She modeled how to be an empathetic person, and when she went to the basement to paint every day, I learned that making art is an important job even if no one pays you to do it.

Three: They gave me money! I really want to acknowledge this, because talent and hard work are only part of the equation. Being able to afford the time it takes to develop as an artist is a rare privilege. That's a problem. We need world-changing stories right now, and so we must do more to support diverse emerging artists who have a vision for change.

Speaking of support, I'm really grateful to the institutions that offered me time, space, and the honor of feeling like my work mattered: the Community of Writers at Olympic Valley; the conferences at Sewanee, Colgate, Southampton, and Tin House; and the residencies at the Kimmel Harding Nelson Center for the Arts, the Gershwin Hotel, and Millay Arts. Thanks to the literary magazines and editors who published my stories, especially my first one at the *Gettysburg Review.* Thanks to my teachers over the years, with a special shoutout to my first workshop instructor, Paul Harding, who gave me the knowledge I needed to grow (and did it with kindness). Thanks to the books that lit me up inside when I really needed it.

I had too much fun in grad school because of my classmates, especially Val, Lynne, Caleb, Jonathan, and Charles—all great writers and great people. Thanks to Alexis Macnab, for being my lifelong best art friend. Thanks to Kimo, for helping me find a home and teaching me about love. Thanks to Naomi, because "Our Country Daughter" wouldn't exist without her. Thanks to my writers group members, past and present: Katie Aspell, Stacey Closser, T. N. Eyer, Kristin Walrod, Kate Weinberg, and Sarah Zoric. It's been so meaningful to navigate this path alongside you.

Thanks to my agents and fairy book godmothers, Michelle Brower and Natalie Edwards, who are so wildly good at their jobs that I can (usually!) write instead of worry. Thanks to the kind and brilliant team at Trellis. I'm so proud to be a Trellis author!

Thanks to the passionate people at Bloomsbury, especially the indefatigable Barbara Darko, Katie Vaughn, and Lauren

Ollerhead. Approximately one million thanks go to my editor, Grace McNamee, who is not only an exorcist-therapist-midwife, but a sorceress who infuses her subtle magic with generosity and wisdom. You made this book better by asking all the right questions.

Thanks to my always-and-forever best friends, Mary Fry and Kelly Mifsud, and to my very first and always-and-forever role model, Jamie Marshall. I am so lucky to have you as the brightest stars and biggest goofballs in my life.

And finally, thanks to my dogs, who make me a better human. You can't read this, but I love you.

A NOTE ON THE AUTHOR

JESSIE REN MARSHALL has an MFA in fiction from New York University. Her work has appeared in the *New York Times*, *New England Review*, *Electric Literature*, *Joyland*, *ZYZZYVA*, the *Gettysburg Review*, and elsewhere. Her play *Hapa Girls* won Kumu Kahua Theatre's Hawai'i Prize and she has received scholarships from Millay Arts, the Sewanee Writers' Conference, the Kimmel Harding Nelson Center for the Arts, and the Community of Writers. She lives off-grid with her dogs on Hawai'i Island.